D1569365

SHOTGUN
MOON

SHOTGUN MOON

MOON

K.C. McRAE

MIDNIGHT INK
WOODBURY, MINNESOTA

FIRST EDITION
First Printing, 2013

Book design and format by Donna Burch
Cover design by Lisa Novak
Cover images: iStockphoto.com/1105240/Chris Downie, 20071989/Kenneth
        Schulze, 7629203/Christian Sawicki, 4733111/Daniel Cardiff,
        14474933/Murat Giray Kaya
Editing by Connie Hill

Midnight Ink, an imprint of Llewellyn Worldwide Ltd.

Library of Congress Cataloging-in-Publication Data

McRae, K.C.
  Shotgun moon / K.C. McRae. — First edition.
      pages   cm
   ISBN 978-0-7387-3684-6
 1. Rape victims—Fiction. 2. Retribution—Fiction. 3. Cousins—Fiction.
 4. Murder—Investigation—Fiction. I. Title.
  PS3613.C5877S56   2013
  813'.6dc23   2013012988

Midnight Ink
Llewellyn Worldwide Ltd.
2143 Wooddale Drive
Woodbury, MN 55125-2989
www.midnightinkbooks.com

Printed in the United States of America

DEDICATION

For Bob and Mark

ACKNOWLEDGMENTS

It truly takes an amazing number of people to get a book into print, and I'm so very grateful to everyone who was involved with this one. The hardworking team at Midnight Ink includes Terri Bischoff, Courtney Colton, Bethany Onsgard, Connie Hill, and Lisa Novak. Without them this would just be a pile of paper on the corner of my desk. My writing buddies Mark Figlozzi and Bob Trott provided advice, detailed feedback, and unstinting support, especially for this book—thanks, guys! The ladies of the Old Town Writing Group—Janet Freeman, Dana Masden, Laura Pritchett, Laura Resau, and Carrie Visintainer—keep me on the straight and narrow, make me laugh, and ask the tough questions. Bizango.net is responsible for my awesome website. And thank heavens Kevin Brookfield is my forever cheerleader, inspiration, and moral support when I'm pretty sure I have no freaking idea how to write a book.

Additional thanks go to Debbie Main and Joe Werner for name suggestions. Maurice Robkin gave me loads of information about guns (pardon the pun), and Leslie Budewitz answered my legal questions early on. The folks at Washington Outdoor Women taught me to tie flies and cast, and Caitlin Hartford taught me how to ride western. Anything I got wrong is my own fault, not theirs.

Then there are the people who read the book—or parts thereof—that contained the seeds for this one. They include Tom Martin, Jeff Weaver, Ed Cattrell, Rod and Nita Lindsay, Margot Ayer, Kevin Fansler, Stacey Kollman, Jody Ivy, Mindy Ireland, Tamera Manzanares, Marjorie Reynolds, Stasa Fritz, and Aimee Jolie.

Finally, let's not forget the real McCoys—my cousins Gary and Marsha, from whom I borrowed the name, and my great-grandmother, Essie McCoy.

ONE

Daylight beckoned from the far end of the dark, cement-walled corridor. It seared her pupils, blinded her to what lay beyond. But she strode forward. Eager. Seeking the light's promise. Then the great metal gate clanged open, and Merry McCoy stepped through to the dusty asphalt outside for the first time in four years.

Her eyes adjusted. A yellow, placarded cab waited fifty feet away, the driver craning his neck to look at her. Ignoring him, she tipped her face to the relentless Texas sun as if the exact same light didn't shine down on the prison compound behind her.

"You got a place to stay?"

The guard accompanying her wasn't a bad sort. Not as bad as most of the others. But Merry wouldn't be adding the woman to her Christmas card list. Or anyone else from inside those high walls, for that matter.

Merry nodded.

"Where?"

"None of your goddamn business." That felt good. Really good. Merry allowed a smile to curl her lips and turned to face her former keeper.

The guard scowled. *Too bad*, Merry thought. Nothing she could do about No. 26492's bad attitude this time. The woman made a noise in her throat and went back inside. As the gate slid closed between them, their eyes met. The smile on Merry's face hardened, then dropped. She turned back to the road.

The cloying, muggy heat pressed against her cheeks. Soon she'd be home in the dry clime of western Montana, on the family ranch outside the little town of Hazel. Some things might be bigger in Texas, but they didn't call where she came from Big Sky Country for nothing. The Last Best Place. The only place she ever wanted to be again.

If only Mama could have been there to welcome her back. Anger flared again at the thought that cancer took her while Merry had been locked away. She hadn't been there to help her mother during the long illness, to be there during her final days, to properly say goodbye. The funeral had been well-attended, but Elsa McCoy's only daughter hadn't been there for that either.

But now, just after turning thirty-two, she was out. Mama's sister, Shirlene Danner, would be waiting for her at the airport in Missoula tomorrow. That would do. That would most certainly do.

It had to.

Plucking at the shoulder of her T-shirt where her cellmate had soaked it with goodbye tears, she straightened her shoulders and strode toward the taxi. She'd leave behind the wasted years in the huge concrete institution. She'd eat whatever she wanted. Get up when she wanted. Go to bed when she wanted. And only be nice to people she actually liked.

She got in and told the driver to take her to the nearest Motel 6. As the car began to roll, sudden fear stabbed Merry's chest. What did the people she'd known her whole life think of her now? She'd heard her ex-husband had lived in Hazel for a while after she'd been sentenced. Who had he talked to? What had he told them?

It didn't matter. Hazel was her home.

Merry stared at the seat in front of her and focused on good memories. The tart-sweet flavor of chokecherry jam on white bread. Green tomato mincemeat pie. Cottonwood fluff floating through warm air, gathering next to curbs and swirling behind passing cars. The perfume of the dry, packed forest floor in the Bitterroot Mountains. The calls of bold camp robbers, tiny striped chipmunks and querulous Stellar's jays. The sound of wind blowing through pine needles and yellow grass.

Soon. She'd be home soon.

———

Aunt Shirlene drove her old pickup down the gravel ranch road and stopped in front of the house. Merry gave her a quick hug and grabbed her duffel from the bed of the truck. Angles plied her aunt's face, which was striking if not conventionally attractive. The nose provided a hawkish air, laugh lines graced her gray eyes, and fine wrinkles from smoking all of her adult life radiated from her lips. Her hair shone the same bottled Titian blonde it always had, only now it was cut quite short. She'd kept her birdlike figure over the years.

Shirlene leaned her head out of the open window. "You're coming for dinner on Sunday." It wasn't a question.

"I promise," Merry said. "But for the next few days I'm probably going to stick around here. Get acclimated." She wanted a few days to settle in by herself before braving the rest of the world.

"Of course, hon. You call if you need anything." She put the truck into gear and waved as she pulled away.

Merry watched her aunt leave, eventually turning west onto the county blacktop. Then she turned and climbed the porch steps, opened the door with the key Shirlene had given her, and walked into the living room. During the whole drive to Hazel, her anxious anticipation to see the house where she'd grown up had increased with each mile marker flashing past. But now she stopped, swamped by the juxtaposition of the familiar irrevocably changed.

They were all dead now. First Daddy. Then Drew. And now Mama.

The furniture was all the same, from the dark green velveteen couch with the crocheted cream-and-rose afghan draped across the back, to the regal sideboard that sat against the opposite wall, handed down from her mother's grandmother. Four well-worn bookshelves filled the remaining wall space. Silky fringes ringed the bottom of the lampshade. But her knowledge of these things was a hollow intimacy. This house no longer had a soul. Absence rode the air.

Daddy had died of a heart attack when Merry was seventeen. Her older brother Drew had been long gone from home by the time he died, working on a freighter that ran up and down the eastern seaboard. It caught fire and went under, taking Drew and several other crewmembers with it. There was no burial, for there was no body. Her mother had arranged a memorial service in the highest meadow on the family ranch, and then life had disconcertingly picked up its usual rhythm. Merry had expected death to have more impact on the living.

And now, in this empty house, she realized it had more impact than she could have ever imagined.

———

Lauri Danner looked up the address in the phone book: Barbie Barnes, 511 E. 8th Street. She waited until after sunset—well after nine o'clock so far north in late June—before she drove by. A white picket fence surrounded the small white house. A tidy porch looked out on a postage-stamp lawn. Unbearably traditional. Barbie doll wasn't home. No one was home, but the door was unlocked. How convenient. The perfect opportunity to further her campaign to get Clay back. Fingering the knife in her pocket, she slipped inside and closed the door quickly behind herself.

———

Later, back home, Lauri couldn't sleep. She lay awake, anxious and angry, watching the fitful dance of light and shadow cast by the two candles burning on her bedside stand. Had Barbie returned home to find what Lauri had done? Or was she spending the night over at Clay's? It would be easy enough to find out. A few peeks in the windows. Just to see. And if Barbie doll wasn't there? Well then, Lauri could go ahead with the other part of her plan. Clay had always been a night owl, staying up late unless he had to work the early shift. Her spirits rose at the thought.

Passing her mother's bedroom, she heard light snoring. A heavy sleeper, Shirlene wouldn't hear the Honda start. Not that it mattered. Lauri was old enough to stay out late, or not come home at all. But she found it easier to avoid the questions. Mom didn't really nag that much, but she kept trying to *talk* to her. Like Daddy had before he died. But it wasn't the same with Mom. She didn't understand like Daddy had. And now she kept talking about her cousin being back. Merry's coming to dinner. Be nice to Merry.

Screw Merry and her bad luck. Lauri had a life to live.

Almost midnight. Empty streets and parking lots, except for the gamblers and drinkers making the most of a Friday night. Lauri guided her little Honda down the street where Clay lived, parking two blocks away. She'd dressed in black. Black stretch pants, ankle boots, a silky long-sleeved T-shirt, and a cute little baseball cap with "Girl Power" stenciled in pink across the front. She slid her keys inside her sock to prevent them from jingling and kept to the shadows as she worked her way toward the duplex. Little moonlight reached the neighborhood, but streetlights shone down at regular intervals, and bright fixtures illuminated some of the doorways. Their reflections littered the wet streets.

A dog barked behind a fence. Adrenaline surged through her extremities as she hurried past. She heard the pop of bottle rockets, and from the next street over came the crackle of a much larger firework. Kids practicing for the Fourth. She'd better be careful; some tight ass would soon call the cops.

At the edge of the driveway running along the right side of the duplex, she paused. His pickup was parked next to the house, and behind it sat an older primer-gray van. She squinted at the dented passenger door. She hadn't realized Clay and Denny knew each other. That couldn't be good.

She slipped between the vehicles, sidled along the front of the house. Blue light from the television flickered against the drawn living room curtains. Standing on tiptoe she could see over the sill, but not through the heavy fabric. A brighter sliver gaped at one end of the window. Craning her neck rewarded her with the view of a shoulder and the corner of the television screen through the gap. She recognized the shampoo commercial playing.

Was the shoulder Clay's? He leaned forward, and she saw it was Denny. A woman sitting next to him got up and walked toward the bathroom, long black hair swinging behind her. Barbie doll had much shorter hair. Lauri had been worried that she'd moved in with Clay but now knew she hadn't because Lauri had been right there in Barbie's own little white house earlier. She'd read the mushy birthday card from Clay. Seen the waterbed in her bedroom. A smile crossed her face as she thought about what she'd done.

She didn't bother looking in the unlit kitchen window. She moved around to the back of the house, to Clay's bedroom. Lower to the ground, this window had easier access. Open to the night, only a screen separated her from the dark interior. Moving close, she peered inside. The red digital glow of the clock on the nightstand revealed the faint outline of a form on the bed. A single form. Good. She kept her breath shallow, silent. He was right there. He was sleeping right *there* on the other side of that window.

Sleeping. If only she'd come earlier. He couldn't deny their chemistry. He couldn't deny the way she'd make him feel. She wanted to do things to him that would make him forget that Barbie doll.

Completely, totally forget her. It would only take one more time. That was all she needed.

————

The first night Merry slept on the porch. Then for four days she'd spent as much time as she could outside. The freedom to do so was one reason, but she was also reacquainting herself with the land. With the sense of her old, yet new, home. Maybe if she could touch the past firmly enough she'd be able to figure out how to make a future.

Outbuildings marched in a clockwise arc northeast of the ranch house, which faced almost due north. Farthest out, the hay barn-turned-shop rose into the clear blue above. One step nearer, the big red horse barn towered almost as large. Then the defunct chicken coop, and closest to the house, the garage constructed of unpainted wood so weathered it glinted silver in the late morning sun. Prairie grass turning from green to yellow ran out toward the blue-gray Sapphire Mountains to the east and to the foothills of the Bitterroot Range to the west. With her eyes fixed on that vista, breathing the sweet dry air felt like inhaling the sky.

The insistent trilling of the phone pulled Merry back inside. The screen door banged shut behind her as she grabbed the telephone off the kitchen counter.

Aunt Shirlene's cigarette-etched voice rasped down the line. "Hey, it's me. I'm down at the police station with Lauri."

A tiny icicle of fear slid up Merry's spine. "Why? What happened?"

"She ... oh, God, you're not going to believe this. She found Clay Lamente dead this morning. Sergeant Hawkins is getting ready to take her statement."

"Jesus. Is she okay?"

"She's a mess." A pause. "I don't know—there's probably nothing you can do. I just thought ..."

"Do you want me to come down there?" *Pleasepleaseplease don't ask me to go into the police station.*

"Well, it's not like she did it, or anything."

Merry's temples throbbed. "Did what?"

"Clay was shot."

Shit. "Call a lawyer. Right now."

"What?"

"You can't let her talk to the police without a lawyer."

"You make it sound like they're accusing her of something. She was just in the wrong place at the wrong—"

"So was I, Shirlene. Wrong place, wrong time. Right side of the law. Look what happened to me."

Not that she'd been thinking about anything except survival. Zeke had wanted to kill her.

Several long seconds passed in silence.

"I'm sorry, honey," Shirlene said. "I wasn't thinking. You just never mind about all this, and I'll call you when we get home."

"Call a lawyer. I mean it."

"The only lawyer I know is Eric Morris, and he only does wills and probate. It'll be fine. This isn't Texas."

Like Texas had the monopoly on wrongful convictions. "Shirlene—"

"I'll call when we get home." She hung up.

Merry cradled the phone. She closed her eyes, leaned her forehead against the cool side of the refrigerator. Through the open window the liquid call of a red-winged blackbird beckoned from a fencepost.

She turned so her cheek lay against the smooth freezer door.

"Shit."

She swept her keys off the counter and into her fist. By the time the screen door slammed behind her, she was behind the wheel of Mama's old K5 Blazer.

TWO

Following the retreating shimmer of early summer swelter rising from the highway pavement, Merry broke the speed limit all the way to town. But when she reached the end of Main Street and pulled to the curb in front of the Hazel Police Station, she switched off the engine and sat unmoving in the heat. Sweat trickled between her breasts.

Lauri really wasn't her problem.

She opened the door and her boots touched asphalt. She walked with slow steps toward the two-story brick building. As her fingers curled around the old wrought-iron stair railing, she looked up at the ancient bars over the windows that had once been part of the original jail. Their Old West grimness now screened wide-open, double-paned inserts that allowed light and air into the main station. The jail proper was now in the basement.

A shriek from inside lacerated the air and she was up the short stairway and through the door.

The sudden dimness slowed her steps, and the clammy, air-conditioned atmosphere smelled of scorched coffee and Pine Sol. Shirlene's angry voice and then another, shorter cry of frustration and fright drew her past the unmanned reception counter and four cluttered desks to an open doorway.

A long wooden table surrounded by chairs dominated a glorified conference room. Lauri sat sideways at the table, black streaks of mascara dribbling down to her jaw line. She didn't look much older than when Merry had last seen her so much as ... harder. Harsher. She wore too much makeup, heat and tears melting and mingling it like a box of crayons left too close to a radiator. In her teens, Lauri's long brown hair had glinted with streaks of gold, but now the chunky layers around her face were dyed a flat, whitish yellow.

Shirlene glowered at the man who stood on the other side of the table. He matched her glare for glare. His pendulous gut hung over the tightly cinched belt of his uniform, and his large flat face radiated a dangerous crimson. He clenched and unclenched his spatulate fingers into meaty fists by his sides.

At one end of the table a skinny woman with large breasts and wide eyes held a pen poised over her notebook. A tape recorder rested on the table in front of her.

"What's going on here?" Merry asked from the doorway.

The beefy man's head jerked around. She became aware of what she must look like: holes in her jeans, dried mud on her battered boots, dark hair a tangle of uncombed curls, no makeup.

"I heard a scream."

His eyes narrowed. "Really."

"Merry?" Lauri sounded like a little girl. "Make him stop?"

She met her cousin's eyes and saw fear and vulnerability beneath the dregs of makeup. When she looked back at the policeman, his eyes narrowed in recognition.

"Merry McCoy." He grated out her name.

She felt the blood drain from her face, then return in a sudden flash. She crossed her arms over her chest and looked around the doorjamb at her aunt.

"What happened?"

Shirlene spluttered. "He badgered her. He threatened her!"

"Sarge?"

Merry jumped at the word, the speaker so close behind her that his breath moved against her neck. Her lips parted in surprise as she turned her head, though in that split second she'd already recognized the voice: Jamie Gutierrez. The muscles across her back eased a fraction, and she found herself able to take a deep breath.

"The girl's hysterical. The mother's not helping, either." The fat guy, who Merry assumed was Sergeant Hawkins, shot a surly look at Shirlene. "She's gotta go so I can finish questioning the daughter."

Jaime took a step to stand next to Merry. He smelled like sage and leather. She took a deep breath as the sudden image of the last time they'd been together flashed across her mental movie screen. "Mind if I sit in?" he asked, giving her arm a surreptitious squeeze.

"Yeah, I mind," Hawkins said. "How 'bout you make yourself useful and get your *friend* out of here instead." He jutted his chin toward Merry.

Jamie's face reddened. Merry looked at the floor and swallowed the retort that rose to her lips.

"Sergeant Hawkins, if I could speak with you for a moment?" The voice came from somewhere behind them, beyond the cluster of desks.

Merry looked over her shoulder, saw a tall figure standing silhouetted in an office doorway. The voice and bearing suggested power.

Hawkins scowled. He lumbered out of the conference room, hitching up his pants and pooching his lips. Merry moved aside to allow his passage, trying not to wince at his sour breath.

She turned to Jamie in the doorway. "Lauri needs a lawyer."

"She's just a witness."

"Bullshit."

"Merry…"

"Don't 'Merry' me. She doesn't have to tell you anything."

Jamie's look held so much sympathy she wanted to smack it off his face. Either that or cry. She set her jaw.

"Officer Gutierrez?" The same voice that had summoned the sergeant.

Jamie turned and walked to the other side of the room. She had to stop herself from reaching out and grabbing his arm as he left, his presence a comfort in this unfortunately familiar and unpleasant environment of law enforcement. In the conference room, Lauri snuffled.

Shirlene hushed her in a maternal tone, raising her eyes to meet Merry's.

Merry leaned in. "You guys okay?"

Mother and daughter both nodded. Lauri's lip quivered, and she snuffled again. Merry looked at the female officer at the end of the table, and she nodded, too, her eyes showing a lot of white.

"Who's the bossy one?" Merry gestured toward the men with her chin.

"That's the chief," the policewoman whispered.

Hawkins raised his voice and Merry looked back at them. He jabbed a stubby forefinger in her direction several times, punctuating what was no doubt a delightful tale about her past. Then he pointed at Jamie, who responded with a threatening step forward. The police chief shook his head and said something to both of them.

Hawkins stomped off. Jamie threaded his way through the gray metal desks, stopping in front of her.

"I'll handle this. But you have to go."

She shook her head. "No."

"Merry. Stop it. You need to leave."

Across the room she saw the tall man watching their exchange. His unapologetic stare never wavered.

"Trust me," Jamie said in a low voice. "Please."

Well, shit. When he put it like that . . .

Sergeant Hawkins reappeared. He didn't smile so much as bare his teeth at her. "Checked in with your parole officer yet?"

She looked at Shirlene, whose face was creased with worry. With the slightest movement, her aunt shook her head. Merry shoved her shaking hands in her pockets and walked to the door.

Hawkins's voice followed her. "I'll be checking in with you, McCoy. Count on it."

She exited the station without looking back at him.

And continued around to the side of the brick building until she was just under the open window of the conference room.

The rough wall scratched the back of her bare arms as she flattened against it, but at least she was out of the hot midday sun. And from the street, no one could see her listening.

Jamie's clear voice came through the screen above Merry's head.

"Don't be frightened, Lauri. I know you've had a shock. But we really need your help. Do you think you could help us?"

Silence.

"If you could just tell us about this morning, then we can get on with doing our job, and your mom can take you home. How does that sound?"

Merry thought she heard Lauri hiccup.

"Can't I do it later? I want to go home now. Please don't make me think about…" A soft sob.

"I'm sorry," Jamie said. "I understand how you feel, but we have to know what happened. The faster you tell us, the faster you can get out of here."

"Just tell him, hon." Shirlene's voice echoed Jamie's firm tone.

"Okay. Jeez." A pause. "I wasn't due at work until one. So I went over to Clay's this morning to talk to him…"

"What time?" Jamie asked.

"About ten. Do you want to hear this or not?"

"Go on."

Lauri sighed. "No one answered. So I got the key and opened the door."

"You have a key to his place?"

"I said I 'got the key.' Why would I say that if I already had one? I knew he kept an extra key under a rock by the side of the house. I got it and went in."

"Okay, you went in. What then?"

"I didn't see anyone. So I went back to Clay's bedroom…"

"You went straight to his room?"

"Well…"

"Yes?" he said.

"I might have gone into the kitchen."

"How about the living room. Did you stay there very long?"

"Does it *matter*?"

"I'm trying to determine how long you were there. And I want to know where to expect your fingerprints in the house."

Shirlene said, "Come on, Lauri. Just tell him. What did you do, shake the place down?"

Lauri hesitated. "Well, no. I might have looked around a little bit. But I didn't take anything, if that's what you mean."

"What? Lauri—"

Jamie interrupted. "Please, Mrs. Danner. If you're going to be in here, you need to be quiet and let your daughter tell her story." Then apparently to Lauri: "So you looked around a bit."

A sniffle. "Yeah."

"Maybe opened a drawer or two, looked in a closet…"

"Um. Yeah."

Merry closed her eyes and shook her head. Not good.

"Nadine? Would it be easier to transcribe from tape?" Jaime asked.

Merry heard the policewoman say, "It sure would. I'm having a hard time keeping up."

"You don't mind, do you, Lauri? Make life a little easier for Nadine? You were saying you looked around Clay's place once you let yourself in…"

"Yeah."

17

"Please continue." His voice became formal, and Merry guessed the tape recorder had been turned on.

"I ... I looked around in the kitchen, opened some cupboards, and looked to see what was in the refrigerator. Just beer and some leftover spaghetti. He really needs ..." A long pause. "... needed ... someone to take care of him. She sure didn't do a very good job."

"She?"

"That woman he hooked up with. Barbie Barnes. Anyway, I checked out the living room. I, um, opened the desk drawer, or maybe more than one. I was looking for a pen and paper so I could leave a note." Lauri sounded defiant despite the tears in her voice. "That's why I looked in the entertainment center, too. Just in case that's where he kept them. I had to go to the bathroom, so I went in there. And I opened the other bedroom door."

"The other bedroom door?"

"Yeah. His roommate's, I guess."

"Who's that?"

"Um, I'm not sure."

"Then what?"

"Then I went into Clay's bedroom." A long pause. "At first I thought he was asleep."

"He was on the bed?"

"Yeah. I thought it was kind of weird that it was so late and he had all his clothes on. It was like he'd passed out or something."

"Did Clay drink much?"

"He didn't drink at all."

"Drugs?"

"He hated all that stuff. Something to do with how his mom died."

"Okay, what did you do then?"

18

"I turned on the light. To wake him up." Lauri's voice quavered.

Everyone waited. Merry picked at a cuticle and watched a beetle circumvent the edge of a puddle near her foot, tensing for what was coming next.

"He was all bloody. There was blood all over the bed. It was so dark! His eyes were open, and ..." Lauri's voice faded as she spoke. The last few words came out little more than a whisper. "*It was awful.*"

Merry's hand crept to her throat as she tried to pushed away the memory of Zeke's blood when she'd pushed him off of her—dark, yes, but also weirdly bright as it soaked into her clothing and smeared across her skin.

"I know this is hard," Jamie said. "There's only a little further to go. Let's just get through it so you can go home."

Lauri took a deep breath. "So I called Mom. I didn't know what to do. I mean, I know to call 911, but for some reason I didn't think of it. I just thought that since Mom volunteers at the clinic and everything she would know what to do about Clay. She told me to stay put and ..." The rest disappeared into choking sobs.

A click. Probably the tape recorder being switched off.

Jamie said, "That's fine. I think we've got what we need. Nadine, will you take Lauri to the restroom so she can recover a little? Then I'd like you to take her fingerprints before she goes."

Shirlene said something Merry couldn't hear.

Jamie said in a gentle tone, "It's standard procedure, Mrs. Danner. Oh, and Lauri? Thanks for your help."

She responded with a fresh bout of weeping. The sound receded, then a door clicked shut and cut it off altogether.

"I need to hurry, Jamie," Shirlene said. "She's a mess, and I want to get her home."

"Just a few questions. When did she call you?"

"At ten fifteen."

"Are you sure?"

"I had my eye on the clock because I was watching for the UPS man. I'm out of solvent and couldn't get started on the dry cleaning until it came."

"And what did you do?"

"Like Lauri said. I told her to go outside and wait for the police. Then I called 911. I shut down the machinery and closed the shop, which takes about ten minutes, and headed over there. The paramedics had already arrived when I got there. Then that dickhead sergeant showed up and told us to follow him here."

"What happened when you got to the station?"

"He put us in here. We waited for a while. I went out front and called Merry. Then he came in and started asking Lauri where she was last night, and what she and Clay had fought about."

Merry swore under her breath. Hawkins obviously disliked her, but that didn't make him a bad cop. Still, she didn't trust him one iota.

"He didn't even give her a chance to answer before he was asking her something else, or yelling at her," Shirlene said. "What the hell is his problem?"

Jamie sighed. "It's just the way he operates. I'm sorry."

"Well, thank God you took over. You need anything else from me?"

"No. As soon as we have her prints, you can take her home. We'll let you know if anything else comes up."

Merry heard them leave the room, but stayed where she was on the off chance she'd overhear Jamie or Hawkins say something about Lauri. All she heard were indistinct voices. Tilting her head, she strained to discern the words. She tried standing on tiptoe and closing her eyes.

"Don't let Rory Hawkins catch you out here."

She whirled at Jamie's words. He stood two feet away from her.

THREE

JAMIE GAVE HER A lopsided grin.

"You're a sneaky one, aren't you?" Merry said, trying to ignore the spurt of adrenaline whipping through her vitals. And more than adrenaline. The tiny kernel of desire shocked her. It had been so long since she'd felt anything like it that she almost didn't recognize the feeling. "How'd you know I was here?" she asked.

"Where else would you be?"

She began to retort, but he held his finger to his lips and led her toward the back of the building. His usual bouncy step was uncharacteristically devoid of bounce. He paused next to a mud-brown dumpster in the alley.

"Eavesdropping can go both ways," he said.

The hot odor of decomposition boiled out of the garbage bin. They moved farther down the alley and stopped behind the Rexall Drugstore.

Merry finally allowed herself to smile. "It's good to see you."

His grin crinkled the corners of his eyes first, then exposed his straight white teeth, bright against summer-dark skin.

"You look great, Mer."

Just in time, she stopped her hand from moving up to her hair, an instinct she'd thought long forgotten.

Jamie's grin dropped away, and he let out an exasperated whoosh of air. "Rory Hawkins could be a real problem."

"Why's he got such an issue with me? I've never even met him before."

"He's a friend of Rand's."

"Oh."

She felt an odd weakness in her legs, and locked her knees so they wouldn't buckle.

"Oh," she said again. "I thought Rand left town."

"He did. He's in Wyoming from what I hear."

She nodded slowly in relief. "Still conning landowners for his father."

Her ex-husband worked for his family's oil company, convincing ranchers and farmers to part with their mineral rights so Daddy could come in and pump out the crude.

"But Hawkins and he got to be pretty good buddies before he left," Jamie said. "So naturally, Rand's side of Zeke's death is the only one he knows."

"Sergeant Hawkins is a misogynistic prick. Rand's side's the only one he could understand."

"Maybe."

"Believe me," Merry said. "I know the type."

He crossed his arms over his chest. "Just be careful, okay?" The platinum band on his left hand flashed in the sunlight. A sudden arrow of jealousy surprised her.

"Yeah. Okay." She tore her gaze from his wedding ring. Reaching out, she touched his forearm with her fingertips. His skin was hot from the sun. "What kind of trouble is Lauri really in?"

He shook his head. "I don't know. Her behavior is suspect—letting herself in, searching the place like that."

"If that's what she was doing. Maybe it happened just like she said. If you know Lauri, that's pretty normal behavior for her."

"You heard all of it?"

She nodded.

"Well, she is kind of a pill," Jamie said. "But hinky behavior's still hinky, whether someone acts that way all the time or not."

Merry was silent. Lauri was a lot of things, but she was also family.

He went on. "We still don't know enough. I'm going over to Lamente's place now."

"Can I come with you?"

Brow wrinkled, he quirked up one side of his mouth. "No."

"But maybe you could call me later and let me know what's going on?"

He hesitated. Then, "I'll try. But we have to play this thing by ear."

She nodded. Between their friendship and his job, Jamie was wedged firmly between the proverbial rock and hard place.

———

Jamie turned and walked back through the alley to the police station while Merry, unwilling to encounter Rory Hawkins again so soon, circled around the drugstore to Main Street. Shirlene's Dry Cleaning was next to the Suds 'n' Fluff Laundromat. Weathered cracks in the blue exterior paint exposed dark red brick underneath.

Her aunt's business, funded five years before by Uncle Al's life insurance, provided steady income, made more so when Shirlene began taking in laundry from local roughnecks and ranch hands. The story was that her career twist began when a young man toted in one of the ranker piles of clothing she'd come across, placed them gingerly on the front counter, and asked in a polite voice if she could see her way clear to helping him out. The laundromat next door wouldn't let him use their machines for his work clothes, and the trailer he was staying in didn't have a washer.

She told him he could have them the next day, naming what she thought was an outrageous price. He kept smiling, nodded, touched the bill of his cap, and left. If he had been dismayed, she might have lowered her price, but he hadn't. That night, she ran the clothes through the washing machine in the laundry room off her kitchen. Twice, with an extra dose of Borax and very hot water, just as she had with her husband's for so many years.

When the roughneck returned the next day, he brought a couple of friends, each with their own garbage bag full of filthy clothes. Word got around. After six months she had enough extra money to buy an industrial washing machine and dryer, which she installed in the back of her shop next to the dry cleaning machinery.

Down the street, Harlan's Hardware, Garden, and Feed still sold a little bit of darn near everything. Further down, the Dairy Shack hunkered in the middle of a large dusty lot, looking abandoned. The teenagers who collected there to eat hotdogs and ice cream wouldn't show up until evening. Between these landmarks, many of the storefronts on Main now held trendy little shops and bric-a-brac dens to satisfy tourist tastes.

The edge of town boasted evidence of new construction: a 7-Eleven, a tiny Kingdom Hall, a Chevron with a drive-through carwash. Ropes of neon tubing, pale in the midday sun, outlined the Lucky Lowdown Casino in flashing magenta. The parking lot behind backed up to a hay field that stretched toward the blue foothills of the Sapphires.

But the changes mattered little to her visceral recognition. At the core Hazel, Montana was still her hometown.

She hadn't lived there for six years. During the first year as a less-than-blissful newlywed, she'd visited often, and she was able to come home twice during the year before her trial. The next four she spent in a privatized Texas prison after a jury of her supposed peers found her guilty of manslaughter. She'd moved to Dallas— flat, humid, drawling Dallas—when she married Rand, but it had never really been her home. She'd convinced the parole board of that, and now that they'd let her leave she'd never set foot in the state of Texas again.

Hurrying to the Blazer, she glanced at her watch. As a matter of fact, she *hadn't* met with her parole officer yet. She'd left a message for her but hadn't received a call back.

Merry had been delighted to learn she wouldn't have to make a weekly trip to Missoula to check in. Though small, Hazel was the county seat and boasted a hundred-year-old courthouse, two judges, and one poor soul to baby-sit the various offenders on parole throughout the county. That same parole officer also contracted to the Montana Interstate Compact Unit, which supervised parolees from other states.

The downside of having her minder so close at hand was that Hawkins would know the woman. But how well? Was he just pawing air, or could he really sabotage her parole? Dread gnawed below her sternum, but the urgent need to assess Hawkins's threat potential overrode it. Merry needed to know if she'd be reporting to an active adversary or merely a weekly annoyance.

She had no paperwork, no appointment, and looked like hell. But she remembered the address.

Good enough.

A block off Main she found the two-story brick home that had been converted into offices. On the lawn in front, a painted wooden slab advertised the Hazel Office Mall. Next to it, a chainsaw carving of a grizzly cub waved at passersby.

Running nervous fingers through her hair, she stepped to the cement walkway that led from the sidewalk to the front door. A slight breeze whispered through the cottonwood leaves above, carrying the sharp scent of hot tar. A road crew was working somewhere nearby.

Inside, a small foyer narrowed to a long hallway that led straight through to the alley in back. The heavy wet odor of carpet shampoo accounted for the vivid yellows and oranges of the ugly paisley carpet. She started toward the rear of the building, examining plaques on the doors as she went.

She stopped and put one hand on the wall when she saw it. Unexpected and unwelcome, the name on the door halfway down the hall had nothing to do with finding her parole officer.

It had everything to do with the past.

Kate O'Neil. Attorney.

No doubt she was an excellent lawyer. Kate had excelled at everything she'd ever tried. Well, everything except keeping Rand faithful. But that was like trying to stop the universe from expanding. His peccadilloes were hardly her fault.

At least she hadn't blamed herself.

She'd blamed Merry.

What was Kate doing back in Hazel? She was smart enough and tough enough to make it in a larger pond. Plus, the money here had to suck.

Merry balked at the thought that this might be the solution to Lauri's problem. She'd wanted an attorney, one with a strong sense of justice and the brains to back it up, and here one had been dumped in her path. That Kate would probably toss her out on her ear for having the sheer nerve to ask for help didn't mean it wasn't worth the risk.

Her hand crept toward the doorknob. A rustle from behind the door made her heart buck, and her hand jerked back. After she'd seen the parole officer. She'd come back then. Kate was probably busy right now, anyway.

Sweating in the dim, humid heat, Merry located the office she wanted by the back door. Not knowing whether she was supposed to or not, she knocked lightly.

"Come on in!" a voice sang out from the other side.

Seated behind a desk piled with neat stacks of files and loose paperwork, a woman with tight iron-gray curls and deep lines radiating from the corners of her eyes peered at her over a pair of half glasses. She stopped typing on the keyboard in front of her and beamed.

"Merry McCoy. Good Lord, girl, what'd you get yourself into?" She finger-walked through several files until she located the one she wanted. "Well, get in here, take a load off. I'm not gonna bite."

Hesitant, Merry advanced into the room, combing her memory. "Mrs. Sonberg?"

"Not anymore, I'm not. Yvette Trager, at your service. Well, so to speak. I finally gave that sonofabitch Sonberg the heave ho five years ago. Don't know what took me so long. But you just call me Yvette, now, okay?"

Merry eased into the chair across from the desk. No wonder she hadn't recognized the name. Mrs. Sonberg had been the secretary at the high school for over two decades. Her hair had been darker then, but the blue eyes remained the same—able to penetrate your bullshit as if she possessed some specialized x-ray vision.

"I called, but when I didn't hear back, I thought I should drop by."

"Glad you did. I've been gone to a conference for the last four days, and I've just gotten behinder and behinder."

Yvette Trager opened the file and sat back in her chair. She wore matching polyester slacks and a long-sleeved tunic the same blue as her eyes. On the floor, a fan moved enough air in the room to make it tolerable without disturbing any of the paperwork. The shrieks of children at play drifted through the open window.

"So what happened?" she asked.

Merry looked out at the street. "I'm sure it's all in there."

"Some of it is. The official stuff. But that's not what I asked. How am I supposed to help you if I don't know the whole story?"

"I didn't know you were supposed to help me at all."

"Just keep an eye on you, huh. Make you toe the line. Watch your P's and Q's. Cross your T's and—"

Merry half-grinned and held up her hands. "Okay, okay."

"—dot your I's."

"So there's an alternative?"

"Well, no. More like a bonus. Icing on the cake. Gravy … I'm starving. Let's go get us some lunch over at the Moose."

"Right now?"

Yvette cocked her head to one side. "Afraid to be seen with me?"

"Of course not."

Silence. Just more of that look.

"Okay, maybe a little."

"Too bad. 'Sides, there's not a soul who gives a damn who doesn't already know all about you. The rest don't care. Might as well face up to that now."

Merry sighed. "Yes, ma'am."

Yvette snorted. "I encourage that kind a talk from most a the dumb shits I work with, but you can skip the formalities."

"That mean you're buying?"

"Dream on, honey."

———

They walked the couple of blocks to the Hungry Moose Diner, where the lunch crowd filled most of the tables and booths. The owner's daughter, Janelle Paysen, who waitressed or cooked as the need arose, stood with one denim-clad hip slung against the counter chatting with a handsome young man wearing a battered seed cap. When she saw Yvette, she waved them toward the back.

Merry inhaled the potpourri of grease, coffee, and toasted bread. Well-worn white tile, red Formica, and chrome gleamed in the bright daylight streaming through the large windows. At a table in the far corner, a disheveled man leaned over his plate, intent on shoveling the mountain of eggs, chicken-fried steak, and biscuits and gravy in as fast as he could. A crumpled pack of cigarettes sat next to his plate.

Heads turned to watch as they made their way through the tables to the back corner. Merry walked quickly, studying the floor. Had people talked about her when she was gone? Did any of them already know that Clay Lamente had been killed? Or that her cousin had found him?

Yvette slid into a booth. "Welcome to my second office."

Merry cleared her throat and sat down across from her. The idea of telling her parole officer about how she'd spent her morning crossed her mind, but she rejected it immediately. No need to volunteer information she didn't have to.

Janelle followed behind with coffee. Not bothering with menus, Yvette ordered the pork sandwich, and Merry asked for a tuna melt. The Moose's tuna melt was on her list of freedom foods. After Janelle left, Yvette extracted the file she'd stuck in her capacious satchel. She pushed aside her coffee cup and silverware and handed Merry a pamphlet.

"These are the rules. Follow them."

Merry glanced through the meager pages. "Looks simple enough." She folded them and tucked them in her back pocket.

Yvette leaned forward and impaled Merry with her gaze. "Well, you're not exactly falling all over yourself trying to tell your side of the story. I'm guessing by now you know how that's usually received and pretty much don't want to bother. But I can figure out some of it—there's a fair amount between the lines in these reports, and I managed to get a hold of the trial transcript, so that tells me the rest, considering that I know a bit about your charming ex. And I know a bit about the company he finds himself drawn to. Got great taste in women, but he doesn't understand them, and rotten taste in friends, and he doesn't understand them either."

She paused and flipped through the file. "So what I think happened is this friend of Rand's—what's his name? Oh, here, Zeke. Anyway, this Zeke fellow was attacking you—" Her voice softened. "—raping you—and you made him stop. For good. Don't know if you intended that or not, but that's what happened. May've gotten a little out of hand, but I think it was self-defense to start with."

Yvette stopped and squinted at her, waiting.

Merry clasped both hands around her cup to hide their slight trembling. She took a careful sip of coffee. Over time she'd woven a veil between the vivid memories and the present. Zeke's contorted face hadn't visited her dreams for more than a month now.

Yvette continued. "But that wasn't the end of it, was it? Well, it wouldn't be. Someone was dead."

Janelle brought their lunch then, and Merry was grateful, both for the fast service and that Yvette had the good sense to shut up, even if it was only for a few moments. She hadn't prepared for this onslaught, had thought checking in with her parole officer would be short and sweet—yes ma'am, no ma'am, I'll see you next week, ma'am. Even the therapist at the penitentiary hadn't made her feel like this. Of course, he couldn't have found his way out of a paper bag with a flashlight and a map, so there was that.

When they were alone again, Yvette squirted mustard on her pork chop sandwich. "You ever see that bumper sticker, the one that says, 'My wife ran off with my best friend, and I sure do miss him'?"

Her first cellmate had made a similar comment, and Merry had managed to force a laugh. But she hadn't intended to talk about what happened, and certainly not here in her hometown diner. But Yvette had created a hairline fracture in her practiced façade. Helpless to stop the widening crack, she struggled to remain silent, but the words tumbled out anyway, raw and awful.

"Yeah. That's about right. Rand was pissed because I killed Zeke, and he refused to believe I wasn't fucking him for fun. 'Cause his best friend might do his wife, but he'd never be low enough to do it if she hadn't seduced him first. That what you want to hear? Does it help you to supervise my parole to know that, Yvette? I got fucked, then I got fucked over, and now I'm fucked up. Does knowing that make your job easier?"

Merry winced and looked away. The words hung heavy in the air. Too late to swallow them now. The elderly couple at the nearest table stared at her in horror.

Yvette took a sip of iced tea, eyes on Merry's face. "Yeah. It does." She picked up a French fry. "And Merry? Don't use those f-bombs around me. I don't like it."

"That's the Mrs. Sonberg I know." Her laugh was bitter.

Yvette pointed the fry at her. "And don't ever, ever call me Mrs. Sonberg again." Now her voice held real warning.

Merry blinked.

She popped the fry in her mouth and spoke around it. "You seeing anybody?"

"You've got to be kidding. Now you want to know about my love life?"

"No. I want to know if you're in therapy."

"Oh. No, I'm done with all that."

"You sure that's a good idea?"

"It's not court ordered, so you can't make me."

"Christ, you sound like a little kid." She held up her hands. "Now, hold on. I've got almost enough from you for this week. You got a job?"

After a few moments, Merry shook her head. "I've got the ranch and some money from Mama's life insurance. It's not like I'm living on the street."

"Are you actually working the ranch?"

"No. Most of the land is leased to Frank Cain."

"Well, then look for something to do, something where you're around people. Part-time is fine. Even volunteer work." Yvette wiped her lips and tossed her paper napkin on the cold remains of her lunch, then scooped up her purse and Merry's file.

"I got to get back, get myself caught up so I'm only my usual day or two behind. Come see me next week."

Merry folded her arms. "When?"

Yvette looked at the ceiling, consulting an internal calendar. "Tuesday's pretty good. Drop by in the morning." She stood. "And while you're thinking about the job thing, I want you to think about what you're going to do about that chip on your shoulder. I know you've been through a lot, but if you don't do something about your attitude, you're going to make more enemies than you can handle."

After she left, Merry poked at the uneaten tuna melt. She'd have to leave it on the list. The Moose's tuna melt. Strawberry shortcake with real whipped cream. Fried egg sandwich. Fresh-caught trout. McDonald's French fries. Sun tea. Chips and onion dip. Moose Drool ale. Peanut butter and chokecherry jam sandwich. Chester-fried chicken. Double-fudge brownies. Freedom foods, all.

Yvette Trager thought she knew what had happened, and she'd been right about a lot of it. But she didn't know the whole story.

Merry picked up the bill. And imagined the accusing eyes following her as she walked up to the register.

FOUR

AFTER UNCLE AL DIED, Merry's aunt had sold their big white two-story just off Main Street and bought a more compact dwelling on the edge of town. She'd painted the neat Craftsman-style house robin's-egg blue with white trim. Her love of gardening showed in the landscaping.

Merry stood on the sidewalk in front, arms folded, wishing she could rabbit back to the safety of the ranch. But Shirlene and Lauri were the only family she had left, and they were in trouble. She trudged up the cement pathway that curved between flowerbeds boasting colorful zinnias, delicate moss roses, and towering holly-hocks. Roses lined the driveway, interspersed with conical evergreen topiaries. In the middle of the lawn, yellow potentilla circled the trunk of a cherry tree. The air smelled green.

Shirlene opened the door and threw her arms around Merry. "Oh, honey. What a mess. What an awful mess."

Merry followed her back into the kitchen. Her aunt lit another cigarette from a smoldering butt then rubbed out the latter in an ashtray on the butcher-block table. The mound of twisted filters among the ashes in the amber glass confirmed her chief activity since returning home from the police station. She shoved aside the piles of paper, clearing the space between them.

"What's all this?" Merry asked.

"Just a bunch of my volunteer stuff. Thought I'd try to distract myself. Didn't work."

Desultory bursts of breeze from the open back door stirred the stuffy air, and the guttural flow of fresh brew dripped from the Mr. Coffee on the counter. Shirlene removed the half-full pot and placed a mug under the stream of dark brown liquid. It slowly filled. She switched it for another and handed the first steaming mug to Merry.

Her parole officer had said she needed to get involved with other people. "What kind of volunteer work do you do?"

Shirlene waved her hand in the air and sat down across the table. "The committee to build the new Hazel Library takes a lot of my time, and I also work with a nonprofit called WorldMed. It Provides medical supplies to third-world countries, places devastated by natural disasters, things like that. They run the local branch out of the Quikcare Clinic, and sometimes I also fill in at the front desk there if they're shorthanded and there isn't too much work piled up at the cleaners."

"Sounds like you're keeping busy."

She sighed and took a sip of coffee. "I try."

Merry picked up a legal-sized sheet that showed the layout of the new library. It said construction was supposed to start in a couple of months. Putting it back, she ran her finger over the stylized world map logo on the WorldMed pamphlet.

She took a sip of coffee. Strong enough to strip tar. Perfect. "Where's Lauri?"

"I gave her a glass of whiskey, to hell with her delicate condition, and put her to bed when we got home. She's asleep upstairs."

"Her what?"

"Oh yes. On top of everything else, she's pregnant."

Merry's eyes widened. "Good God. How did that…?"

Shirlene's eyebrow arched.

Merry shook her head. "Never mind. Why didn't you say something?"

"I was going to, but it seemed like you had a lot on your mind when we were driving down from the airport."

True enough. "How far along?"

"Doctor says six weeks."

"Do you believe her?"

"She's puking most mornings. No real reason to lie about the timing."

Merry raised a skeptical eyebrow. It wouldn't have been the first time her cousin had tried to pull something. "So who's the father?"

"She won't tell me. But she's still hung up on Clay. Hasn't really dated since they broke up last year."

"It's got to be him. Why else would she be over there this morning?"

"That's what I thought, though he didn't seem the type to fool around on his girlfriend. Damn it. I was pretty glad when he and Lauri broke up. I mean, nothing against him, he was a nice enough kid—clean cut, upstanding sort. And I know his stepmom pretty well, of course." She nodded toward the pamphlet by Merry's cup. "She's the one in charge of the WorldMed operation here in Hazel."

Merry nodded. Olivia and Bo Lamente owned a chunk of property that adjoined the McCoy place where they ran a small horse training operation. But like many rural people, they needed town jobs in order to pay all the bills. She remembered Olivia was a nurse.

"Bo still teaching?"

Shirlene nodded. "At the high school."

"Right." She'd been a decade too old to hang out with their son but knew he'd been an only child. Like Lauri.

"I thought it'd be good for that daughter of mine to be on her own, toughen her up a bit." Shirlene snorted. "Yeah, on her own in my house. Lot of good that was. And he still managed to knock her up. I wonder if his girlfriend knows."

"What's her name?" Merry asked.

"Barbie Barnes. Another nurse over at the clinic. Nice girl."

How nice would she be if she found her boyfriend cheating?

Merry hesitated.

"What?"

"I know you worry about Lauri, want to keep her safe …"

Shirlene rolled her eyes.

"… but she needs to fend for herself. She needs to get a job—"

"She has a job at the Dairy Shack."

"That's not a rent-paying job, Shirl. That's a buy-yourself-more-clothes job." She paused. "All I'm saying is, you've got to let her grow up."

"Oh, for God's sake. I'm not stopping her."

"Well, maybe she needs a little push."

Her aunt's hands gripped the handle of her coffee mug so hard her fingers turned white. "You want me to kick my pregnant daughter out into the street?"

39

"No, of course not." Merry looked out the window at the backyard. "Has she thought about adoption? Or ...?"

Shirlene closed her eyes and shook her head a few inches back and forth. "I can't even get her to talk about it." When they opened, her gaze snapped with anger.

Merry dared another sip of coffee. "It didn't look good, her snooping around over there before she found the body."

A pause. "I know. You know how she is."

"Yeah. I do."

"You think she'll get in trouble for it?"

Their eyes met. "I hope not." Merry couldn't quite keep the doom she felt out of the words.

Shirlene looked away and reached for another cigarette. She sat with it in her hand, staring into space before lighting it.

A loud banging on the front door made Merry almost drop her cup. She jumped up to answer before Shirlene could rise. Through the window, she saw a police cruiser parked in the driveway and another one cozied up to the curb in front.

She opened the door, and the frame filled with Sergeant Rory Hawkins's considerable bulk. Enmity crackled between them as they stared at each other.

"Now what?" Merry said.

"Police business." Hawkins managed to sound both gruff and smug. "Get out of the way."

She winced at the rank halitosis that gusted out with the words. "I don't think so."

He spoke with cartoonlike formality. "Unless you're the owner of this property, stand aside. I've got a warrant to search the house."

"Search for what?" Indignation increased the volume of her words.

"What's going on?" Shirlene said from behind her.

Hawkins pushed the door open, and Merry shifted a half step to the side. The sergeant had to suck up his sagging gut as he sidled past, pooching his lips and scowling. He clutched a folded sheet of paper and, ignoring Merry's outstretched hand, thrust it toward Shirlene. She unfolded it and began to read as Hawkins headed for the stairs.

"Wait a minute!" Merry said. "Shirlene, what's he looking for?" She leaned over her aunt's shoulder, trying to make out the words on the warrant.

"Footwear, it says." She looked up at Merry. "They want our shoes."

What? Then she realized Hawkins had disappeared. "Shirlene, get up there. Watch every move he makes. Don't let him take anything except what it says here. Don't let him snoop. Hurry!"

Shirlene ran to the stairs.

Merry rushed over to Jamie, now standing in the doorway. "What the hell is going on?"

Shirlene's angry voice echoed down the stairwell. "What are you taking those for? They're bedroom slippers, for God's sake!"

A masculine murmur, then Shirlene again. "Well, try using some common sense, then."

Jamie grimaced. "I didn't know about this until just before we came over here." He sounded defensive.

She gripped his arm and pulled him into the kitchen. "This is nuts! It's only been a couple hours since you guys let Lauri go."

41

"Hawkins is in a lather about this one. He got Judge Vander-heeve to sign the warrant."

"What are you looking for?"

"Shoes. And/or boots. To compare to the footprints we found under Clay Lamente's bedroom window."

"Why would you think Lauri made the footprints?"

Jamie hesitated. "Someone saw her over there last night. Walking around, looking in windows—" He stopped as Merry's gaze flicked over his shoulder.

A very angry Shirlene approached. "Don't you have some idea what you're looking for? You people are taking every pair of shoes in this house. We won't have any to wear!"

"Don't mention that. Hawkins'll want the shoes off your feet." Jamie glanced down at her Keds.

Her lips thinned into a grim line.

"Is Lauri still upstairs?" Merry asked as she and Jamie joined Shirlene in the living room. "I don't want Hawkins up there by himself."

"She's up there watching. Barefoot, I might add."

Another uniformed policeman came in the open front door. A long, tall plank of a man, his skin glowed pale under a cap of fine orange-red hair. Freckles dusted his nose, and his cheeks carved parentheses on each side of his mouth.

Jamie said, "Merry, this is Lester Fleck."

"Hey, Merry. Good to know you."

She nodded at him and gave Jamie a perplexed look. Then she saw the welts her fingers had left on his forearm when she'd dragged him into the kitchen.

He hadn't said a word.

Shirlene glowered. "I'd better get all those shoes back and in exactly the same condition as when you took them. I can't afford to go buy all new ones, you know."

"You'll get them back. All except the ones that fit the prints," Rory Hawkins said, lumbering down the stairs with a lumpy green garbage bag.

How much had he been able to hear from upstairs?

"We got 'em all. Let's go." He handed the bag to Jamie, directed one last smirk at Merry, and went out the door.

Jamie, looking apologetic, shouldered the bag and went outside. Lester Fleck followed.

Shirlene slammed the door behind them and reached for her Camels. Her hands shook, so Merry tapped one out and lit it for her. The acrid flavor made her regret it. Her aunt moved into the living room, slumped into the recliner, and dragged on her cigarette in silence.

Merry paced in front of her. "Remember that lawyer I wanted you to get?"

Shirlene sighed. "I don't know." She chewed on a fingernail. "Once they check our shoes against those footprints and they don't match, that'll be the end of it." She looked up. "Won't it?"

"Oh, for crying out loud. You *know* better than that. They can't get a warrant on a whim. They had a reason."

Shirlene blinked worried eyes. "Like what?"

"Like they have a witness who saw someone who looked like Lauri sneaking around Clay's place last night."

"What? Lauri!" Shirlene called toward the stairs.

A shuffle, then a thump upstairs.

"What is it?" Lauri called from the top of the stairs.

"Get down here. I want to talk to you."

Lauri picked her way down the steps. Barefoot, she'd changed into a short skirt and sleeveless top in periwinkle blue. She acknowledged Merry's presence with a wave of her hand.

"What *is* it, Mom?"

"Get over here and sit down."

She wrinkled her brow, but did as her mother told her.

"Did you go over to Clay's last night?"

She frowned. "Why would I do that?"

"Good question. Did you?"

She shrugged in response.

"Lauri."

"Stop yelling at me!" she said. "I've been through a lot, you know. You don't have to be so mean!"

"I know," Merry said. "It's been one rough day for you already. And I'm sorry to have to—"

"I want an answer," Shirlene interrupted. "Were you there last night?"

Lauri's eyes darted to the side, and she bit her lip. "Yeah! Okay? I went by his place."

Merry broke in. "Did you drive by? Or walk by?"

Lauri wouldn't look at her. "Does it matter?"

"Someone *saw* you," Shirlene said, leaning in. "The police know you were there. Now, tell me …" she swallowed, "… tell me why you went."

Her head jerked up. "Someone saw me?" Fear flickered behind her eyes.

"Lauri," Merry urged.

44

"Well, I just went by—walked by—" She looked between the two women. "—to see what Clay was up to. I didn't want him to hear my car. I wanted to look in the window to see if he was alone, is all."

Shirlene sank back in her chair, pale. "Oh my God, Lauri. Those shoes they took. They were your footprints, weren't they?"

"What footprints?" She looked blank.

"They found footprints outside his bedroom window. That's why they took the shoes. I thought they were barking up the wrong tree, but they weren't, were they? You actually left those prints."

"Is that why they cleared out my closet?"

Shirlene's listened to her daughter with narrowed eyes. "What about the footprints?"

"Well, I guess they might be mine. But I didn't *kill* him, Mom." She looked at Merry. Nervous. Pleading. "I mean, come on. I didn't even go inside 'til this morning. I looked in the front window, and tried to see into Clay's room, but it was dark. I thought I saw him sleeping in there. I'll just tell the police why the footprints are there. They'll yell at me for being a Peeping Tom, is all."

Shirlene gaped at her daughter.

Merry sat on the arm of the sofa and put her hand on her cousin's shoulder. She could feel her trembling. "This is serious, Lauri. Look at me."

Lauri raised her face and met her gaze.

"Are you telling us the truth?"

Lauri nodded vigorously.

"The whole truth?"

"Yes!"

Merry dipped her chin. It had been years since she'd seen the girl—woman now, despite her sometimes flippant behavior—but she believed her.

Had to help her. No one else would.

"What shoes were you wearing last night?" she asked.

"I don't remember." Lauri got up, shot Merry an enigmatic look, and traipsed out the back door. A moment later she was back, a pair of strappy white sandals in her hand.

"What?" Lauri asked in response to their stares. "You didn't think I'd let them take my favorite pair of sandals, did you? I dropped them out my bedroom window." Shaking her head, she ran up the stairs.

Shirlene turned to Merry. "Oh, my God."

Merry got up and leaned against the arm of the recliner, put her arm around her aunt. "It'll be okay." But even as she said it, the clenched fist in her chest gave another squeeze.

"No. No, it won't be okay." Shirlene jerked her head back and forth. "I know she didn't kill anybody. I know it. But they won't believe…" Her voice broke. "Oh, my God. What am I going to *do*?"

"First of all, you're going to face what's going on and stop hoping it just goes away. Then, you're going to call a lawyer."

"Who?"

Merry sighed. "Do you know Kate O'Neil?"

FIVE

MERRY SAT A HALF block down from the Hazel Police Station in the Blazer. The air conditioning had stopped working long ago, and Mama had kept putting off getting it fixed. Then the cancer started gnawing on her insides and such mundane chores fell by the wayside. The interior temperature had risen five degrees in the half hour Merry had been waiting for Jamie. He'd gone out to his Jeep once and returned to the station. She had no idea when he might get off work, but she'd follow him to a call if she had to.

Twenty minutes later, at four o'clock, he came out again and this time got into his Wrangler and started it up. She followed him three blocks down Main. He pulled in next to the curb, and she parked three spaces behind him. He got out and went into Harlan's Hardware, Garden, and Feed.

Bright shards of late afternoon sunlight reflected off a car window, blinding her for a moment as she walked up the sidewalk. She went through the propped-open door into the relative gloom of the store, pausing so her eyes could adjust. Short aisles of shelves held a mixed lot of tools and hardware, painting supplies, and electrical and plumbing accessories. Straight ahead, on the wall behind the counter, locked cases enclosed an assortment of guns, most of them rifles. The air smelled of dust and machine oil. A smooth-faced youth gave her one desultory look from under the bill of his John Deere cap and went back to the comic book spread beside the register.

Daylight streamed in through an open door at the back. It led to a covered loading dock where she knew she'd find tack and sacks of feed. In the lot beyond that, piles of gravel, sand, topsoil, and bark mulch could be purchased by the yard. Rolls of fencing, posts, and a collection of gates crowded into that area as well. Harlan had a little of everything but not much selection of anything.

Eyes adjusted to the dim light, Merry located Jamie looking at packets of fishing hooks hanging with the fly-tying paraphernalia along the wall by the front window.

"I just keep running into you, Gutierrez. Arrested any little old ladies yet today?"

"No, but there's still some daylight left." His tone was acerbic. "You followed me."

"Wow. You really are a cop." More sarcasm than she'd intended leaked out around the words.

He opened his mouth, then closed it. He looked at his feet, then up at Merry, his expressive face suddenly wretched. "I wish all this stuff wasn't going on with your cousin, so soon after you got home."

Well, that really made her feel like a bitch. "It's not your doing." He was a cop, sure, but more importantly he was *Jamie*.

"I know. I just ... what are you doing tomorrow?"

"Shirlene wants me to be there when she meets with Lauri's attorney first thing in the morning."

"She got one? Good for her. Who?"

She looked at him. "A Ms. O'Neil."

"Oh. God. Well, there aren't that many choices around here. And she's good."

Naturally. "Why didn't you tell me she came back and set up in town?"

"Didn't seem … relevant."

She sighed. "No. Don't suppose it was."

Merry couldn't bear the way he looked at her, like he wanted to bundle her up and feed her chicken soup from a spoon. She tore her gaze away, shifting attention to a barred Plymouth Rock cape, traditionally used for grizzly hackle by those who tied their own flies, hanging from the edge of a shelf. Her fingertips traced the half-plucked feathers, skimming over the gaps that exposed the withered bare skin beneath.

When she looked back, her friend had turned toward the street. She followed his gaze, wondering what infraction had caught his eye.

It wasn't an infraction at all, unless you counted the length of her skirt, which probably should have been illegal. She wore it well, along with the straight blue-black hair that fell to her waist, the vermilion mouth, and the impossibly high-heeled sandals. A woman of extremes.

"Your wife know you still wander around town leering at sexy young things?"

"Leering? I'm just looking. Which is still allowed, as far as I know. In fact, it's kind of a requirement when she walks by."

The woman turned a corner and Jamie's focus returned to Merry. "That's Anna Knight. Hangs out with Clay Lamente's roommate. Lives with his girlfriend."

"Barbie Barnes?"

"Yeah. There's something hinky about Anna."

"Like what?" He'd said Lauri acted "hinky," too.

"Just a feeling."

"So, who's Clay's roommate, the one she hangs out with?"

"Name's Denny Teller."

"Did they get along?"

"Him and Clay? As far as we've been able to find out. Merry, what are you doing? This whole thing will only mean trouble for you. Stay clear."

"I wish I could. I really do, but I can't. In one day you've all decided Lauri killed Clay—is anyone looking for who really killed him?"

"She admitted to knowing where they kept the key and entering without either Clay or Denny's knowledge. She just happened to find the body, despite the fact that they hadn't dated for over a year. Someone saw her outside the house the night he was shot. If any of her shoes match the footprints outside his window…"

"So he was definitely shot."

Jamie sighed.

"What about the girlfriend?" Merry asked. "Barbie."

"She has an alibi."

Merry made a get-on-with-it gesture. "And?"

Jamie looked over her shoulder and lifted his chin in greeting. "Harlan."

She turned to see Harlan Kepper approaching. In six years he'd aged fifteen. Though it was late afternoon, he appeared hungover: red-rimmed eyes squinting against the daylight streaming in; a couple days' worth of white stubble on his dry, sallow cheeks, and hair that might have been combed with a piece of buttered toast.

"Jamie," he said. "Good to see you're back, Merry."

She nodded at him. "Thanks. It's good to be back."

"Can I help you folks find anything?"

"Nah," Jamie said. "Stopped in for some size eleven hooks, but I just remembered where I have another pack. I'll see you later."

He sketched a wave and walked out to his Wrangler. Merry stared after him.

"How 'bout you? Gonna let me sell you something?" Harlan's face was transformed by a sweet smile, and she felt herself returning it.

Then his expression became sorrowful. "Awful thing about your mom."

"You two ran around a bit back in the day, didn't you? Before my dad came along."

Harlan looked uncomfortable. His eyebrows drew together. "She was a special lady."

Merry felt her own smile begin to slide. "Hey, Harlan—do you know the Lamente kid?"

"The one who got shot?" News in Hazel apparently moved as fast as she remembered. His eyes narrowed and he looked like he wanted to spit. "Shit. Yeah, I knew him. Little cocksucker."

She raised her eyebrows in surprise.

He shook his head. "Never mind. Don't want to speak ill of the dead."

"You have a run-in with him?"

"Let's just say, as of this morning, he's whole lot more likeable."

And though she tried, she couldn't get the old man to say another word on the subject.

———

Merry gratefully headed back to the ranch. Funny how it had come to represent the ultimate comfort in a mere four days.

Between the late breakfast Shirlene's desperate phone call had preempted and the tuna melt she hadn't eaten at the Moose, she was more than ready for dinner. She consulted her mental list of freedom food, then checked the contents of the refrigerator. A fried egg sandwich would fit both criteria. White bread, one side smothered with mayonnaise, the other with catsup. Sliced dill pickles laid on top of the catsup, sliced cheddar cheese on the mayonnaise. Two eggs swirled together in the pan, not exactly scrambled, but cooked through and laid hot on the cheddar. Put the whole thing together and wash it down with a glass of cold milk.

Ambrosia.

She made a fresh pot of coffee, poured a steaming cup, and went outside. As she sipped, the pungent taste mingled with memories of bacon-and-egg breakfasts eaten out on the porch on summer mornings. She stepped into the yard. Around back of the house, a quarter-acre vegetable garden reached south, a six-foot wire deer fence encircling the barren ribs of dark brown earth. One corner held a patch of garlic and onions growing up through the winter mulch Mama had spread over them last fall. The bare earth emphasized her mother's absence: by this late in June the space should have been crowded with sprawling squash plants, neat tomato cages, rows and rows of cabbages and carrots, beans and greens, radishes nearly spent, and peppers just setting their compact white blooms.

A rose garden, also surrounded by deer fencing, snugged alongside the vegetable patch. The dirt strips on either side of the back steps where Mama had always planted the old-fashioned annuals—marigolds, geraniums, petunias—lay empty except for the tall, self-sown hollyhocks leaning their dark pink heads against the hip-high stones of the foundation and the white boards above. The drowsy sound of bees working among the flowers grew louder as she circled back toward the outbuildings.

Merry hated the old K5 Blazer, always had. But there was an alternative.

Dust coated the shiny paint of Daddy's 1956 Chevy stepside, hazing the teal to bluish gray in the unlit interior of the wooden garage. Trellises and a wheelbarrow leaned against the passenger door. Moving the garden implements aside, she popped the hood. The battery was still connected. Corrosion bloomed white and grainy around the terminals.

Mama had taught her what to do about that when Merry was only fifteen. In the house she opened a can of Coke, sipping it as she walked back to the truck. She poured the Coke over the battery, where it frothed and bubbled like a science experiment. When she rinsed the foam away with clear water, the corrosion had vanished.

On her way home she had filled two containers with gas and picked up some starter fluid. Now when she thumped on the gas tank and received a hollow response, she leaned hard on one side of the truck bed, listening for the sloshing sound of liquid as the vehicle rocked. The gas tank was empty or near enough that she wouldn't have to drain it before putting in the fresh gas.

The rattle of metal and the sound of an engine on the ranch road announced a visitor. She came out of the garage, wiping her hands on an old rag. Parked in front of the house, dust still swirling behind it, was an F350 king cab pickup with a dingy white two-horse trailer hooked on behind. The driver's door opened and disgorged Frank Cain. Of medium height and with a slight paunch, he wore jeans, a blue western-cut chambray shirt, and beat-up cowboy boots. His sweat-stained Resistol sat atop a head of hair more salt than pepper.

The lined face split into a lopsided grin as he approached her. They exchanged greetings, and Merry led the way inside to the kitchen and the coffeepot.

Steaming cup in hand, Frank stood at the kitchen sink and indicated the horse trailer in the drive. "I brought Izzy."

"I was going to call you, find out what I owe you."

"Don't owe me nothin'."

"Now, don't be like that. You've been boarding her for over six months. That's not cheap."

"It's not expensive, either. And the kids loved having her around. They've been riding her every day, almost, so she's in pretty good shape."

"You should charge me exercise fees, then."

"Your Mama would've kept her in shape for you. It was the least I could do."

If she kept pushing, she'd offend him. "Well, that's awful nice of you. Let's go see how the old girl's doing." The words required effort. She didn't want to owe anyone, and at the same time she didn't want anyone depending on her. Not even a horse.

A smile creased Frank's face, and he put his empty cup in the sink.

Outside, he opened the gate on the horse trailer and attached the ramp. Composed and deliberate, Izzy backed down the incline. Her nostrils flared to receive the scents that had meant home for most of her nineteen years.

A chestnut mare with a white star on her forehead and three white socks, she was well muscled from her recent stay at the Cains'. Glossy highlights along her sixteen-hand shoulder and down her flank gleamed in the sunshine. Whether she smelled or saw her first, Merry couldn't tell, but Izzy snorted and shifted toward her. Frank let her begin moving, then used her own momentum to turn her toward the fenced area along the east side of the barn, two finger-tips hooked under the chin strap of her halter. The big horse followed, looking back over her shoulder at Merry.

"I'm coming, baby," she murmured.

Inside the paddock, she closed the gate and moved to take the lead rope from Frank. She unbuckled the halter and slid it down the mare's nose. Free of any encumbrance, Izzy stretched her neck and shook her head, then turned to face Merry. Planting her nose on Merry's chest, she pushed against her. Merry instinctively leaned into her. The mare let out a soft snuffling whuffle and blinked slowly. The old ritual flowed over her and, without thinking, she reached up with both hands and began to scratch Izzy's face, beginning at the ears and working her way down to the tender nose. The mare's eyelids drooped to half-mast, and she sighed. Merry grinned wide and looked over at Frank, who smiled with his eyes and headed back out to the trailer.

He lugged a bale of alfalfa hay into the barn. Merry left Izzy in her paddock and followed him. "Hell, Frank, you don't need to do that."

"I got one more to bring in. Then you're on your own."

Shaking her head, she pushed the bale he'd dropped into the corner of an empty stall. He returned, dumped the second bale on top of the first, and turned to her.

"I got to tell you something."

She started to bite her lip but stopped herself. Nodded once instead. "All right."

He looked out through the open door to the yellowing grassland running up to the foothills. "I hate to do this when you just got back and all, but I wanted to give you as much warning as I could."

She latched the stall door and leaned against it, waiting.

"I don't think I'll be able to keep leasing from you next year."

She took a careful breath. "I see."

"I got a good deal on those six sections that run along the north side of my property."

Six sections. 3,840 acres. A few more acres than he currently leased from the McCoy ranch.

"That's good grazing up there," she said.

He nodded.

"I appreciate you telling me."

"I'm sorry. I know the timing's bad."

Bad didn't begin to describe it. Those leases were what had enabled her mother to keep the ranch solvent. To keep the ranch, period. When Daddy had died, Mama had the good sense not to try to work the place by herself and offered to lease the land to their neighbor who wanted to expand his herd of Angus cattle. It had worked out well for everyone for years.

Merry nodded and clapped him on the shoulder. "I'll figure something out."

Frank left, the empty trailer bumping and rattling along the gravel road behind his truck. Merry swept out Izzy's stall before spreading old but clean straw in it. She considered going for a ride but decided the day was getting away from her. Let the mare settle in a bit. She'd try to fit in a ride before the meeting with Kate O'Neil the next morning.

Yvette Trager's instructions to get a job had just taken on a whole new urgency. The drugstore had displayed a Help Wanted sign in the window this morning. Couldn't hurt to try.

Izzy watched with interest as she stuffed a flake of hay into the rack on the wall and filled a water bucket, stepping close and nuzzling Merry in hopes of getting another good face scritchin'. Merry indulged her once and finished setting up her quarters. When she was done, she stood watching Izzy eat, listening to the loud, scissorlike grinding of hay between her teeth and breathing in the distinct scent of horse: musk, sweat, and honey.

"Welcome home, baby."

———

Merry brought jumper cables from the shop and parked the Blazer outside the garage. The trick was gaining access, since Lotta—so named because she took a lotta money and a lotta work to fix up—was nosed into tight quarters. The smells of old dust and motor oil tickled her nose as she pushed into the hot, dingy interior of the garage. She cleared a mass of sticky cobwebs from around the old truck, rolling their white gossamer off her palms and letting it drop to the dirt floor. Wedging herself between the wall and the rounded front bumper, she leaned her back against the grille. She grunted with effort. The vehicle slowly began to roll out into the yard.

A voice close at hand startled her, and she stood up, losing a foot of ground she had just gained. She picked her way around to the back of the truck and found the speaker peering around the other side.

"Hello?" he said again in a tentative voice.

He swiveled and saw Merry watching him. A few dozen long hairs sprouted above the man's left ear, arranged in elaborate denial above a childish face, pasty white and soft as newly risen bread dough.

"Hi there, hi there. My name's T. J. Spalding. You must be Merry Green."

He reached out and she reluctantly shook his hand.

"Merry McCoy," she said. "Randall Green is my ex-husband."

"Just so, just so. Well, I'm sure your mother told you all about me."

A breeze caught the man's hair, lifted it whole, as if it were a cap attached to his scalp by a hinge, and laid it back down again. Merry studied him, trying to tamp down her instant dislike for T. J. Spalding.

"Nope. What would she have told me about you?"

"Why, I'm the one handling the sale of this ranch. Yep, yep, she was pretty happy to be rid of the place."

A few beats while that hung in the air.

"Excuse me?"

"Well, hell yes. I'm the one taking care of the whole transaction, kit and caboodle." He shoved a business card at Merry.

"My mother wasn't selling this ranch."

"Sure she was, you betcha you bet." He lowered his voice. "The deal's almost done."

Crossing her arms, she leaned against the tailgate of the truck and considered him. "Is that so? And who, exactly, is under the impression that they're buying my land?"

The real estate man shuffled his feet, hesitated. He spoke through the grin frozen on his face. "Well now, my client—" He waggled his eyebrows. "—prefers to remain anonymous. Doesn't want to bring a lot of attention to himself."

His theatrics ground against her already raw nerves. "Mister, you are so full of shit."

"I beg your pardon?"

"Mama never would have sold this ranch."

"Well, she must not have told you about it, I guess. That's a shame, it really is. Hard to find out when you come back after … being gone for so long and all. But trust me, you don't want this big ol' patch of land. Too much trouble to take care of, hasn't been a working ranch for well over a decade. And I'm getting you a great deal." He named a figure.

Merry stared at him. "You're kidding."

"Nope. That's what they'll pay. You'll be able to live the life of Riley."

"I mean you have to be kidding to think I'd ever sell this land. Thanks for stopping by, but don't let's do this again."

Patches of red mottled the pale sponge of the realtor's face. His jowls quivered.

"Your mother gave her word!"

Red fury swept up her neck and through each follicle on her scalp, hovering on the verge of explosion. With effort, she clenched trembling fingers into fists at her side.

"Get off my land."

Spalding backed toward the shiny silver Cadillac parked in the drive. Merry paced him, step for step. He jumped in the car, started it with a roar. Running over a corner of the lawn, he left behind a cloud of dust as he raced away from the ranch.

An hour after Frank Cain tells her he got a great deal on prime grazing land adjoining his own, this real estate guy shows up with a mysterious buyer for the McCoy ranch. Mama hadn't known about Frank buying the land along his north property line—she'd have at least mentioned it in one of their monthly phone calls—so she'd have no reason to sell the land that had been in her family for four generations.

What the hell was going on?

SIX

WITH SWEAT AND THE luck of a slight incline away from the building, Merry finished pushing Lotta out of the garage. She fed gas into the tank, hooked up the jumper cables, sprayed starter fluid into the carburetor, and fired up the Blazer. The older Chevy's big engine tried a few times, then caught. She left the two vehicles running, still connected by the snaking umbilical cord, and went inside to do her dinner dishes.

Jamie had hightailed it out of the hardware store, but if he thought she wouldn't hunt him down to find out more, he was dead wrong. She glanced at the clock. Once she was sure they'd be done with dinner, she'd call.

Lauri couldn't have killed Clay. She might be a kooky, narcissistic little brat who tended to view the world in direct relation to her own version of how things ought to be, but she wasn't a murderer. She'd been genuinely upset about finding Clay. Okay, she'd recovered pretty quickly from the experience. People who didn't know her could see that as suspicious, but Merry saw it as evidence that Lauri had quickly come to see Clay's death as being all about her.

That was just how Lauri worked.

Was she pregnant with his child? For that matter, was she pregnant at all? If he was the daddy, then they'd been seeing each other again. For how long? Jamie had run from Merry's questions about the girlfriend like a scared bunny. Lauri wouldn't have a reason to kill the father of her baby, whereas any girlfriend would be spitting mad about her boyfriend knocking up an old flame.

Find out what her alibi is.

Wiping her hands on the dishtowel, she went back outside, disconnected the jumper cables, and left Lotta running in the yard. The Chevy coughed. Merry ran her finger through the thick dust on the hood, remembering the new carwash on the north side of town.

With an old rag, she wiped the interior of the old truck free of the little dust that had sneaked around the windows, and drove it over to the shop. Fluorescent bars overhead illuminated an assortment of well-organized tools and a small, ancient blue tractor at one end of the mostly empty space. Replacing the jumper cables in the cubbyhole on the wall where she'd found them, she peered around and located the air compressor. She filled the one very low tire on the old truck and topped off the rest. Every movement, every tiny clank, echoed off the walls.

Her driver's license had expired the year before, so any trip to town courted disaster. Driving without a valid license could get her parole revoked. But the dust nagged at her. At least that was what she told herself. The truth was, she loved driving and had missed it, and loved driving the old stepside in particular.

Back in the house, she stuffed some cash in her pocket and headed back out the door. Hoping the gas would last to town, she babied the elderly Chevy down the gravel road to the highway.

Lotta ran pretty smooth once she opened her up. At the Chevron station Merry filled her tank, indulged in a Brushless! wash, and checked her tires again.

What about the roommate, Denny Teller? Had he and Clay had problems?

Find out.

And the woman with the long black hair and impossible heels? What about her?

Find out.

Harlan had acted like Clay himself was an axe murderer when Merry had brought his name up at the hardware store. What was that all about?

Ask Shirlene about Harlan.

Tomorrow was going to be a very busy day for an unemployed ex-con who just wanted to sit on her porch and work her way through a list of foods she'd been forbidden to eat for four years.

———

She got back to the ranch around eight and called Jamie at home. His wife, Gayle, answered.

"Is Jamie there?"

"Um, yeah, hang on." A pause. Then in a slightly different tone, "May I ask who's calling?"

"Tell him it's Merry."

"Merry. I see." The voice turned frosty. "Hang on."

Through the window she watched Izzy roll on her back, then stand up and shake off a cloud of dust.

"Um, Merry?" Gayle again. "He can't come to the phone right now. May I take a message?"

He was avoiding her. It was one thing for him to take advantage of Harlan's arrival in the middle of their conversation that afternoon, but now he was actually avoiding her. She was unprepared for the empty feeling in her gut.

"No. No message. Thanks anyway."

Gayle hung up.

Merry stood with the phone still pressed to her ear for a few moments until it occurred to her to replace the receiver.

———

"Do you have any retail experience?" the owner of Rexall Drugs asked as Merry leaned against the counter and filled out the application the next morning.

"I worked for a used bookstore while I was in college," she said.

"Oh. Well, this would be a little different than that, but it's not hard to pick up. You've got a degree?" The words had a Minnesota rhythm. He seemed impressed with her college experience.

She chose to view that as a good omen. "A B.A. in English Lit."

He smiled and took her completed application. "We haven't had much luck finding the perfect fit for this job. When would you be available?"

Jobs in Hazel were scarce and plenty of people were willing to work. What kind of "perfect fit" was he looking for?

"I could start in two weeks," she said. She wanted this thing with Lauri figured out before she started a full-time job.

He frowned but didn't respond as he scanned the form. She watched his eyes travel down the page, then snag where she knew they would. He looked up.

"You're a convicted felon?"

She tried to swallow, but her mouth had lost all moisture. "Yes."

"What did you do?" he asked.

Her lips parted in surprise. "What?"

"Oh, I don't get to ask that?" Sarcasm replaced friendliness. "You come in here looking for a job and expect me to leave you around the drugs in the pharmacy and in charge of a bunch of money, but I don't get to ask why you're a felon?"

Her neck grew hot, and then her cheeks. She should have lied on the application. But someone would have spilled the beans sometime. This guy wasn't going to give her a job now, no matter what she said.

So she turned around and walked away.

"Hey!" he called.

The ding-dong of the door opening drowned out whatever he said next.

———

"I'm glad you made it in time to catch Kate before she leaves," Shirlene said as she opened her front door.

Her brows drew together when she saw Merry's expression. Merry had half-hoped that renewing her driver's license and applying for the job at the Rexall would take so much time that she'd miss Kate altogether.

No such luck.

The house smelled like stale cigarette smoke had burrowed its way into every square inch of paint, every twist of carpet, every fiber of the upholstery. She followed Shirlene into the kitchen. Kate sat at the butcher-block table, tapping a pile of papers on edge to even the corners before sliding them into her open briefcase. Across the table sat an open pack of Camels, a green Bic lighter, and the usual amber ashtray half full of crushed butts. The back door was open, and a fan whirred on the counter.

Kate had plaited her luxuriant black hair into a thick braid that hung over one shoulder. She wore jeans and a dark peach silk blouse with the sleeves rolled up. The color glowed against her tan forearms. Her ski-jump nose sat between wide, high cheekbones, and when she looked up, her eyes were dark brown under long lashes.

Shirlene held out a cup of coffee.

With horror Merry realized her hands were shaking. "No. Thanks anyway, Shirlene."

Her aunt's eyes narrowed a fraction as she poured the coffee back into the pot on the counter.

"Merry." Kate stood up. "You're looking well."

"You, too." She cleared her throat. "You haven't changed a bit."

Kate didn't smile. "Oh, but I have."

Merry hesitated. "I guess we both have."

Their eyes locked for a long moment. Shirlene watched them both over the flame of the Bic as she lit a cigarette.

"So," Merry said, easing into a chair. "How do things look?"

Kate sat back down. A wedding ring glinted on her left hand. She must have kept her own name, at least for her practice. And Merry would bet her husband was a better catch than Rand had been. By a long shot.

"Well, it could be worse. From what Shirlene tells me, the main problem is they may match the footprints they found outside the house with some of Lauri's footwear."

Not if she was wearing those silly sandals. "And someone saw her there that night," Merry said.

"And someone saw her there that night. Still, not enough for an arrest warrant."

"She found the body."

Shirlene looked as if Merry had turned on her.

"I'm just playing the devil's advocate," she said.

"We need that," Kate said. "Anything else they might throw at us?"

"Where's Lauri?" Merry asked. "She knows a whole lot more about what's going on than I do."

"She supposed to be here." Worry sapped some of the anger from Shirlene's tone. "I don't know where she's got to."

A wave of anger at her clueless cousin threatened to swamp Merry's good intentions. What was she thinking, dealing with people and authority she didn't want to have anything to do with in order to help someone who didn't even know she needed help? She should get up and walk out. Why bother with this bullshit?

She sighed. Precisely because Lauri didn't know she needed help. Rory Hawkins could—and probably would—railroad her into a conviction unless someone stood up and prevented it. Convicting Lauri was the easiest way for him to snap the file shut on the case. The path of least resistance. And Hawkins was the sort to take the path of least resistance.

She looked up to find both Kate and Shirlene watching her.

"Anything else you think might be relevant?" Kate asked.

Merry glanced sideways at Shirlene. "Have you told her about the baby?"

Shirlene rubbed at a spot on the tabletop and shook her head.

Kate looked displeased. "Baby?"

"Lauri's pregnant. Or at least she says she is," Merry said. "She won't say whose it is. She and Clay broke up a while back—how long, Shirlene?"

"A year, at least."

"But the fact that she was over there at all suggests Clay was the father."

"Well, shit." Kate sat back. "Shirlene, I wish you'd told me this."

Shirlene looked uncomfortable. "She could be seeing someone else entirely."

Merry wanted to shake her. One look at Kate confirmed she had the same inclination.

"Clay had a girlfriend, you know. She's a nice girl, too," Shirlene said.

"You know her?"

"Oh, sure. Barbie Barnes. We've done some volunteer work together."

"At the Quikcare?" Merry asked.

"Yeah, plus for WorldMed, which runs out of there."

Kate nodded. "I've heard of it. You guys do good work. And I know who Barbie is. She's involved with WorldMed, too?"

"Pretty much everyone at the clinic is."

Merry rested her chin on her hand. "What would she do if she found out Clay was cheating on her?"

"Oh," Shirlene said, her eyes widening. "You don't think..."

"Someone killed him. The police aren't looking at anyone but Lauri."

"I can't believe Barbie would shoot anyone," Shirlene said. "She's too level-headed. Even if Clay really hurt her, she'd never do anything like that."

Kate didn't look convinced.

———

Merry paused in the doorway of the Hungry Moose. Janelle was behind the counter filling salt shakers. A few customers lingered over their coffee, but the lunchtime rush was over.

After Kate had left, Merry asked Shirlene where she thought Lauri had gone.

Shirlene had shrugged. "She called in to work and told her boss she couldn't make it."

"Then where? A friend's?"

"She doesn't have that many friends. Except ..."

"Who? She's in a lot of trouble. I need to talk to her."

"Janelle."

"Payson? Over at the Moose?"

Shirlene had nodded.

Now Janelle looked up. "Hey, Merry."

"Hey. Seen Lauri?"

"She just left."

"You know where she was going?"

Janelle nodded out the window toward the drugstore. "Said she needed to pick up some eyeliner."

No way was Merry going back in there today. But sure enough, her cousin's car was parked around the corner from the drugstore. Merry walked up the sidewalk, glanced around to see if anyone was looking, and tried the passenger door of the little beige Honda. It was unlocked. She slid in.

Dozens of bright yellow Juicy Fruit wrappers littered the floor and back seat. Lumps of foil wrapped around huge wads of chewed gum were wedged in the ashtray and filled the cup holder. She rolled down the window to let out some of the thick, sweet air.

Ten minutes later, Lauri turned the corner. She raised her head, saw her cousin sitting in her car, and paused. Merry smiled and waved. Lauri heaved a big sigh. She trudged over, opened the driver's door, and got in, tossing a small paper bag into the back seat.

"What are you doing in my car?"

"Your lawyer was just over at the house. Think maybe you ought to meet her?"

"Oh, God! Why can't everyone just leave me alone?"

Merry gritted her teeth. "Listen—this is a big deal. You better hurry up and figure that out."

Lauri glared at her even as her eyes filled with tears.

Merry tried to imagine the girl in prison. She wasn't good at making friends, and inside you needed friends. As many as you could get. Merry had bunked her first three years with Vonda Dubuque, a tall black woman with a quick smile, Cajun accent, street smarts, and a genius IQ. She'd also been slightly insane, a fanatical animal rights activist who had been caught with four others trying to blow up a beef processing plant full of workers.

But Merry had worked with it, downplaying her family's cattle ranching background and finding common ground in books and music. She knew she was extraordinarily lucky. If she'd had to bunk with Tally White or "Snickers" Montrose, those three years would have been pure hell. A few months into her fourth year, Vonda had been transferred, and Merry got a new cellmate.

The new girl hadn't been a threat, but she had been one hell of a drain. A recovering addict, she'd moaned and wailed her way through both waking and sleeping hours, nightmares taking over after each complaint-filled day. But by then Merry had carved herself a place of respect, if not admiration, with the other women. And she'd known she'd be eligible for parole in a matter of months.

Even with Vonda as a bunkmate, it hadn't been a cakewalk.

Any privacy was imaginary. Merry tried to see her cousin being rousted from her hard, narrow mattress at six every morning, showering with three dozen other women—women brittle from abuse, bewildered from addiction, and often with a hate-on at the world that Merry had understood even as she did her best to deflect it away from herself—and then off to breakfast and the rest of the day.

Jaw set, Lauri stared straight ahead as Merry struggled for the words to convey the enormity of what could be waiting for her if she were actually convicted of Clay's death.

"I've been in prison, Lauri."

"No kidding."

"Not something I'd recommend. The food's bad. Every minute of every day is scheduled."

"Sounds like home," she grumped.

Merry gripped her shoulder and turned her so they were facing each other. "The guards would come into our cells. We didn't have much—mostly children's drawings and family photos, some books and magazines, a few other things. But they'd search our stuff any-time they felt like it. And they felt like it a lot. Whenever some-thing caught their attention, they'd just take it."

Her cousin tried to twist away, but she didn't let go. "Mama's pecan double fudge brownies were a big hit. She sent me a batch every single month until she died, but I haven't tasted one for three years." Merry's voice cracked, but she cleared her throat and went on. "You have few privileges, hard earned. You never know what the guards are going to do, but you can be sure they don't like the pris-oners on simple principle. They watch everything you do. *Every-thing.* You can't even pee in private."

Lauri blinked.

"If it's not the prison authorities, there are always the other prisoners to make life difficult." An unspoken protocol existed within the hierarchy that naturally developed among the inmates. "You're never alone. You're always afraid."

They'd break her in less than a week. Some women emerged from prison stronger, but Lauri wouldn't be one of them. She'd be unrecognizable. It would break Shirlene's heart.

Lauri jerked her shoulder away. "Stop trying to scare me! I'm not like you. I'm not going to jail. I didn't *do* anything."

"Neither did I."

"Sure you did. You killed a guy, didn't you?"

Merry licked her lips. "You know I didn't have a choice."

"Fine. Whatever. But I didn't kill Clay *at all.* I loved him, and now he's dead." Her throat worked and her next words came out a whisper. "I didn't kill him."

"Lauri—"

She sniffed hard and blinked back tears. "I've got stuff to do." She crossed her arms over her chest.

"But—"

"A lot of stuff to do."

Hell. Let her rot, the little brat. Merry opened the door and got out. She started to slam it shut, but stopped herself. Took a deep breath. Leaned back into the car.

"Let me know if you want to talk, okay?"

"Yeah, okay." Lauri waved her away.

This time Merry did slam the door.

———

Merry's first trip to the grocery store had been for staples: bread, milk, butter, eggs, and the like. Now it was time for a more thorough shopping expedition. She was halfway to the local IGA supermarket when the police prowler pulled out from a side street and the blue and red lights began flashing.

She pulled over, thinking it might be Jamie.

It wasn't.

Rory Hawkins heaved his bulk out of the driver's seat. As he approached her open window, she switched off the ignition and placed her hands on the steering wheel at two and ten so they'd be visible.

Hawkins leaned his elbow on the doorframe and the smell of onions filled the cab. "Now, what do we have here?"

In her rearview mirror, she saw Lester Fleck get out of the patrol car and lean against it, watching them.

"What can I do for you, sergeant?" She kept her tone light, despite his hard stare.

"License and registration. For starters."

She reached for her wallet on the seat beside her and saw his hand move toward his hip in her peripheral vision. She extracted the license and handed it to him.

"The registration's in the glove box." Moving with slow care, she opened the box and took out an envelope, silently grateful for her mother's foresight in signing the vehicle over to her before she died.

He examined the documentation. "Just got this, I see." He looked up from her license. "But what were you using when you drove to the station to bust my chops yesterday? Wouldn't have been driving on an expired driver's license, would you? Not a law-abiding girl like you."

She knew she didn't have to answer that. "Why did you pull me over?"

"You wouldn't be carrying any contraband, would you?"

"Of course not."

"No drugs? We've been having some problems with that in town, and I mighta got a tip that I'd find some in this very vehicle."

A thread of fear wended its way up her spine. She took a gamble.

"Officer Fleck," she called.

Lester pushed himself off the car behind her and ambled toward them. He nodded to her over Hawkins's shoulder. "Ms. McCoy."

"Your sergeant here says he 'mighta got a tip' that I have contraband in here. You know anything about that?"

Lester glanced at Hawkins. Chewed the inside of his cheek. "Can't say that I do."

She looked at Hawkins and raised her eyebrows. "Now what?"

If he insisted on searching the Chevy, she couldn't very well stop him. Did he have this planned, have something illegal already stashed up his sleeve to "find"? Would Lester stand by and let him do it?

After a long moment, Hawkins looked away. He shoved the paperwork in his hand toward her. "Watch your step."

He turned and walked back to his patrol car. Lester hesitated, then followed him.

She waited until they had driven past her before she let out an explosive breath and started the engine.

SEVEN

AMONG THE NECESSITIES IN her cart, Merry tossed in a T-bone steak, a couple potatoes, a six-pack of Moose Drool ale, beef ribs, new peas still in the pod, a quart of fresh strawberries, a half-pint of whipping cream, and vanilla extract. At the last minute, she went back and added a ten-pound bag of carrots. Izzy deserved a treat, too.

Emerging from the IGA, she saw an old white RV at the edge of the parking lot, BLOOD MOBILE stenciled in red on the side. A green awning shaded five metal folding chairs. A corner of bright white fabric fluttered through the propped-open door.

And there in the shade sat Anna Knight, wearing a sky-blue nursing uniform and sipping one of the Cokes from the cooler beside her. The woman of extremes who had caught Jamie's eye the previous afternoon. Barbie Barnes's roommate. Today she wore her glossy dark hair piled up on the back of her head. Even from this distance, Merry could see dark-rimmed eyes and lipstick the color of Merlot. Anna caught her staring and smiled.

Merry loaded the groceries into Lotta, parked where two horse-chestnut trees cast a bit of shade, and headed toward the awning. A gaunt, gray man who looked like he didn't have any of the red stuff to spare leaned back in the folding chair on the end. Anna sipped her Coke and watched Merry's approach. Her coif glistened smooth and sleek, and her almond-shaped green eyes narrowed as her smile touched them. White teeth gleamed in a Cheshire grin against the tan of her face.

Merry stopped in front of her. "Hi."

Anna cocked her head to one side. "Hi. You want to give blood?" The nasal voice whined and twanged through the words, startling Merry.

"Um, sure. What do I need to do?"

"You haven't given blood before?"

"Not intentionally."

Anna giggled, high and staccato. "Fill this out, and then I'll hook you up inside," she said, handing Merry a clipboard and a pen.

She sat down and began filling out her name and address.

The thin man rose to his feet and spoke in a rich bass. "Watch her. She stuck me four times before she found a vein. Hurt like hell. You'd think they'd send somebody out in this thing who knows what they're doing." He turned and walked across the parking lot.

Great.

Reading the form, Merry realized she had to provide an awful lot of information. She sketchily answered questions about travel, sexual history, and medications, skipped the rest, signed the release, and returned the clipboard. Anna drained her Coke while reviewing what Merry had written. She absently dropped the empty aluminum can onto the asphalt beside her chair with a metallic clank and made a notation.

"You don't know your type?" she asked without looking up.

"No."

"You want me to mail that information to you later?"

"Nah. I like a little mystery in my life."

Anna giggled again. Then the sound suddenly stopped, as if her amusement had run full tilt into a wall. She pointed to the clipboard.

"McCoy. Aren't you related to Lauri Danner?"

"She's my cousin."

She bit her lip, then rose and gestured Merry into the RV. Inside the cramped space, a recliner backed against one wall. A sheet, crisp and bleached, draped over the chair in folds hanging to the floor. On one side, a metal chair the color of putty faced a small stainless-steel table with a shelf below and wheels that allowed it to roll from one side of the recliner to the other. A small oscillating fan moved the hot air but failed to cool it.

"Seems kind of warm in here," Merry said.

Anna indicated she should sit in the recliner. "It's a freakin' oven in here, is what it is. I'm shutting down soon. I don't care what they say at the clinic. I'm about to pass out."

Great.

Perching on the edge of the metal chair, Anna gripped both of Merry's hands, pulling them toward her and examining the veins running up her arms. She nodded once and unwrapped a cellophane packet, removed a cotton swab presoaked in alcohol. Selecting the arm closest to her, she rubbed the alcohol onto the inside of the elbow while gazing at her watch.

"Idiots," she said. "This blood mobile is so stupid. Who wants to donate blood in the IGA parking lot, for God's sake? I sit here all day, and only two donors have come in. Most people only want to ask stupid questions."

"You're making me feel really good about doing this, you know."

"Oh God. I'm sorry. I get kind of carried away."

"How long are you going to rub that stuff on my arm?"

She looked back at her watch and bit her lower lip. Dark lipstick smeared across her teeth. "Five more seconds."

Moments later she tossed the swab in a wastebasket and struggled into a pair of thin disposable gloves from the box on the counter running along the wall behind her. Finally flexing her rubber-clad hands, she began dabbing a three-inch, purple-red circle of iodine on the inside of Merry's arm. Two drops ran down and dripped off her elbow and onto the white sheet.

Sweat beaded in tiny glistening dots on Anna's forehead. Merry felt a trickle herself, inching down her left side under her T-shirt. Anna unwrapped a needle and a coil of clear tubing attached to a thick plastic bag. She poked the needle at a vein. Merry clenched her teeth. Anna poked again. She managed to slide the needle in on the third try and taped it in place. Then she attached the tubing, almost dropping it once in the process, and twisted the cap to allow the transparent pipeline to fill with deep maroon.

"Sorry if I made you nervous. Just sit back and relax. It won't take long." She placed the slowly filling bag on the shelf under the table, a few inches above the floor.

Just like siphoning gas.

Merry watched her heart pump blood into the bag. "You didn't make me nervous," she lied.

"Good. Squeeze this." Anna handed her a rubber ball.

"So you know my cousin Lauri?"

Anna nodded. "She gave my roommate a hard time."

"Your roommate?"

"Another nurse at the clinic. Barbie."

"She the one whose boyfriend got shot?"

Anna gave her a speculative look. "Don't play dumb. Everyone's heard about it. And Barbie's having a real hard time."

Merry felt a little chastened. "It's got to be hard. I guess he and my cousin used to go out, too."

Anna snorted. "Yeah. Used to. Too bad she couldn't get that through her head."

"What do you mean?"

"Oh, I bet you know exactly what I mean. Practically stalking Clay, breaking into Barbie's house and vandalizing her stuff. She left my things alone—good thing, too, because I don't put up with that shit."

Merry said, "I just got back into town this week. I'm a bit behind on what's going on around here."

"Well, get this. Lauri pushes her way into Clay's house, asks him to marry her, and then throws a fit when he says he doesn't want to have anything to do with her! He had to throw her out. Thought he was going to have to call the cops."

Asked him to *marry* her? How many people had this story been through before making it to Anna Knight?

"I don't know what Barbie saw in him, anyway," the nurse said.

"Clay?"

She nodded. "He was such a stick in the mud. Didn't like to party, didn't even drink. Didn't like it when other people had fun, either. 'Anna,' he said one time, 'sometimes people *can* have too much fun.' 'Not this girl,' I told him. 'Stop being such a downer.'"

"What about your friend? What did Lauri do to her?"

Anna removed the needle and tube. "Hold this gauze here, and keep your arm straight up. No, all the way up, from the shoulder." She unrolled more gauze. "That Lauri's a real piece of work, you know? I mean, she's scary."

"Really?"

"She's your cousin. You ought to know."

Merry shrugged. "I never thought of her as scary." Bratty, yes.

"Well, you haven't been paying attention, then. After that visit to Clay, she breaks into our house ... well, I might have left the door unlocked, but that doesn't mean someone should just walk in. She poked a big hole in Barbie's waterbed. Flooded her bedroom and part of the living room. The carpet's still drying out."

Jesus. "How do you know it was Lauri?"

"Who else would do something like that? I mean, she didn't leave a note or anything, but Barbie's sure it was her."

So they were guessing. But Merry's stomach began to roil.

Anna pulled her arm down and removed the gauze. She fixed more folded gauze against her skin with iridescent lime-green tape. It crinkled like crepe paper, and, as she wound it in an elaborate figure eight around the elbow, it stuck to itself. She tore off the end and tucked it in, but it immediately flipped back out, and the tape began to slowly unwrap. Anna didn't seem to notice.

"And Clay told Barbie he'd spotted Lauri following him twice. Like I said: *stalking* him." She gazed out the open door to the gray asphalt and blue sky outside, her expression pained. "And then she went too far. He wouldn't marry her, so she killed him. I guess she figured if she couldn't have him, then no one else would, either."

Oh, God. How movie-of-the-week.

"Maybe she just wanted him to take responsibility," Merry said.

Anna looked blank. "For what? Breaking up with her?"

Either she didn't know Lauri was pregnant or didn't see a connection to Clay. Merry changed the subject. "I bet Barbie was mad about her waterbed."

"Well, she wasn't very happy about it. Or about Lauri elbowing her way into Clay's house to talk to him."

Merry tried a sympathy nod. "How long had Barbie and Clay been together?"

"Six, seven months."

"She must feel awful. But it's a good thing she wasn't with Clay that night."

"Oh, I *know*. Her and Olivia—that's Clay's mom—were working at our house on some stuff for this volunteer thing we do."

It shot a big hole in Merry's jealous girlfriend theory if Olivia was Barbie's alibi.

"Did you and Barbie report the break-in and the waterbed, um, stabbing to the police?"

"Not then. I mean, what would they do, right? And Barbie figured if she ignored Lauri she'd eventually stop being such a little pain in the ass. But when your cousin shot Clay, well, of course Barbie told the police that Lauri had broken in. She's pretty scared."

"She thinks she's in danger?"

"Wouldn't you?"

Merry shook her head, baffled. "Are you frightened?"

"A little. You know, I was actually at Clay's the night she shot him."

Merry's heart tripped in her chest. "You saw her?"

She shook her head. "Nah. I was out with Clay's roommate, and we got back late." She shuddered.

The roommate would be the Teller guy Jamie mentioned.

"But then you were there all night?"

A suspicious look crossed Anna's face. "You know, I already told the cops everything yesterday."

Merry shrugged. She'd learned enough. "Whatever. I was just curious. My family and I aren't very close, so I don't always hear what's going on." She stood. "I better get going. I've got groceries in the truck."

"I didn't mean to be rude," Anna said. The pink skin of her lips showed through in patches where she had licked off her wine-colored lipstick. "And I'd appreciate it if you don't talk about me seeing Denny. We're trying to keep it quiet because, well, he's kind of married."

At the rate this one talked, everyone in town already knew.

Wait a minute. "If he's married, why is he living with Clay?"

"He's here working on a drilling rig. His wife lives in Kalispell. He goes back when he has days off."

Merry nodded her understanding. "Well, I can see why you don't want to talk about it. I wouldn't, either."

"Do you feel at all dizzy? Maybe you should sit outside for a while before you leave."

"I'm fine. I'll take a Dr Pepper, though."

Merry ducked through the doorway and stood on the top step. After the stifling heat of the RV, the middle of the late June day felt like walking into air conditioning. A slight breeze cooled the sweat on the back of her neck and along her ribs. For some reason, the air held the cloying scent of lilies. Chartreuse leaves pulsed against the painfully blue sky, and fifty feet away a car throbbed a sickening red. Wild, surreal colors assaulted her eyes.

Her head floating somewhere in the vicinity of her shoulders, Merry heard Anna intone her parting script, going from gossip to public service announcement without missing a beat.

"Well, thanks for donating blood. It's very important to the community. Don't lift anything for at least an hour using that arm. Don't drink any hot beverages for at least an hour. And make sure your next meal ..." she trailed off, and Merry felt rather than saw her reach out.

"Are you okay?" Anna said from far away, and the charcoal-colored asphalt reached up. Everything went dark.

EIGHT

SHE'D BE LATE FOR morning count, and one more time would mean being banned from the commissary for a month. Merry struggled toward consciousness as panic over this minor infraction seized her. But the voices that woke her murmured from above. Puzzling. A thumb lifted one eyelid, and she saw a man peering down at her. A piercing brightness brought her to full awareness.

"Knock it off," she said, and shook her head away from the man's hand and the beam of the tiny flashlight. A wave of pain stopped her movement, and she retched.

"Now that wasn't really what you wanted to do, was it?" the man said.

She put together the white uniform shirt, the rocking sensation, and the sound of an engine. Moving her eyes only, she took in the interior of the ambulance.

"Apparently not," she said. She remembered now, giving blood to Anna Knight, her exit from the stifling hot RV into the Daliesque parking lot outside the IGA supermarket. "Did I pass out?"

"I'm so sorry," a female voice said, all twang and twitter. Merry carefully turned her head to see Anna hovering nearby. "I shouldn't have let you give blood in that heat. You just looked so healthy …"

Embarrassed, Merry said, "Why does my head hurt so much?"

"You fell on it," the paramedic said.

"We'll be at the clinic soon," Anna said. "Then we can take a better look at you and make sure you'll be okay."

"Her pupils are even. She'll probably live."

Merry closed her eyes. "Good to know."

The ambulance stopped at a red light, and the paramedic adjusted the gurney so she wasn't lying flat on her back. He frowned, reaching down and lifting a bag of blood. It sloshed in his hands.

"Sheez, Anna, how much did you—"

He stopped as Anna's eyes widened. He shook his head and reached below the gurney, popped the top on a drink can, and stuck a straw in it.

Merry craned her neck and tried to see where he'd put the bag. "What's wrong?"

"Nothing. Here, this'll make you feel better," he said. Merry took the can and sipped a little Dr Pepper. The sweet syrup trickled down her throat, leaving behind the stale flavor of fake fruit on the back of her tongue. It was wonderful.

The ambulance pulled up beside the Hazel Clinic, and Merry started to sit up. Anna put a hand on her chest and pushed her back. "Let us roll you inside."

"What for? I can walk, for God's sake."

The paramedic gave her a sympathetic look. "Liability. Besides, you're still wobbly, whether you realize it or not."

"Shit," she said, falling back. *Ouch.*

They wheeled her into a large room painted a cheerful yellow with blue cupboards lining the walls. A stainless steel sink sat in one corner and a large window looked out onto the tiny parking lot. Three hospital beds with curtains hanging from circular bars in the ceiling above crowded into one end of the room. The air reeked of antiseptic.

The paramedic sketched a salute to Merry and left. Anna hovered by the window while an officious male doctor she'd never met before poked and prodded at her, finishing off with x-rays. He told Merry she had a mild concussion and handed her a couple of Tylenol, which she washed down with a little more Dr Pepper. The doctor rattled off a list of symptoms to watch out for and darted out of the room.

Merry swung her legs down, and Anna rushed over.

"Quit fussing. I'm fine."

"Don't worry, I'll take care of her," Shirlene said from the doorway.

"What are you doing here?" Merry asked.

"Anna called me."

Merry turned to Anna, who said, "You listed her as your emergency contact."

"Oh, Jeez. Shirlene, I'm sorry. You didn't need to run down here for this. I'm fine."

Shirlene shook her head. "You *are* hard-headed. In this case that's probably just as well, but you're not getting rid of me yet." She looked at Anna. "How is she, really?"

"Gave me a good scare, I can tell you that. But she'll be all right. Her head hurts, and she'll want to take more painkiller later. And she needs to eat something, but it might be hard to find something she can keep down."

Shirlene nodded and turned to Merry. "You have Tylenol at home?"

"I don't know. The truck's at the IGA. I can run in and get some when we get there."

"Nah. We'll grab some out front."

As she followed her aunt out to the waiting room, Anna whispered, "You're awful lucky, you know. To have someone like Shirlene to take care of you. She reminds me of my grandma, God rest her soul. You'd better not take her for granted."

And you'd better not let her hear you comparing her to your grandma, Merry thought.

She followed Shirlene through an empty waiting room to another door. It opened into the clinic's pharmacy. Four gray plastic chairs lined one wall, and a potted ficus tree twisted toward the ceiling in one corner. The only other decoration was a print of a Norman Rockwell painting, wrinkled under the cheap acrylic frame and crooked on the wall.

Olivia Lamente stood behind the counter talking with a younger woman who leaned against the wall. Clay's mother had pulled her white-blonde hair into a rough ponytail, flyaway wisps forming a halo around her face. No makeup, but thin lips and generous eyes and cheekbones a model would kill for. Looking all of her forty-eight years, she wore black slacks and a wrinkled white shirt. The shirt had a small stain on the front. She broke off the conversation when she saw them and held her lower lip clamped between her teeth.

"Olivia! What are you doing here?" Shirlene asked.

"Someone has to be here."

"Well, why didn't you call me?"

Olivia looked away. "I'm okay."

Shirlene asked for Tylenol in a subdued voice. Olivia opened a drawer and pawed through a mess of sample packets. The younger woman hadn't said a word. Now she turned to go.

Shirlene took a step toward her. "Barbie."

The woman hesitated, then turned back. She wore running shorts and a navy T-shirt. Long tan legs showed well-defined muscles and her long brown hair was held back with a stretchy headband. Under her eyes, blue-gray half moons emphasized lids pink and swollen.

"Shirlene." Her voice was tired and flat.

"I'm so sorry about Clay, hon. How're you holding up?" Shirlene said.

"Okay." She turned to go.

"You take care of yourself," Shirlene said as she opened the door.

She didn't respond, already beginning to jog as the door eased shut on its pneumatic hinge.

Merry watched her go. If the red eyes were any indication, she was taking Clay's death hard. Harder than Lauri seemed to be. Merry still wanted to talk to her.

Not now, though. Too hard to concentrate.

Olivia handed Merry six sample packs of painkiller.

Shirlene continued to stare after Barbie, her face drawn in concern.

"Anything else?" Olivia asked.

Merry glanced at her, saw the barely concealed hostility. But her stomach, now rebelling against the Dr Pepper, had joined her throbbing head, and she couldn't think about it.

As they walked outside, she said, "So that's Clay Lamente's girl-friend."

Shirlene sighed. "Yeah."

"Close to Olivia?"

"Treats her like a daughter. You know how Olivia takes in strays, and Barbie doesn't have any family close." She sighed again. "Olivia. I wish . . . I don't know. Never mind."

"It's not personal, Shirlene. They're just upset."

Her aunt opened her driver's door. "They think my daughter killed someone they love. Of course it's personal."

———

Her aunt parked her little Toyota truck in the IGA parking lot and they both transferred to Lotta. Shirlene slid through the Chevy's gears as they picked up speed on the highway. Clouds piled like clotted cream on the horizon, but overhead only a few stray mares' tails streaked the clear blue. Wild mustard speckled the barrow ditches along the sides of the road with their vivid yellow. Merry leaned her head on her hand, her elbow propped into the V where the half-open window met the door. The painkiller had kicked in, but only dulled the throbbing in her head to this side of unbear-able. Behind them, the paper sacks of groceries in the pickup bed quivered and rattled in the wind. Merry wondered what she'd have to throw away.

She gazed out at a clump of white-faced cattle. "Tell me more about this WorldMed you volunteer for," she said as a distraction. "Olivia runs it?"

Shirlene's eyes cut toward her, then back to the road. "The head office in Denver coordinates the four processing sites in the Rocky Mountain region, lets us know what to pack up and for which area of the world, helps keep track of inventory. We send out everything from aspirin and bandages to morphine." She snorted. "Without a medical background I'm pretty much on the aspirin and bandages end of things."

"Where do you get the stuff?"

"It's donated by the pharmaceutical companies and manufacturers. Or people donate money and we use that to purchase supplies. Some of the money is used for overhead, but even the medical personnel donate their time."

"You mean Barbie and Olivia?"

"And Dr. Finley and Dr. Parsi. Anna Knight." She paused. "Barbie's very organized, efficient, you know? Not like that roommate of hers."

"Good Knight Nurse?"

"Mmmm. Not the best prize in the Cracker Jack box."

"She's very …," Merry said, looking for the right word.

"Yes. She is," Shirlene said.

Merry laughed, then winced. "And she volunteers with World-Med, too?"

"Like I said, they all do, to varying degrees."

"Why would a big organization like that operate out of a little place like Hazel?"

"All the distribution sites are in small towns. It keeps the operating costs down, so more money can be directed to getting the medical supplies out." Shirlene downshifted.

A silver Cadillac was pulling out on the highway from the McCoy ranch road. Plumes of dust hung in the air behind it.

"Merry?"

"Goddamn it!"

T. J. Spalding, hunched over the wheel, swiveled his pale round face toward them as the car went by.

"Who's that?" Shirlene asked.

"No one."

Another sidelong glance. "Merry."

She sighed. "Real estate agent. Says Mama wanted to sell the ranch. Says he has some bigwig buyer."

"Whaaat? She never said anything like that to me."

"Me either. I don't know what he's up to, but I don't like it."

They turned off the blacktop. Merry sat up, unwilling to jostle her sore head any more than necessary.

At the ranch, they unloaded the groceries. Shirlene poured the milk down the sink, and mixed up the no-longer-frozen orange juice concentrate, but everything else seemed to be okay. Shirlene insisted that Merry sit still while she made toast and smeared it with peanut butter. At least her stomach didn't do the foxtrot at the very thought. She took it out to the rocking chair on the front porch and ate it in tiny bites. Through the open window she heard the comforting bustle of water running and cupboard doors closing as her aunt fussed around the kitchen.

Izzy wasn't in her paddock, and Merry had assumed she was waiting in her stall for dinner. The distinct sound of an equine sneeze from around the back of the house belied that. Setting her plate on the railing, Merry walked around the corner to find the mare standing at the edge of the defunct vegetable garden. She ripped out a mouthful of long grass by the roots and stood gazing at Merry while she munched.

Merry's grimace turned to a smile at the sight of the stalks sticking out around the horse's mouth in a comical starburst. Izzy eyed her approach and continued to chew, powerful teeth pulverizing the greens. She ran her hands down the mare's legs to check for injuries, squatting on her haunches because leaning over seemed like a bad plan. Leaving Izzy to her appetizer, she retrieved the halter from the barn and ducked into the kitchen for a few carrots and a quick explanation to Shirlene, who quirked one side of her mouth and shook her head.

The sweet carrots proved to be more interesting than the fresh grass, and Izzy crunched and munched as Merry slipped on the halter and led her back to her stall. The horse nuzzled her, pushing against her chest, and her headache ebbed as she rubbed the long face, breathing in musky horse and sweet alfalfa and dry dust. She stuffed a flake of hay into the wire rack and went out to look at the gate.

It stood open about a foot, swinging on its oiled hinges with a touch of a fingertip. The latch wasn't damaged in any way, and designed so that even a clever horse couldn't somehow flip it up and push the gate open.

That goddamn real estate agent. Anger pounded through her temples, and she took a deep breath. Trespassing was one thing, messing around with her horse another.

Who could want her land that badly? She determined to talk to Jamie about it. Maybe she could get a restraining order on T. J. Spalding. Maybe the law would work in her favor for once.

But she wouldn't hold her breath.

Shirlene had cheese and crackers on the kitchen table when she returned. Merry picked at them a little and returned to the porch. After a while, her aunt joined her, settling into the other rocker with a sigh.

Merry told her about Hawkins pulling her over earlier that day.

"Prick," was her aunt's response.

Merry didn't have much to add to that.

"I'll take your Mama's room tonight if that's okay," Shirlene said.

"Oh hell, you don't have to babysit me. I feel bad about taking up half your day as it is."

"You weren't paying attention at the clinic. Someone has to wake you up every two hours tonight."

"So I'll set the alarm."

"I'm staying."

"What about Lauri?"

"I left her a message on the answering machine. She insisted on going out with Janelle Paysen tonight, said she needs to do something to cheer herself up. So it won't make any difference whether I'm home or not. Frankly, I'd just as soon be here."

The melancholy in her voice kept Merry from insisting. They sat in silence, listening as the calls of meadowlarks gave way to the songs of hopeful crickets serenading their prospective mates.

"Sure is nice out here," Shirlene said.

Merry put one boot up on the porch railing. "When I was gone, I spent a lot of time thinking about these summer evenings."

"Winter's a bitch, though."

"Yeah. I missed that, too."

She turned to see her aunt smiling at her in the fading light.

"Say, Shirl?"

"Yeah."

"Why did Harlan Kepper hate Clay so much?"

Shirlene half-turned in her seat. "I didn't know he did."

"I talked to him yesterday afternoon, and he seemed pretty happy Clay was dead."

"That's weird. Far as I know, Harlan and Clay barely knew each other."

———

"Hello?"

"I'm pregnant."

"Who is this?"

"You know damn well who this is," Lauri said. "And I'm pregnant."

Sigh. "Yeah. I heard."

"It's yours."

"The hell you say. We only had that one little ol' romp."

"You're the only romp of any kind that I've had. Can't be anyone else's. Congratulations, Daddy."

"Well, that didn't work out quite the way you planned, did it, babe?"

"What do you know about it?"

"Even if he hadn't died it wouldn't have worked, you know."

It would have. He only had to sleep with me once and he would have believed the baby was his. "Clay would have married me once I brought him to his senses."

"Wrong, baby doll. Not with Barbie around."

"I don't believe you."

"Doesn't much matter if you do or not. But I think you do believe me. In fact, maybe he told you the same thing himself. Must have made you mad. Maybe even mad enough to kill him."

"You're so full of shit. And I didn't call about Clay, anyway."

"Yeah? Wouldn't be about money, would it?"

"You owe me something."

A snort, then, "Oh, really."

"I thought you might want to avoid all the drama and legalities—and publicity—and give me a lump sum up front."

"A lump sum, you say. For child support, of course."

"Of course."

"What kind of 'lump' did you have in mind?"

"Twenty grand."

"Twenty grand, huh. Which you would wisely invest for your baby's future?"

"Exactly." This was going better than she'd thought it would.

"Why not fifty?"

"I don't think you have fifty."

"But you think I have twenty? You're wrong, babe. I so don't."

"You could get it."

"Maybe. Yeah, maybe I could."

"Good."

"But I'm not going to."

"You don't want me to tell your wife, do you?"

"Tell her whatever you want. What makes you think she'll believe anything you say?"

"She must know the kind of man she's married to."

"Yeah ... well, in that case what makes you think she'd care?"

"Couldn't hurt to find out."

"I think a better question is whether you want the whole town to know what you're trying to do. How you fooled around and got knocked up, tried to rope your old boyfriend in, and then, when that didn't work, moved your sights a little to the left and came up with his roommate. See, nobody's going to believe you, babe. Not a soul."

"We'll see about that!" Lauri slammed the phone down.

That son of a bitch. He'd pay. Somehow, he'd pay.

NINE

MERRY HAD FLOATED BACK into the melted warmth of sleep after another one of Shirlene's wake-up shakes when the jangling phone jerked her back to consciousness.

Shirlene caught it on the second ring.

The bedside clock glowed 2:37 in the dark. Couldn't be good. No phone call in the middle of the night could be good. Merry struggled out of bed and stumbled through the living room to the dimly lit kitchen. The bulb over the stove washed half of Shirlene's face in its yellow glow while casting the other half into shadow. Her aunt pressed the phone to her ear while her other hand gripped the back of a kitchen chair. Wearing only one of Merry's T-shirts and a pair of startling purple underwear, she stared at nothing, intent on the caller's words.

"What is it?" Merry whispered.

Shirlene flapped her hand at her in a *be quiet* gesture, while at the same time sending her a look of urgency. "I'll be right over. Call Frank and get him and the kids over there, too—they'll be able to help with the horses...Oh?...That was a good idea. Is their trailer still okay? He might have to take a couple back to his place."

Now Merry could hear a woman's tinny voice from the receiver, talking loud and fast.

"Okay, hon," Shirlene said. "Thanks for calling."

She cradled the phone and rushed into Mama's room, where the crumpled bedclothes said she'd at least tried to get some sleep. As she struggled with her jeans in the near dark, Merry followed and flipped on the overhead. They squinted at each other for a few seconds, Shirlene balanced on one leg like a bird, half in and half out of her pants.

"That was Missy Ganner—she's covering 911 dispatch tonight. There's a fire at the Lamentes'. The horses are terrified, and they need help getting them into the far pasture or off the property altogether. The fire department is on its way, but they're worried about the gas tanks. If those go, so will everything else, and the horses will go nuts. Plus, nobody wants this to turn into another wildfire."

"Shit. That's just what we need."

"Frank's already on his way. Missy called everyone she knew who lives out this way. I've got to get over there."

"Let's go." Merry turned from the doorway as Shirlene started lacing up a pair of tennis shoes. "There's a pair of paddock boots in the mudroom that'd fit you. Better than those things."

Shirlene stood. "You're not going anywhere."

"The hell I'm not. My head feels fine." Well, fine was a relative term. But she could function.

"No, hon, you just stay..." Shirlene's words trailed off as Merry went back into her bedroom and began getting dressed. Merry heard her mutter, "Well, hell. I guess I can't stop you."

"Isn't there a road straight through to their place?" Shirlene asked. She'd insisted on driving.

"Used to be, just an old dirt track. No telling what kind of shape it's in. Better take the county roads."

Shirlene nodded and turned onto the pavement, tromping on the accelerator. At least the Lamentes' property wasn't far. In fact, it had been the eastern tip of the McCoy ranch until Mama and Daddy had sold that sixty-acre parcel in 1985.

The truck slewed a little on a curve, and her aunt slowed.

Flashing lights painted the night as they crested a hill. A county sheriff's deputy directed a tender truck loaded with water around the last corner before the Lamentes'. The truck had "Hazel Fire Department" emblazoned on the side. An ambulance waited by the side of the road. Shirlene waved to the deputy as he motioned them to follow the fire tender into the little valley below.

The house and barn still burned, flames lapping at the ashes whirling upward from the structures. Two of the smaller outbuildings already slumped in dreary charcoal defeat to the ground, smoke burping out of black crevasses in the debris. None of the electricity seemed to be working; other than the firelight, the only illumination came from the ladder truck and water tanker, and from the headlights of a dozen vehicles parked strategically around the yard.

Several had parked around the covered riding arena behind the barn. To one side, a beat-up Nova aimed light toward the propane tank. Bo Lamente had placed it far away from the buildings, common sense winning out over convenience. The diesel tank stood even farther out, on a concrete pad. White foam covered both, and four firefighters worked the house fire from that direction, pushing the flames away with streaming hoses connected to a portable tank that looked like an above-ground swimming pool. The fire tender they had followed into the ranch yard began backing up to the porta-tank to replenish the water supply. They seemed to have given up on saving the barn. The east side was fully engulfed in flames.

As Shirlene maneuvered the truck through the other vehicles, Merry lowered the passenger window. The burning stink assaulted her nose and eyes. The homey smell of wood smoke rode above the stench, confusing her associations; this base note was meaner, with a chemical bite.

The air shimmered with heat, even some seventy yards away from the fire. In the distance, two small sets of headlights jittered across the dark landscape; they were using four-wheeled ATVs to round up already skittish horses. She could hear the distant bee-hive buzz of the engines, and closer, the flapping sound of the fire, flames like medieval standards snapping in the wind.

The horses must be used to their motorized replacements by now—ATVs and pickups were used for far more ranch work than horses. Of course, Bo and Olivia didn't ranch—they ran a training stable. Most of those horses belonged to their clients.

Frank Cain appeared in Lotta's headlights, his arms full of halters and lead ropes. He motioned the pickup forward until they reached a pile of lumber on the far side of the burning house. Shirlene tumbled out and looked around for something to fix.

The older man took the Colorado Rockies cap off his head and wiped sweat away with his bare forearm. Merry caught a glimpse of the startling white forehead above the deep tan of Frank's face before he put the cap back on.

"Might as well try to keep this stuff from burning," he said, gesturing at the pile of boards.

"You got it," Merry said.

"I'm going back down to the horses."

"I'm coming with you," Shirlene said, taking the tangle of halters from him and climbing on the back of his four-wheeler.

"Where are Bo and Olivia?" Merry called.

He shook his head. "Olivia's with the horses. Haven't seen Bo." He revved the engine and they went bouncing back out to the pasture.

She turned to the stack of lumber.

Barbie Barnes stood with her hands on her hips. "Bo was going to use this stuff to build a new deck on the back of the house. Guess that'll be kind of hard without a house to attach it to." Bitterness edged her laugh.

Merry turned to her. "Where is Bo?"

"I haven't seen him. Probably down with the horses already."

"I'm Merry McCoy, by the way."

"Figured you were, after seeing you with Shirlene at the clinic. And I imagine you know who I am."

Dipping her chin in acknowledgement, Merry said, "And I imagine you know a few things about me, too."

"A few."

They locked gazes. Barbie was the first to look away. "Guess I can't really blame you for something your cousin did. And this wood isn't going to move itself."

Together, they began loading lengths of two-by-six cedar onto the truck bed. They made several trips, unloading in a dirt paddock well away from the fire. Splinters slid into Merry's hands, despite the calluses formed by working the prison garden. She swore when a particularly large bit of wood, more of a slab than a sliver, slipped deep into her left palm.

Barbie ignored her.

As they lifted the last of the lumber into the truck bed, a loud creaking and groaning issued from the house, followed by a crash as the upper floor collapsed. No saving the structure, or anything still in it. A fresh stink rose on the air, a sourness riding on the smoke that stung Merry's eyes anew and made her cough. Beside her, Barbie's eyes watered, tears bleeding down her cheeks, her expression one of a bewildered child.

The fire crew shifted their attention to the barn. "Move back!" shouted one of the firemen, and Merry and Barbie complied, climbing in the truck and hauling the last load of cedar to the pile they'd formed several hundred feet away.

"I've got to find Ginger," Barbie said when they finished.

"Mare?"

"Dog. Yellow Lab. Have you seen her?"

Merry shook her head and watched her leave, then moved Lotta away from the fracas. The volunteer firefighters began to douse the west side of the barn.

Why was Barbie here? She might have come in on the ambulance in her capacity as nurse. Or someone could have called her when they found out about the fire. After all, she'd know Bo and Olivia if she'd been dating their son. And Shirlene had said Olivia treated her like a daughter. Or—

An explosion rocked the ground, sucking all the oxygen out of the atmosphere for a split second. The roof of the barn burst open with fire. Pain lanced like shrapnel through Merry's skull. She shook her head, instantly regretting it as her vision doubled for a moment. She bent and threw up a stream of thin, acrid bile.

As she stood and wiped her mouth with the sleeve of her flannel shirt, a hand gripped her other arm.

"What are you doing here?" Jamie pulled her away from the blaze. "You've got a concussion, for God's sake!"

"How'd you know that?"

"Shirlene told me. I just came from up in the pasture where they've taken all the horses."

As he said it, she made out the scream of a horse through the roar in her ears.

"Are they hurt?"

"Just panicked."

"We've got to get down there." She moved toward Lotta.

"No. I'll go back. You get in your goddamned truck and stay there."

"Screw you, Gutierrez. What the hell do you know about horses?"

"What you taught me."

"That's not enough. They need me."

"You're not fucking indispensable. Everybody got along just fine while you were gone."

She stared at him.

"Oh, come on. I didn't mean it like that."

"Ginger!" Barbie's terrified voice yanked their attention back to the barn.

She stood in the barn's double doorway, looking in. A firefighter yelled at her to move as he wrestled with the muscular arm of the hose, but she ignored him. Suddenly, she ducked and ran inside.

"Jesus." Merry took off at a run, Jamie on her heels. The fire-fighter continued to grapple with his hose, yelling at them to stay away.

Peering through the smoke inside, she made out a figure bending over a lumpish form on the floor. The figure seemed to be pleading with the animal to stand up. Merry saw a leg move.

A small piece of roof fell, glancing off Barbie's shoulder, and she screamed. She kept screaming as she ran out of the barn, one side of her T-shirt and hair ablaze. She dropped to the ground and began rolling in the dirt. Together, Jamie and Merry helped to rapidly smother the flames.

Jamie called for help, and the uniformed paramedic that had been in the ambulance with Merry that afternoon came loping up. He did a double-take when he saw Merry, and disapproval quickly replaced the surprise on his face.

But Barbie demanded his immediate care, and he turned to her. Jamie stood back to give him room to work.

"The dog's still in there," Merry said.

"The dog's dead." Jamie's response was flat.

"I can hear it. It's whining."

"You can't hear shit with all this racket. If it's not dead, it's unconscious. There's too much smoke in there."

She glared at him. He was being a real bastard. It meant he was worried, and knowing Jamie, he was worried about her. But she hated it when he got like this.

And besides, he was wrong.

Shrugging, she moved away. When she was far enough from him, she took off at a run.

"Merry! No!"

She ran as close as she could to the powerful stream of the fireman's hose, letting the spray saturate her hair and shirt. Didn't even pause at the door of the barn, jumping over a fallen beam still burning on the ground and slowing only when she couldn't see in the choking, roiling smoke. She felt her way with her feet toward where she thought the dog lay.

A tiny canine whimper came from below, and she realized she'd almost stepped on the Lab. Merry squatted and ran her fingers through fur, discerning the animal's outline. Struggling not to pass out, she sipped shallow breaths and slipped her arms under the dog. With a loud grunt, she picked her up and turned toward where the door should be.

Snaking steps, low to the ground, helped her avoid the scattered detritus, but did nothing for her speed. She didn't dare stoop to avoid the smoke because she'd drop the dog, now a silent, motionless weight in her arms.

A wall loomed in front of her. For a split second, her mind scrabbled in wild terror as she tried to decide which way to go.

"Merry! Where the hell are you?"

Jamie had followed her into the barn. She saw a shadow of movement beyond the wall, and realized she'd nearly trapped herself in a stall. Keeping one shoulder along the partition, she found the opening and reoriented herself.

"I'm over here." Speaking made her cough and gag.

"Where?"

"I can see you. Guide me out—I'm right behind you."

"Thank God."

The shadow moved away, and Merry followed. The smoke cleared as they approached the open door, and she found herself panting in the relatively sweet air. The flames had died down a little as water saturated the old building. She squinted at the dog in her aching arms, willing it to show some sign of life.

A moaning above and to her left was the only warning before the charred section of wall fell. Instinct propelled her forward, toward the open doorway and the people gathered beyond it.

She almost made it. The edge of something heavy hit her across the shoulders, sending her and her charge sprawling and trapping her right foot.

The dog's yelp shot an arrow of joy through her pain and weariness. Hands came out of nowhere, grabbing at her, easing the pressure on her foot, taking Ginger, pulling her to safety.

"Well, this is a first. Twice in one day." The paramedic squatted beside her and did that thing with his little flashlight. It made her eyes water more than the smoke did.

She jerked her head to the side. "Quit it."

He gave her a look. "Does this hurt?" He moved her ankle.

"Ow!"

"Hmm. It's not broken, but you're going to want to stay off it for a while."

"How long is a while?"

"Let me rephrase that. You're going to *have* to stay off it for a while. It won't be as hard as you think. After snorting all that smoke on top of the concussion, you're not going to be feeling too whippy for a day or two, anyway. Just go with it." He began wrapping her ankle. "Keep it elevated. Put some ice on it. If it doesn't feel better in a week, come in and get an x-ray."

"I thought you said it wasn't broken."

The paramedic opened his mouth, then shook his head. "Get it x-rayed tomorrow, then. Can't hurt."

Jamie's ashen face replaced the paramedic's. "Don't you *ever* do that again."

His tone took Merry aback. She struggled to a sitting position. "Is the dog okay?"

He sighed. "I don't know. Someone took it to the vet."

Something in his expression made Merry wonder if his red eyes were due entirely to the smoke and fire.

"I'm sorry," she said, "if I scared you."

"Damn right." His voice was rough. Of course, that could be from the smoke, too.

"This wasn't an accidental fire, was it?"

"We don't know yet. There'll be an investigation and—"

"Oh, for crying out loud. How you people could think this disaster and Clay's death are all a big coincidence is beyond me. Jamie, you know they're related, and you know Lauri didn't have anything to do with the fire."

"'You people?'"

"You police. You cops. You bastards who take other people's lives in your hands and fuck them up as if we're just—oh, God." Her hand flew to her mouth. "I'm sorry. Not you. I know it's not you."

He blinked and glanced away, but not before she saw the look in his eyes.

Shit.

She sighed. "We've gone all haywire, haven't we?" Was it her conviction, she wondered, or his wife? "You're even avoiding my phone calls now."

"Phone calls?" His eyes still didn't quite meet hers.

"Last night. Well, I guess technically it was the night before. After I saw you in the hardware. You don't usually avoid me like that. I mean, you get pissed, sure, but at least you're up front about it."

He looked confused. "I didn't even know you called."

Oh.

Merry remembered the tone in his wife's voice. So that's the way it was.

Jamie said, "What time—"

"What the hell do you think you're doing, young lady?" Shirlene stormed up to them, hair sticking up in all directions and a smear of horse manure down the side of her leg.

Merry laughed.

Which, by the looks on their faces, didn't go over very well with either of them. But then, they couldn't know how wonderful it was to be free to do what you wanted to, just because you wanted to or because it needed to be done. The glory of making choices, even bad choices, and acting on them.

So she changed the subject. "Barbie okay?"

Shirlene said, "She looks like hell, but the burns aren't too bad. Thank God. She wouldn't let the paramedics take her because she was afraid they might need the ambulance for someone else." Her eyebrows drew together. "Good thing, too."

Merry was too tired to defend herself. "Any chance we could go home now? Everything seems to be under control. Unless they still need some help with the horses?"

"No, that's all handled. We can go."

Olivia ran up to them. "Have you seen Bo? I found his truck parked behind the arena. He has to be around here somewhere." There was panic in her voice.

They all shook their heads. Dread settled across Merry's shoulders.

"Oh, God. Barbie! What happened?" Olivia took off toward a car, where Merry could now see Barbie sitting sideways in the passenger seat, the door open and her feet on the ground. Bright patches of gauze on one side of her face and along one arm delineated her injuries.

The roar of engines captured their attention as two vehicles turned in the driveway, coming faster than necessary and spraying gravel when they stopped. Given the twin light bars and official logos, Merry figured the speed was more out of habit than anything else.

One was the deputy she'd seen up on the road, directing traffic around that nasty curve, and the other was Rory Hawkins, looking half hungover and mean as hell.

Shirlene gave her a look. "We're out of here." She started toward the truck. Jamie bent, picked Merry up, and followed.

"Put me down."

"Shut up."

He deposited her into the passenger seat. "I'll call you tomorrow—today, whatever. I have to tell you something."

"Tell me now."

He shook his head. "Later. Be careful going home."

And with that he turned and ambled toward his sergeant.

———

"I wondered if Bo was with that woman he's been seen around town with," Shirlene said as she drove back to the McCoy ranch. "Now I hope he was."

Merry turned to look at her, but her aunt's face was in shadow. "What woman?"

"I don't know. Herb Paysen said they were together at the Moose."

"Bo's having an affair?"

She could barely make out the movement of Shirlene's shoulders against the back of the seat as she shrugged. "Maybe. All I know is Herb said she had long black hair."

"Long black hair? Like Anna's?"

Shirlene made a sound in the back of her throat. "Oh. No. You don't think … no, not her. He's way too old for her. Hell, he's almost too old for Olivia—he's in his sixties. I just can't see it."

Merry didn't know Bo well enough to speculate on whether he'd be interested in Anna or not. But she wouldn't put anything past the sharp-featured nurse.

"Does Olivia know?"

The shrug again. "It's hard to keep something like that secret around here. Especially if you go flaunt it in the Moose."

TEN

BEFORE SHE EVEN MOVED, Merry let out a groan, which started her coughing, which sent shards of pain through her bruised shoulders. It wasn't until she tried to sit up that the pangs started in her head and swollen ankle. She flinched as her fingertips probed the goose egg just above her hairline. Easing the covers back revealed her foot twisted inward as if trying to escape the bulging bruise-stained ankle. A soggy bag of once-frozen peas lay on the wrinkled sheet.

God. She hurt in places she hadn't even known she had.

"Nice job on the alarm clock," Shirlene said, entering the room with a glass of water and one of the sample packets of Tylenol from the clinic. "About scared me to death when it hit the wall."

Merry spied the pieces on the floor. It had been almost six a.m. by the time they got to bed, and she'd promised her aunt she'd set her alarm for every two hours. It had gone off once. Immediately after realizing she didn't have to muster forth for some prison foolishness, she'd flung the thing across the room. Must have put a little English on it, judging by the fragments.

She turned her attention to the painkiller. "I need more than that."

Shirlene glanced down at her hand, then back up at Merry. "Yeah, okay. I'll get another one."

Handing the water and pills to her, she left and came back a few moments later with more Tylenol and a package of frozen corn. She replaced the bag of peas with the new makeshift ice pack.

"Does it hurt?"

"If it's mine, it hurts. What time is it?"

"Almost one."

"Jesus. How long have you been up?"

"Got up around eleven. Stuck around in case you needed me."

Merry removed the corn and eased her feet to the floor. She tried putting her weight on the damaged one. The sudden, sharp pain felt like someone had shoved a red-hot blade into the joint. With a sharp intake of breath, she transferred all her weight to her other foot and stood, flamingo style.

Pulling a handful of hair around to her nose, she sniffed. "Yuck. I'm in desperate need of a shower. Go ahead and go home. Take Lotta."

"How're you going to get around?"

"Hop, I guess."

"Hang on." Shirlene disappeared around the corner, and Merry heard her rummaging in Mama's room. In a few moments she returned with a polished stick of beautifully gnarled wood.

"What's that?"

"Your mother's cane. She used it quite a lot, toward the end."

Merry took it, angling it in her hands to catch the light from the window. The smooth, warm grain twisted and flowed down its length, suggesting the vibrancy of living wood. She tried to imagine Mama leaning on it, her calloused hand wrapped around the burl at the end, fingers gripping its solid presence as her own existence faded day by day, finally winking out in the early morning hours as Merry lay on her bunk two thousand miles away.

She looked up to find Shirlene watching her, eyes shiny.

Lowering the end, Merry tried leaning on the cane and taking a step. Still hurt like a son of a bitch. Not something she'd be doing a lot of today.

"I'll be okay. Do me a favor, though?"

"Sure."

"Feed Izzy and open the gate to the pasture just outside her paddock. Check her water."

Shirlene agreed and went out the door. Merry half-hopped, half-hobbled to the bathroom and took an awkward shower. Her head felt better as the double dose of Tylenol kicked in, and discovering more in the medicine chest cheered her considerably. Dressed in loose cotton hiking pants and T-shirt, she left her hair to air dry and made a sandwich with peanut butter and chokecherry jam Mama had made the year before. Check that one off the list. She carried it and the phone back into the living room and propped her foot up.

She called Jamie at the station. Nadine, the woman who had been taking notes when Lauri had first told them about finding Clay's body, put her through to him.

"Hey, McCoy. How are you feeling?"

"Like hell. Listen, did you guys ever track down Bo?"

A long silence, and then she heard him exhale. "The sheriff's department is investigating the fire. This morning they uncovered a body in the debris of the barn."

"Oh, no."

"They don't have a positive identification yet ... but it's him."

"No wonder that dog wouldn't leave the barn. She was trying to save him."

"He was already dead. Blunt force trauma to the skull."

"Damn it. I told you there was a connection between that fire and their son's death. This has nothing to do with Lauri."

He hesitated. Then, "What are you doing this evening?"

"Well, I had some elaborate plans. Thought I'd sit on my ass with my foot up for a while in the kitchen, then move to the living room and see what was on TV, sit on my ass with my foot up for a while in there."

"How 'bout sitting on your ass with your foot up by a river?"

"What did you have in mind?"

"I come and get you, we go fishing."

"You know what?" she said. "That sounds fan-fucking-tastic."

"I'll be there around four-thirty."

———

Merry was watching *Dr. Phil*. She professed to hate the show, had seen more than enough for her lifetime in the prison rec room, but couldn't tear herself away from the woman who had been convicted of child abuse. Now, teary-eyed and repentant, she tried to convince her hostile in-laws she was off drugs and taking responsibility for her life. It wasn't Kylie Lynn, Merry's second cellmate, but the woman sure looked a lot like her, down to the rabbity teeth and big blue eyes. She hoped the woman didn't have a husband like Kylie's, who beat the crap out of her on a regular basis. Kylie had told her it was too hard to stay straight when you were afraid of dying all the time.

"Hello?"

With a sense of relief, Merry turned off the TV, calling toward the screen door, "It's open."

Barbie Barnes stepped into the living room. "Hi."

"Hi yourself," Merry said. "You look awful."

Barbie's laugh sounded like it could spill over into tears any moment. "I know." A thin bandage ran along her hairline on that side, and down in front of her ear. The skin around it glowed bright red and shiny with salve. Her jeans were tight, but the long-sleeved T-shirt she wore was at least two sizes too large. To cover the bandages on her arm, no doubt. Her hair had been shaved to a scant inch all over her head. The circles under her eyes looked like they'd been carved into her face.

"The haircut's nice," Merry said.

"The haircut's terrible. But it's not like I had any choice."

"It'll grow back." Merry waved at the couch sitting against the wall to the kitchen.

Barbie perched on the edge of the cushion. She moved with care, favoring her right side.

"How bad are the burns?"

"First degree, like a really bad sunburn. I'm lucky—blistered up pretty bad, but at least I won't need skin grafts."

"That's good."

"I guess I owe you a thank you."

116

Merry shook her head. "No need."

"It would have been a lot worse if you hadn't helped, you know, pull me out. But I wanted to thank you for saving Ginger, too."

"Is she okay?"

Barbie pressed her lips together. "She has a broken rib, and her lungs were damaged by all the smoke, but the vet says she's going to be all right. You know, that dog just showed up out of nowhere one day, and Olivia can't turn away a stray. Now Ginger's a little something for her to hang onto, I guess."

Lowering her voice, Merry said, "I heard about Bo."

The tears finally spilled over, and Barbie quickly reached up to wipe them from her cheeks. "I can't believe it. First Clay. Then this. And Olivia losing her home, maybe even her business."

Merry winced. "How's she holding up?"

"Horrible. I mean, she's tough, you know? On the outside she seems okay, but I know better. It's just too much for anyone to take all at once. She's staying with me and Anna for the time being. I didn't want her in some skanky motel."

Merry nodded. "That's good."

They sat in awkward silence for a few minutes, Barbie gazing out the window.

"You've got a nice place here."

"Thanks. It's been in the family for four generations."

"My family had a place like this, too," Barbie said. She sounded angry. "Well, they lost it before I was born, but I've always thought of it as my family's place. Up north of Frank Cain's."

"Really?" Merry asked, surprised. "Frank told me the other day he's buying that spread."

Barbie stared at her, her face going white. She got up and walked to the window.

Without turning around, she said, "I've been saving up my whole life to buy that land back."

"I'm sorry. Maybe Frank'll sell to you when you get the money."

"It's all I've ever wanted. To have some real roots. My dad's military, and we always moved around a lot." She turned. "I guess that's partly why I was so attracted to Clay. Because he was so solid, like he was part of the earth. And Olivia and Bo treated me like I was their own daughter." Her eyes filled again, and she turned back to the window.

Merry didn't know what to say, so she didn't say anything. After several moments, Barbie wiped the sleeve of her T-shirt across her face and turned back around.

"Sorry. I seem to keep leaking."

"I think you're entitled."

"Anyway, I wanted to say thanks." She took a step toward the door.

"Glad you stopped by."

Barbie nodded, but seemed to have difficulty speaking.

"Really," Merry said. Watching the other woman struggle to keep it together made her whole chest ache.

She nodded again. "Maybe I'll see you around."

"I hope so."

And as Barbie left, Merry realized she really meant it.

———

It took Merry a while to dig her tackle box, Daddy's old fishing vest, and a dusty bamboo fly rod out of the basement. She'd bought the rod from the Sears catalog the summer between her freshman and sophomore years in high school with money she earned haying. Jamie, a serious fisherman, would probably laugh his head off when he saw it.

The Wrangler pulled up in front of the house, a pair of waders slumped against the rear window, and at least three poles growing out of the tumble of other equipment in the back seat. Her friend bounced to the ground and strode toward the porch. She met him at the door.

"Got enough stuff with you?"

"Never." Jamie grinned. "Wait 'til you see what Gayle got me last Christmas."

"New toy?"

"Oh, yeah. Spey rod. The thing is so light you hardly know you have it in your hand. You gotta try it."

"Sounds like she did good."

"And I only had to hint around about it a couple dozen times or so."

"What did you get her?"

He shrugged. "Some bracelet she'd been wanting." He looked around. "Where's your stuff?"

She nodded toward the front door. "You just walked by it."

He eyeballed the meager pile. "I brought extra gear, just in case."

But fishing was just an excuse for her. Running water soothed: the motion of it, the sound of it, the way light became fluid within its flow. The more she'd thought about going fishing the more she craved time by the river. She couldn't even remember the last time she'd been near water.

They headed to Troublesome Creek, a tributary feeding into the west fork of the Bitterroot River. The radio blasted country music that competed with the rushing currents of cool air flowing through the open windows as they drove 93 out of town. Jamie drummed the steering wheel and sang along.

Merry indicated a Richardson's ground squirrel, called a picket pin because it sat up so still and straight at the side of the road. Jamie nodded that he saw it, though he looked surprised that Merry would even think it worth pointing out. She thought about the car game she and Drew played as children, sitting in the back seat and counting the picket pins on their respective sides of the road. She never won because Drew cheated.

There had been more of them to count then. Farming, ranching, oil wells, mines, and the ubiquitous onslaught of people seeking out refuge in Montana, "The Last Best Place," had taken their toll. She felt the undercurrent of the coming change move through her with a pang. Watching for more picket pins, it felt as if yet another element of her childhood had been irretrievably lost.

She shook it off. "What were you going to tell me last night?"

Jamie looked grim, then seemed to make a decision. Reaching under his seat, he handed her a folder.

"You never saw this."

She glanced at him and flipped open the brown cover. Wire tabs clasped a single page inside. No photos, just the one form filled out by hand in blue ballpoint ink. She tried to decipher the scrawled handwriting.

"It's not the final report, just a preliminary to give us something to work from. The rest of the autopsy'll be done tomorrow. I had to go up to Missoula yesterday afternoon, so I stopped by and got that."

She looked up. "So this might not be accurate?"

"Theoretically there could be changes. But all it says is, big surprise, Clay Lamente died of a gunshot wound to the heart. Additions will likely be the results of the toxicology report, information on stomach contents, things like that. But with a gunshot they don't have to get too fancy, once they make sure it's the cause of death. Medical examiner says he died sometime between nine thirty and midnight."

Leaning back and stretching her legs as far as she could in the somewhat cramped quarters of the Jeep's passenger seat, Merry looked out over the green-gold fields flowing by.

Suddenly she turned back to him. "What about the gun that was used to shoot him? Do you know what kind it was?"

He looked sidelong at her, then back to the road. "We may even have it."

"What does that mean?"

"We found a thirty-eight revolver. And a bullet in the mattress —there were two shots, but one just winged him—and the bullet was a thirty-eight caliber. Found the gun in the desk drawer in Lamente's living room. Belongs to the roommate, Denny Teller. It'd been fired, but we don't know when because he said last time he used it at the range he didn't clean it afterwards." Jamie's voice was disapproving. "I bet he's never used it at the range. He's more the type to shoot rats at the dump."

"When will you know if that's the murder weapon?"

"Hawkins put a rush on the ballistics, so we should know soon. And I understand Lester got some fingerprints off the gun itself. He does most of our in-house crime scene stuff, though the state takes care of some of it."

"So you think the murderer left the fingerprints?"

He shrugged. "Don't know. But if it's the weapon used to kill Lamente, and if the prints don't belong to Denny Teller, I'm hoping they belong to a guy named Gus Snyder."

"Who's that?"

"Maybe the closest thing Lamente had to an enemy besides your cousin."

"I don't know if you could really call Lauri his enemy."

"It sounds like she was stalking him. But listen, Denny Teller and Clay Lamente both roughnecked on the Hi-Sho well, out at Red Bennett's place. Teller told us Lamente found out this Gus Snyder was doing coke while he was working on the oil rig with them. He managed to get Snyder fired. Apparently Lamente had absolutely no tolerance for drug use, especially at work. And after he got fired, Snyder had no tolerance for Lamente, either."

"Have you talked with the guy?"

"We're having some trouble tracking him down."

"What about the footprints? Have you matched those yet?"

"Lester's still working on it."

Soon enough, the Jeep growled along the final dirt access. The river sparkled through the trees. They parked in the shade of cottonwoods and a few red-barked pines. Beyond, low scrub straggled to the narrow river beach, exposed now that the spring runoff had receded. Good fishing, with small boulders interspersed with smooth-flowing, crystalline water reflecting distorted portions of the cloudless sky above. Deep pockets, and hopeful-looking riffles. Downstream, a snag of branches and brush formed a handy hide-out for lurking trout.

They got out and stretched. Jamie reached past the jumble of gear and pulled out a pair of waders. He shrugged into a mesh vest covered with a complicated array of pockets and zippers and opened a slick, brushed-aluminum box lined with foam. Inside, dozens of flies nestled, hooked into the pad. He selected one and passed the box to Merry.

"Stonefly?" she asked, squinting down at the water. A hatch was in progress. In the early evening light, the winged insects fluttered through the air, mating and dropping their eggs into the water below.

"Sofa Pillow." He named a particular fly pattern.

She chose a Goofus Bug. Together, they moved down to the river's edge, Merry managing to hobble along with the help of Mama's cane.

"So, how's Gayle?" she asked, keeping her tone light.

Jamie squinted at the uni-knot he'd just tied in his leader. "Fine."

"What's she think of this little fishing trip?"

He shot a quick sideways look at her.

She set her pole on the rock beside her. "Jamie."

He shrugged. "I went fishing. Go all the time."

"But not with me."

"So, you going to call her up and tell her?"

Rolling her eyes, she picked up the pole again. "Someone might."

His jaw tightened, and he turned to face her. "We're not doing anything wrong. Just a couple friends out to hook some brookies."

Their eyes locked. She hesitated, then nodded once.

"Let's get to it, then." He turned toward the water.

He moved upstream, casting toward the opposite bank and working the fly back. He stopped to finesse a riffle corner. Merry stayed perched on a boulder with her Sears rod, alternating casts between a boulder pocket and an area along the water's edge where the flow gentled under the shade of a large willow.

An hour later, he had two rainbows, and she'd caught a fourteen-inch cutthroat. She thought of them rolled in cornmeal with salt and pepper, and fried in butter. He settled on the rock beside her.

"Someone supposedly wants to buy the ranch."

Jamie swiveled his head toward her, eyebrows raised. "Really? When did this happen?"

"Yesterday, guy shows up, says Mama was going to sell." She related her conversation with the realtor.

He shook his head. "I can't believe it. You set the little ambulance chaser straight, right?"

"More like a hearse chaser. I think he got the message. What can you do about people like that?"

"Not much." He looked rueful. "They're skirting fraud, but the county attorney wouldn't take something like that to court, so all you could really do is file a complaint for harassment."

"Not even worth it."

"Not really. But if you ran him off the other day, you're probably rid of him for good."

Maybe.

She thought of Spalding exiting the McCoy ranch and Izzy loose at the back of the house.

Probably not.

"Any news on what caused the fire?"

"They brought in dogs this morning, found evidence of accelerants. Took samples—carpet pad and some other stuff—and sent them off to the lab. Haven't heard back yet, but from what I understand arson's pretty certain."

She watched the leaves of a large cottonwood twist silver and green against the azure sky, moved by air currents beyond her reach. Of course it was arson.

Jamie began assembling his gear. As she watched the way his muscles moved under his skin, she became aware of affection for his familiar form, for the body she'd shared so much with in their late teens. God, they'd had fun. The affection, of course, was really for the whole man. For her friend. For possibly the best friend she'd ever had.

He looked up. "What's wrong?"

She shook her head and blinked rapidly. It was as if his steady presence brought her other losses into sharp focus.

"Merry?" He stepped toward her, hesitantly, and then with his quick trademark strides.

She shook her head again and put her hand up. He stopped. His gaze softened, and he sidestepped her hand, bending to wrap his arms around her.

She flinched and he drew back, dismay on his face. But he didn't remove his hands from her shoulders, and after a few moments she looked him in the eye, stood up, and hobbled forward with a kind of determination. If she couldn't let this man, this one man in the world that she still felt safe with, touch her, she might never feel normal again.

The embrace felt awkward at first, and she willed herself to relax. One by one, her muscles unclenched until she gave herself up to the human comfort of his warmth.

And without warning she felt ... need. Physical desire. She couldn't have said whether that delicious feather touch began in her body or her brain, but she recognized it with a kind of hopeful joy. They stood immobile, Merry with her bad foot held behind her like some black-and-white movie heroine, while the feeling divided and increased, a mitosis turned to contagion, consuming both her will and her good sense.

She pressed her lips against the moist skin where his neck met his shoulder, parting them just enough to taste his salty sweat. She opened them further to slowly run the flat of her tongue up his neck.

And found herself being held at arm's length, slack-jawed with surprise. She closed her mouth, feeling a little sheepish. "Sorry."

"What the hell was that?"

"I ... I don't know. Old habit?" What was the big deal? He'd made it clear he still had feelings for her. It wasn't like she'd tried to ...

She saw Zeke's face, twisted and ugly, looming above her ...

... she'd only wanted ... she'd only *wanted*. Having any kind of physical desire had felt like a victory. Now it tasted like sawdust in her mouth as she registered Jamie's furious expression.

"Old *habit*? You're the one who decided 'old habit' wasn't good enough anymore. You're the one who decided we should be 'just friends.'"

"I decided?"

126

"You fell in *love*—remember that wonderful conversation? About how you were going to marry that son of a bitch Green? Well, you made your choice, and it turned out to be one hell of a lousy one, didn't it? But I dealt with it. And I found someone else. Now you think we can just start again where we left off?"

She stared at him, confused and ashamed, until the anger came to save her.

"Fuck you, Gutierrez."

She turned and would have stomped off, but had to be content with grabbing her fishing pole and her cane and limping to the Jeep. Putting too much weight on her sore ankle sent pain stabbing up her leg, and that helped some. By the time she reached the Wrangler, her world had narrowed to putting one foot in front of the other, opening the door, and pulling herself into the passenger seat.

It was a long ride home.

ELEVEN

MERRY PUT HER CREEL on the dresser in the guest room where she'd been sleeping. A lace runner draped white and delicate across the top of the dresser to protect the surface of the wood. The mirror hanging on the wall above reflected the room behind her and her own wary eyes.

It was the larger of the two spare bedrooms. But this room, tidy, barely decorated, sterile save for the flowery fragrance of the candle on the bedside table, had been her bedroom growing up. It bore little resemblance to the messy room she remembered: windowsill overflowing with Breyer model horses, corners full of fishing gear and softball equipment, books crammed into the little bookcase, leather crafting tools in a chest on the floor.

Clothes tumbled out of her duffel bag onto the rug by the bed. Merry bent and started to shove them back in, then paused. She moved to the closet door and opened it. Stacks of sweaters neatly encased in plastic marched along the top shelf. Two coats—one a long wool dress coat, the other a thick down jacket—hung next to wool slacks, two blazers, a knit dress, and several thick flannel shirts.

Thinking of pushing the garments aside in order to hang some of her own, she reached out to grab a handful. But instead of sliding the hangers down the rod, Merry found herself stroking the sleeve of the dress. Black and buttery soft, the cashmere offered up a trace of her mother's scent in response to her touch. She slid the dress off the hanger and buried her face in it, breathing in the aromas of horsehair and cinnamon. Her knees bent until she was sitting on the side of the bed.

Cinnamon.

When she was eight years old, Merry had told her third grade teacher she would bring cookies the next day for the class Christmas party. Mama had promised to make the cookies that evening, but before she could start, a horse went down with colic. She'd spent the whole night in the barn, bundled up in sweaters, fur-lined boots, and Daddy's big Carhartt coat. With the temperature around zero, Merry and Drew had walked out through the bitter cold to say their goodnights. It was a little warmer in with the horses, musky and sweet.

She remembered coming to breakfast the next morning. Mama told her she hadn't been able to make the cookies for her class. She understood why, knew a horse's health was more important than some dumb old cookies. Sparks, the horse, was doing better, and that was what counted. Still, she dreaded telling her teacher that she didn't have the treats. She'd promised to bring them. Her teacher lived in town and didn't have horses, so she might not understand.

At school that day she didn't say anything about the cookies, putting it off as long as possible. Finally, it was time for the party.

She began to tell the teacher about Mama and Sparks the night before, when she heard a familiar voice. Mama stood in the doorway of the classroom with a big Tupperware container full of colorful shapes. She'd baked and decorated all morning.

Merry flopped back onto the chenille coverlet, her feet still on the floor. With a sigh she tossed the dress aside. Stared at the ceiling, remembering. Tears blurred her vision, streaked hot and silent across her temples, and soaked into her hair. She welcomed them as another version of the river: washing, soothing, altering the light.

They faded. Stopped. She breathed deep, got up, went into the bathroom. Splashed some cold water on her face. Took some more Tylenol.

She went back into the bedroom and hung the dress, now slightly rumpled and damp, back on the hanger and took it and another armful of Mama's clothes out of the closet. In Mama's room she laid them on the bed. As she left, she closed the door behind her.

Back in her old bedroom, the mirror gauged her available courage. Merry looked away, feeling as if she was made of glass and the slightest jostle might shatter her into a thousand pieces.

The rest of the evening stretched out ahead of her, blank and lonely. She thought of the six pack of Moose Drool in the fridge, considered getting good and properly drunk, but figured it was a poor plan so soon after a concussion. Despite her mood, she wasn't quite ready for suicide.

At least the Blazer was an automatic, she thought, driving toward town.

———

Merry spied Lauri sitting on a stool outside the Dairy Shack and pulled into the parking lot that had been beaten down to hard-packed, dusty earth. Lauri's elbows rested on the counter, her head bent over a magazine laid open in front of her. She glanced over at the sound of the vehicle, and went back to her reading.

Squatting at the north end of Main Street, the Dairy Shack couldn't really be called a restaurant, not even of the fast food variety. Rather, it was the permanent version of the kind of food booth lining the walkways at county fairs. You could walk up to the window and buy espresso and soft drinks, and ice cream in the summer. Behind a dirty pane of glass, glistening lengths of hot dogs and sausages constantly turned on their heated metal rollers. Their greasy aroma filled the warm evening air.

Outside, where Lauri sat on one of the four stools bolted to the concrete below the counter, customers could enjoy their tasty treat and stare at the brown wood siding. Sliding onto a stool next to her cousin, Merry tried to see the magazine article holding her attention. Lauri checked off boxes, answering multiple-choice questions. The part of the headline Merry could see read, "How You Can Tell If He's…"

She waited. Minutes passed without either of them saying anything, and Lauri gave a good impression of being immersed in her magazine, except that she'd stopped checking the little boxes. Merry could see a smudge of fingerprint ink still staining the edge of one of her thumbs.

"Lauri."

A quick sidelong look, then back to the page in front of her.

"Lauri. Look at me."

She sighed the long dramatic sigh Merry was beginning to associate with her reluctance to deal with anything she found the least unpleasant.

"What?"

"I want to talk to you."

"Well, I don't want to talk to you."

"You don't know what I want to talk about yet."

"You want to talk about Clay. Or about me going to jail. Or else my mother sent you."

"Why would she send me?"

Her eyes cut to Merry again. "To find out who knocked me up." One shoulder rose and dropped. "She got real upset when I wouldn't tell her this afternoon."

"Nobody sent me. I stopped by to see how you're doing. I know Clay's death really shook you up, and I wanted to see if you were okay."

Lauri turned and faced her. "Really? You were worried about me?"

The hope on her cousin's face arrowed pity through her. "Sure I was. I know you're upset. In fact, I'm a bit surprised you're back at work already."

"Yeah, it sucks. Mom said it would be good for me to come back to work instead of just moping around. What does she expect? I just lost the man I was going to spend the rest of my life with." She shook her head.

"You were going to spend the rest of your life with Clay?" Merry asked, careful to keep her voice mild and nonchallenging.

Lauri nodded.

"So if he was the father, why are you being so secretive about it?"

Her cousin looked away.

"Lauri?"

She shrugged, still avoiding Merry's gaze.

"Clay was the father, wasn't he?"

"It doesn't matter now, does it?" Bitterness dripped from her response.

"I don't understand."

"No. You don't."

"Well, help me out," Merry said, wondering if the girl was even capable of straightforward conversation.

"Clay might not have technically been the father, biologically, I mean, but he would have been a great daddy, once we got everything straightened out."

It was like trying to maneuver in a swamp of conundrum without a map. "What did you have to get straightened out?"

"Barbie, for one thing. If it weren't for her, he would have given in, slept with me one more time, seen things my way. I'm sure of it. He was an honorable man." Lauri's gaze willed her to see things her way.

Merry didn't see what honor had to do with Lauri and her pregnancy unless Clay was the one responsible for it. Wait a minute. "What do you mean, 'slept with you one more time'?"

She looked away but not before Merry saw the shimmer of tears in her eyes. "I wanted him to think he was the father. Then he would have married me and taken care of me and I could have moved out of Mom's house."

Stunned, Merry stared at her for a long moment. "So who is the, uh, biological father?"

"Why does everyone care so much about that? It was just a one-night thing. What matters is that Clay and I were going to have a family."

Rubbing her face with both hands, Merry tried to take in what Lauri was saying. Apparently, she got pregnant from a one-night stand and had been trying to convince Clay it was his so he'd marry her and be a father to the child. But he had to sleep with her for that plan to work, and he hadn't gone for it. It sounded like Clay *had* been an honorable man.

"So, are you mad at Barbie?" she asked, wondering if Lauri had gone in and slashed the woman's waterbed like Anna hads aid.

Lauri clenched her jaw. "She's such a snot. Just because she's a nurse and works at the Quikcare doesn't mean she's any better than I am. I don't think she even loved Clay, not like I did. She just wanted to be part of that whole family. She started going around telling people I was stalking her boyfriend, so I made a point of letting her know not to mess with me."

Merry sighed. "I take it that means you messed with her?"

"Just a little."

"Good God, why?"

"So she couldn't just blow me off. So she'd have to think about what she was screwing up. So she'd …"

"So she'd get scared?"

"Yeah. So she'd know I was serious." The tears had vanished.

"How serious were you?"

She squinted at Merry as if trying to read small print. "What do you mean?"

"I mean you're under suspicion for Clay's death. I mean Barbie's waterbed was slashed and flooded part of her house. I mean

134

you've been acting strange, and if you don't 'fess up to what you *have* done, there's a strong possibility the police will assume you did all of it, including killing Clay."

Lauri's mouth fell open.

"Well?"

She closed her mouth. Blinked. "Whose side are you on, anyway?"

I'm trying to be on your side, you infuriating little ninny. "What were you doing at Clay's house the night he died?"

Silence.

"Were you going to try to seduce him?"

Lauri clamped her lower lip between her teeth before nodding once.

Merry held her hand up. "Okay, okay. Now tell me something. What time were you there?"

She shrugged.

Merry struggled to keep her irritation from showing. "It's important."

"Around midnight, I guess. It had stopped raining."

"Were you wearing those sandals?" She indicated her cousin's feet.

"No. A pair of Mom's boots."

Merry closed her eyes. They'd match the footprints for sure. "Why didn't you *say* that when I asked you before?"

"She gets mad when I borrow her stuff."

Christ. "Did you see anything? Hear any shots?"

"No. Just fireworks. You know, bottle rockets, some of the bigger stuff. I'm surprised someone didn't call the cops."

"Yeah," Merry said, thinking.

"His name is Denny Teller."

Lauri's words startled her out of her reverie. "Who?"

"Denny Teller. The one-night stand guy."

"Clay's roommate? He's the father?"

"I didn't know he was Clay's roommate, not then."

"You didn't go to his place, to, um …"

"No."

"Your mom's house?"

"No."

"A motel?"

"A van, okay? We did it in the back of his van. Would you like a blow-by-blow?"

"Uh, no. I shouldn't have asked. It's not any of my business."

"No, it's not." Still, Lauri looked mollified by her apology.

"You know he's married?"

Lauri sighed. "Yeah, I know." She watched an eighteen-wheeler rumble by. "It doesn't matter. I just wanted to have the baby and be with Clay. I don't care about Whatshisface anyway. The only reason we got together in the first place was because I was lonely and drank too much beer, and one thing led to another … whatever. None of it matters now."

"It matters to the baby."

"No, it doesn't. Denny told me he wouldn't pay child support."

"You can take him to court. Force him to take a blood test to prove he's the father."

Lauri didn't say anything.

"You'd better tell your mom about Denny."

"Why? It doesn't make any difference."

"Because she thinks it was Clay. Because if you don't, I will. And I think it would be better coming from you."

136

Lauri turned on her. "You lied. You said you wouldn't tell her."

"I did not. I said she didn't send me. And she didn't."

"Shit."

"Lauri, if it really doesn't matter, why not tell her? It would mean a lot to her to know that you trust her."

"She doesn't trust me."

"You keep secrets."

"Whatever."

"It's up to you. Tell her or don't. But she's going to find out."

A car full of teenagers pulled into the parking lot, country pop thumping out of the stereo. Merry stood to leave. She put her hand on her cousin's shoulder. Lauri stiffened for a moment, then went slack. After a few moments she turned and looked up. She blinked slowly.

"I miss him, you know?"

Merry patted her cousin's shoulder. "I know."

"Nothing turns out the way you plan it, does it?"

"Sometimes it's worse. Sometimes it's better. Sometimes it's just different, and you don't know whether it was better or worse until a lot later."

Lauri nodded. "Okay."

Merry was surprised. "Will you be all right?"

She shrugged. "I guess."

"I bet you'll feel better if you talk to your mom."

Lauri held up her hands in mock surrender. "Okay. I'll tell her tonight."

Walking back to her vehicle, Merry wondered how much of what Lauri had said was true. Her gut said most of it was. In fact, all along her cousin seemed to be pretty up front when asked direct questions. But what about the things she left out? Then Merry realized Lauri had neatly deflected the question about the waterbed, before she even got a chance to ask it.

TWELVE

MERRY FELT GUILTY THAT Izzy had been getting so much more exercise at the Cains'. The next morning she decided she could manage a placid ride, sans stirrups. Then a run into town to see this Denny Teller character. Have a little talk about child support. But before she could saddle Izzy, before she'd even washed her breakfast dishes, the phone rang.

"Call Shirlene." The voice spoke just above a whisper, but she could tell it was Jamie.

"What the—"

Merry heard conversation in the background, and he hung up. Well, hell.

She dialed Shirlene. After four rings she answered, sounding subdued.

"Jamie just called me. What happened?"

"Oh, God," her aunt said. "They came and arrested Lauri. That asshole Hawkins. She was in the bathroom when he got here, and when she came out he arrested her. He was going to take her in her pajamas and bathrobe, but I raised holy hell at that, and finally he let her go get dressed. Then he tried to handcuff her, and she started to fight him—she managed to smack him a good one across the face before he grabbed her hands. That other one came in then, the skinny one who was here the other day? Well, he came in, and he took her out, and then Hawkins went out and shoved her into the back of the police car. She was screaming at them, Merry." She took a shaky breath. "She was in handcuffs and screaming at them."

"Jesus. Are you okay?"

"I tried to go out and calm her down, but Hawkins stood in my way, wouldn't let me by. God, he was mad! When she hit him, I thought for a moment he was going to lay her out. But he decided to take it out on me instead."

Merry grabbed the edge of the counter. "What did he do?"

"He told me, real sarcastic-like, not to worry about trying to visit Lauri today because the only person he'd let in to see her would be a lawyer. He's not even going to let me take her a toothbrush. Can they do that, Merry?" Her voice wavered.

She'd never heard Shirlene like this. "Sure, when they first arrest her. What about bail?"

"I don't know. They just left."

"Call Kate."

"I was just about to. I'll talk to you later."

They said goodbye. Merry finished the dishes and sat at the kitchen table with a second cup of coffee, thinking hard. She'd really been looking forward to that ride on Izzy.

She placed another call.

"Hazel Police. May I help you?" Nadine again.

"Hi. Is Jamie around? This is Merry McCoy."

"Oh, hi. How's it going? No, he left already... um, can you hang on a minute?"

Merry heard a male voice, and pictured Rory Hawkins's bulk looming nearby. Nadine returned, sounding official.

"No sir, I'm sorry. Officer Gutierrez is not in. May I take a message?"

"Can you tell me where I could track him down?"

"I'm afraid Officer Gutierrez will not be in until tomorrow."

"He's off today?"

"That's right."

"So he's probably at home."

"Yes, sir."

"You're a gem."

"That's true, sir. You have a good day now."

———

After that fat jerk hustled her into back of the police car, Lauri endured the ride to the police station in silence, scarcely able to breathe since his B.O. reeked so bad. God, what a pig. She coughed and he shot her a menacing look in the rear view mirror.

Then they asked her questions in the same long room as before, lots of questions, but Lauri wouldn't answer them because she imagined Merry would tell her to keep her mouth shut. She tried to find out why they were so sure she'd killed Clay, but they wouldn't tell her anything.

Then they asked about the gun.

She'd wondered when that would come up. She'd already told Officer Gutierrez about looking around Clay's house the morning she found the body. Now she wished she'd said something about touching the gun, too. It would've been better if she'd slipped that information in then, instead of having to answer for it now.

Of course, she hadn't thought they'd ever suspect her. Stupid nosy neighbor, spying on her in the dark. Her mom had better get on the stick and get her *out* of here.

She waited while they filled out forms. The skinny chick with the big boobs—what was her name … Natalie? No, Nadine. She searched Lauri and made her turn out her pockets, took her stuff away. Then she led her downstairs to the jail.

Lauri peered into the first doorway they passed and saw a long room with one big cage on the left side of a walkway, and facing it on the right, four smaller spaces enclosed by low-tech black iron bars. The two men sitting in the big cell looked up when she walked by, and one of them grinned at her.

The women's jail was the same, but smaller. There were only two mini cells across the aisle.

The poured-concrete floor sloped to a drain set into the walkway. As she walked over it, an oddly fruity smell wafted from it, cloying and putrid at the same time. She held her breath and hurried past.

The cinderblock walls reflected pale hospital-aqua like an underwater cave. The absence of windows intensified the feeling; claustrophobia pressed around her throat when Nadine shut her inside the big cell with a clang. Though it had been warm when the police took her out of her house, down here the walls held a damp chill the sun never touched. Fluorescent light glared down from parallel tubes over the center aisle, casting the room into starkness that made her eyes hurt.

Lauri shivered as she turned to survey the space. The only seating was a thick wooden bench bolted to the back wall. There wasn't even a toilet. Good thing she'd been allowed to go the bathroom before coming down here. At least the little cells had bunk beds.

On one end of the bench, a large woman reclined on her back with one leg bent, forearm resting over closed eyes. She wore jeans and a black T-shirt, and her greasy brown hair was pulled back into a lank ponytail. Her beer belly peeked out from under the T-shirt, all soft and pasty. Lauri's lip curled.

It was spooky quiet. No television or radio. No voices or traffic noises. The light bulbs didn't even hum, as if the water-colored walls drank in every vestige of sound before it could strike human ears. For just a second, she wondered if the walls could suck in the sound of a scream, leave the husk of it hanging in the air, less than a whisper.

The woman on the bench shifted her arm and opened her eyes, looking her up and down without moving from her prone position. Even though the look was downright rude, Lauri didn't look away. The woman slowly sat up. She might have been fat, but upright she looked like she could wrestle a bull to the ground.

Her clothes rustled when she moved, and even though she knew it was silly that made Lauri feel a little better.

"What're you here for, princess?" the woman asked.

She didn't answer. Hugging herself she walked to the other end of the bench and sat down.

"Not very talkative, huh? That's okay. I can respect that." The woman leaned against the wall and closed her eyes.

"I don't know why I'm here," Lauri said.

The woman opened her eyes again. "Whadaya mean you don't know?"

"Well, I shouldn't be in here," Lauri said.

"Honey, nobody should be in here. I'm Val, by the way. I shouldn't be in here, either."

"What did they mess up and arrest you for?" Lauri asked.

"Oh, just because I shouldn't be in here doesn't mean I didn't do it."

"Do what?"

Val narrowed her eyes. "Took a baseball bat to my ex-husband's truck."

"How come?"

"It was my truck, but the bastard got it in the divorce. I loved that truck, did all the work on it myself. I'll be damned if he hauls his new little piece of ass around in it."

"Huh," Lauri said, not understanding why anyone would love a pickup. Sounded like Val should have taken the baseball bat to her ex-husband.

"So? Whadabout you?"

She looked away. "They think I killed my boyfriend. Well, ex-boyfriend."

Val whistled. "No shit?"

Lauri sighed. "No shit."

"So what did he do to you?"

"Nothing. He didn't do anything. We broke up a year ago. We'd been talking lately, but he had this new girlfriend …"

"Did you do it?"

"Of course not."

"So why'd they arrest you?"

Lauri bit her lip. "Some stupid footprints I left under his window."

"Under his window."

"Yeah. His bedroom window. I looked in his window late one night, and suddenly they decide I must have shot him."

"Shot him, huh. Wow."

"I don't even know how to shoot a gun—and I wanted to *marry* Clay. Just because it happened the same night I was there, they think I did it. I mean, I'm the one who found him dead, right? I wouldn't have done that if I'd killed him, would I?"

"Unless that's what you want them to think."

"Hey. Whose side are you on?" Lauri said.

"I'm just saying. And it's what those cops upstairs are saying, too."

"Well, nobody asked you."

"Sensitive little thing, aren't you?"

"Leave me alone."

Val raised one eyebrow, and her expression turned hard. Without another word she resumed her horizontal position on the bench.

Lauri pulled her legs up and rested her chin on her knees. She was cold. She was scared. And she was getting really pissed off. The slick soles of her sandals wanted to slide off the bench. She took them off and cupped her fingers over her cold toes. What she wouldn't give for some warm socks and a pair of tennis shoes right now. And a sweatshirt. A nice fuzzy, snuggly sweatshirt. If her mom didn't hurry up, she could freeze to death in here.

God, what a bunch of jerks the police were. Merry had warned her, and maybe she should have listened. Cousin Merry, poking around, asking her questions, handing out advice like she was some big sister or something.

Lauri had told her about Denny, after he'd bailed on the money he owed her. *Owed* her, damn it. Maybe Merry would get all high and mighty and get something out of him. Her cousin was like that: a girl version of a white knight. A sucker. Lauri could smell them a mile away. And prison had made her cousin tough, too. She bet that if Merry did talk to Denny, the guy would listen a lot harder than he had when she'd talked to him. Little creep.

Her thoughts swerved from anger at Denny to Clay as she'd last seen him. He'd been so still. It had frightened her, badly. She'd thought dead people were supposed to look like they were sleeping, but once she'd seen him in the light, Clay had looked *dead*. And not just because of all that blood, either. It was like he didn't have any bones left, only skin holding in the soft parts he'd left behind.

The tears felt hot on her cold cheeks. She wiped them away.

Stop thinking about it. Just stop. Don't think about the smell of blood that left a taste in the back of my throat like when Becky Ostler dared me to chew a piece of tinfoil in the fourth grade.

After a little while, Nadine brought in another woman. She had mascara circles like a raccoon around her bloodshot eyes, bits of dried grass sticking out of blonde curls in desperate need of combing, a dribble of yellow mustard down the front of her soiled white shirt. She staggered to the bench and sat next to Lauri, leaning against her arm and muttering under her breath.

And, oh, what breath it was. Dismayed, Lauri looked over at Val, who watched them with a small, enigmatic smile, ignoring the silent plea in her eyes. She edged away from her new companion, sliding off the bench as she propped the woman against the wall. As she stood, the woman leaned over and vomited on Lauri's bare feet.

146

Lauri shrieked. Val grinned. Nadine came running. The woman stretched out along the bench and went to sleep, stuttering snores rising with her sour breath. Nadine took in the situation and left, to return with a roll of paper towels. She passed them through the bars, said she'd come back when she wasn't so busy upstairs.

"I need to go to the bathroom!"

"I'll be back as soon as I can," Nadine said, and hurried out.

Lauri cleaned up as best as she could, blinking back tears of disgust. This was police cruelty. They'd put that revolting woman in the jail with her on purpose. That Val person was probably even in on it.

She threw the dirty paper towels through to the walkway.

After an hour, Nadine returned with lunch: Cokes, cheeseburgers, and fries in waxed food boxes Lauri recognized from the Hungry Moose. Ignoring the food, she demanded to go to the bathroom again.

Nadine took her upstairs and left her in there, giving her time to balance on one foot at a time and wash her feet in the sink. Then she scrubbed her sandals where the splatter had reached them until the soles began to split from the water. They made soft wet noises when she put them on and walked out to where Nadine waited to lead her back to the jail.

"Hasn't my mom paid the bail yet?" Lauri asked.

"She can't. Your bail hearing isn't until tomorrow morning," Nadine said.

"Tomorrow morning!"

"I'll move you out of the holding cell to one of the bunks across the hall."

Lauri tried her most beguiling smile, the wide-eyed one she reserved for other women. "I'm pregnant. Do they know that?"

"Does who know?"

"The judge, or whoever. Whoever's in charge of getting me out of here."

"With a murder charge the judge might set the bail too high for your mom to pay. You could be here a lot more than one night. So you might as well make the best of it," Nadine said.

Lauri gaped at her. Nadine opened one of the smaller cells, conducted her inside, and handed her the cold cheeseburger. She sat on the edge of the bed and ate half of it, trying to ignore the gross smell from the cell across the aisle. She kept the Coke and set the food wrappings on the floor outside the bars.

Nadine moved Val into the other bunk cell. Then she used a hose with a spray nozzle to sluice down the floor under the bench where the drunken raccoon-eyed woman continued to snore. The drain in the floor emitted loud, throaty gurgles as she worked.

Lauri removed her soggy sandals and crawled into the narrow bottom bunk. She shivered until the thick blanket began to reflect warmth back to her. Her muscles began to unclench.

She wasn't getting out of here today. She still had a hard time believing she'd be stuck here all night. As for Nadine's warning about bail, her mind refused to go there. Just tonight, she told herself. That was all she had to get through. Her mom would help her. Merry would help her. At least she had a blanket. And no one could barf on her in here. There was even a little toilet in the corner, hidden behind a concrete partition.

It still totally and completely sucked.

THIRTEEN

MERRY RANG THE DOORBELL and moments later heard footsteps. Jamie opened the door but didn't step back.

"I'm sorry," she said. "You were right, and I was wrong, and I'm sorry. Can we put all this stuff between us aside for now? I need your help."

His eyes held hers for a long moment, then he blew out a breath and gestured her in. She limped along behind him, through the living room and kitchen and down the basement stairs. She knew the way well; Jamie had grown up in this house, had bought it from his parents when they moved to Arizona to escape the frigid Montana winters.

"Is Gayle here?"

"She's at work."

Merry realized she didn't know where Jamie's wife worked. And didn't really care.

"Why were you at the station on your day off?" she asked.

"Had to pick something up and managed to stumble into the Hawkins and Lester show."

Lester Fleck seemed to spend an awful lot of time with Rory Hawkins. Shirlene had said he'd been there when they'd taken Lauri.

In the basement they passed a finished guest bedroom and tiny half-bath, ending up in a large open room. One wall held fishing rods, each supported horizontally on pegs. In the corner a pair of waders hung from a rack, along with a couple of pocketed canvas vests and an assortment of hats. A shelf at eye level boasted an assortment of books on fishing, maps, and an ancient metal tackle box. The painted concrete floor and cinderblock walls provided at least a ten-degree drop in temperature from upstairs.

An old sofa with tattered brown cushions caught her eye. Gayle must not be aware of the history in that thing or it wouldn't still be around. Merry smiled to herself. When she looked up, Jamie was watching her, and her smile faded.

She pulled the chair out from a small table fitted with a vise for fly-tying. A large compartmentalized box covered the rest of the table, the sections filled with floss and tinsel, a dozen sizes of hooks, fur and feather hackle materials, and three different whip finishers. Jamie sat at the industrial-looking table in the middle of the room. He'd been installing guides on a bamboo fly rod.

"Is Lester the sergeant's toady?"

He turned so his chair faced her and tipped it back on two legs. "Lester's not bad, actually, and I can't blame him for playing Hawkins to make his life easier." He paused. "So have you seen Shirlene?"

"I talked to her on the phone. She's calling Kate."

He nodded.

"So why did they arrest Lauri?" she asked.

Jamie's eyes slid to the side. "Screw the apology, huh. You just came over here to grill me."

"No. The apology is real. But my cousin's in jail for murder."

He let out a puff of air. "Yeah. Okay. I guess it's not a big secret. Or at least it won't be, and Kate will find out sooner than later anyway. You remember yesterday when I told you Hawkins put a rush on the ballistics?"

"Yeah."

"Well, we got them back. The gun we found in the duplex was the gun that killed Clay. And guess whose fingerprints are on it?"

"Not the guy with the grudge because Clay got him fired for doing coke."

"Gus Snyder. No, they aren't his."

"You're shitting me. Lauri's fingerprints are really on the gun?"

He nodded. "It's confirmed. Actually, I guess they knew there was a fingerprint match last night, but they had to know for sure it was the same gun used to kill Lamente before the county attorney would let them move on it."

"You keep saying 'they,'" she said.

He rubbed his hand along the back of his neck. "Well, I'm sorta on the edge of this thing now. Hawkins is doing as much of the investigation with Lester as he can. He knows you and I are friends, and he doesn't trust me."

She shook her head. "So what does she say about the fingerprints?"

"Lauri?"

Merry nodded, trying to hide her impatience.

"I don't know if she's said anything," Jamie said. "In case you haven't noticed, I'm off today."

She ignored him. "When you talked to her after she found the body, she admitted to snooping around before going into the bedroom. She could have touched it then."

He gave her a look. "And the footprints we found outside the window match a pair of the boots we took from the house."

She grimaced. "They're Shirlene's."

He raised his eyebrows.

Merry shook her head. "Lauri borrowed them."

"She tell you that?"

She hesitated, then nodded. "Back to the gun—she'd have to be stupid to leave her fingerprints if she used it, right? And if the murderer wiped it clean and Lauri touched it when she was snooping around before she found Clay, hers would be the only prints on it. Did you find anyone else's? Denny's?"

"Just hers. Hmm. That's something to think about. Anyway, Gus Snyder? Admits to hating Lamente, but has an alibi. He was in Lewiston, staying with family for three days. Had relatives around him the whole time."

"Shit." She'd been planning to go see Snyder next.

He watched her for a moment. "Everything points to her, Merry."

She studied the floor. "It sure looks like it." She thought of Shirlene's face when talking about her daughter's pregnancy. How would it affect her if Lauri were convicted of murder? Merry shivered in the cool air, unable to get her head around the idea of her cousin inside a prison.

"Could she have done it? In your mind?" Jamie asked. "I know she's your cousin and all, but—"

She looked up, shaking her head. "No. I mean, she *is* my cousin, and I don't have a lot of family to spare, but I really believe she's innocent. There must be other possibilities. Besides Snyder, I mean."

He humored her, running through the list of people around the periphery of the crime. He'd spoken with most of them before Rory Hawkins had pushed him aside. He told Merry that barring another ready suspect, the police looked at the spouse.

"Clay Lamente didn't have a spouse, but he had a girlfriend," he said.

"I know. Remember, we put her out when she was on fire."

"Right. She seems pretty shaken by his death."

Merry reached over and fingered the feathers of a rooster cape. "She could be acting, I suppose." But she didn't really believe it.

"Sure, and I'm not saying it's impossible to fool me. But why would she do it?"

Merry sighed. "I don't know."

"And Clay's mother provided her alibi. Barbie said she and Clay were supposed to get together that night, but he called her and said he wasn't feeling well. So he went to bed, and she stayed home. Olivia came over, and they worked on some volunteer stuff."

"WorldMed."

"Right." Jamie's chair creaked as he brought the front legs down.

"Was Olivia there the whole time?"

"From seven until about eleven."

She put both elbows on the table and laced her fingers together. "But you said he was killed between nine thirty and midnight."

"Yes. But Anna was over at Clay's, with Denny Teller, from about ten thirty on."

"And they didn't see anyone."

"Nope. They went to bed about eleven. But they still would have heard the shots. He must have been killed before they got home, between nine-thirty and ten-thirty."

"Did Barbie have a key?"

"No. But she knew where they kept the extra. Just like Lauri did." He picked up a whip finisher and twirled it absently between his thumb and forefinger. The silver metal shone in a small patch of sunshine angling through the basement window.

"Could she have used a silencer?" Merry asked.

He raised one shoulder and let it drop. "Silencers are hard for the average Joe—or Joanna—to come by. And they aren't designed to be used with revolvers like the thirty-eight we found, but with semi-automatics. So it would have to be specially made for the gun, and even then a silencer—sound suppressor, really—might muffle the shot a bit, but it would still be pretty damn loud. They just don't *work* on that kind of gun. And there was no evidence that the killer shot through anything like a pillow to muffle the shot, either."

Merry considered. "Lauri said she was there around midnight. Anna and Denny still would have heard the shots if she'd done it."

"She *said* that's when she was there. The prosecution will say she's lying, that she was there earlier."

She remembered staring at the puddle by the police station while eavesdropping on Lauri. "It rained that night, but she said it had stopped by the time she got there. If Lester could identify the foot-prints, they must have been distinct. No water in them, right?"

"Right." He thought for a moment, then quirked his lips. "Still, and this is just looking at it from the prosecution's standpoint, she could have come back."

"After he was dead? Why?"

"Merry. Why does she say she was there in the first place?"

There was no point in sharing that Lauri had been planning to seduce Clay. Explaining away Lauri's inexplicable behavior with a different kind of inexplicable behavior wouldn't go over well with a jury, and might even support the idea that she had been stalking him.

A jury. Christ. She took a shaky breath remembering how hope had turned to horror as her own trial progressed. She forced herself to focus. "Well, it's still not likely she'd come back."

"It's certainly something for Kate to bring up. I guess you'd call the evidence they have circumstantial. But it's some of the best circumstantial evidence I've ever heard of."

"God." She rubbed the back of her neck. "Could Anna and Denny be lying? About hearing the shots?"

He held up his palms. "Anyone can lie. But why?" He cocked his head to one side. "You know, we had some reports of fireworks going off in that neighborhood that night. They could have heard it and just didn't realize what it was. They were pretty drunk."

"Anna didn't say anything about being drunk." But she had made it pretty clear she liked to imbibe.

"Anna didn't . . . when did you talk to her?"

Merry explained about her visit to the blood mobile.

He looked unhappy. "I should have known." He paused. "She didn't tell us they'd been drinking, either. But Denny wasn't shy about telling us how many black Russians they drank over the course of the evening. It was enough to at least dim their hearing."

"That's what he told you. What if they didn't drink that much? What if they killed him?"

"Why?"

"Shit, I don't know. Maybe Clay found out Denny fathered Lauri's baby. Maybe he disapproved."

"Wait a minute. Denny and Lauri?"

She nodded. "She told me yesterday."

He sat forward in his chair. "Well, that's an interesting development."

"So Clay got angry, and Denny killed him, and Anna is covering for Denny."

"But why would Clay get angry? And why would Lauri's fingerprints be on the gun?"

"Well, I'm pretty pissed at Denny, and I've never even met the guy. He told Lauri he's not going to give her any money for the baby. And like I said, Lauri could have picked up the gun when she was snooping around the duplex. *And*, it's Denny's gun in the first place."

He nodded. "It's a thought. What's your scenario for Anna shooting Clay and Denny protecting her?"

She looked to see if he was making fun of her. He didn't seem to be. "What if Clay didn't like her seeing Denny, seeing as how Denny is married? It sounds like he was kind of a tight-ass. Maybe he threatened to tell Denny's wife."

"That sounds more like a motive for Denny than for Anna."

Merry considered. "Whatever. They'd have to be in it together anyway."

"Anyone else you'd like to pin this on?"

She hesitated. "Harlan."

"Harlan *Kepper*?"

She shrugged. "He was awfully happy to hear Clay was dead that afternoon we saw him in the hardware."

Jamie looked puzzled. "You want me to tell Hawkins?"

She shook her head.

He frowned. "You're not going to do anything stupid, are you?"

"Of course not. But I can talk to the guy. Hell, Hawkins probably wouldn't bother following up, even if you did tell him."

"Yeah. Okay. But maybe I should go with you."

"I'll let you know when I do it." But she knew she wouldn't. She was pretty sure he knew it, too.

They sat in silence for a minute.

"You know, there's always the possibility that there's someone else, someone we know nothing about," he said.

"What I really don't get is how Bo's death fits into all this."

"It might not fit in at all. There's no proof he was murdered."

"'Blunt force trauma to the skull,' you said."

"That doesn't mean someone whacked him over the head. Something could have fallen on him. Shit was flying everywhere, if you'll recall."

"Why would he be in the barn once it was on fire?"

"Well, that damn dog seems pretty popular."

She ignored that. "Pretty weird that no one saw him the whole time we were there, then."

"I don't know. They had insurance. Hell, Bo could have set the fire himself, and then been caught in it. I can't think why Lauri would have it in for him."

"Hmm." Merry stood up. "Well, thanks for letting me pick your brain. But I'd better get over to Shirlene's."

Jamie walked her upstairs.

At the door, she stopped and turned around. "I really am sorry."

He sighed. "Me, too. I overreacted."

"No. I never realized how you must have felt when I married Rand." She started down the steps.

"Merry?"

She stopped and looked over her shoulder.

"Yeah?"

"I ... nothing, I guess." He bounced a couple of times on the balls of his feet, then fell still.

"Sure?"

"Yeah. I'll talk to you later."

She nodded and continued out to the Blazer. He was still standing in the doorway when she pulled away.

FOURTEEN

MERRY WALKED INTO HER aunt's house and found Shirlene and Kate seated together on the sofa. The shades were half-drawn and the atmosphere was gray and musty with worry. Kate waved her in, still talking to Shirlene. "I'm surprised they arrested her on what they have. Right now our main focus has to be on getting the judge to set a reasonable amount of bail and then coming up with it so you can get your daughter out of jail. I don't know what will come after that yet—I'm sorry, Shirlene, but I really have to talk to some people and see whether there's anything else in the mix we don't know about."

"There is." Merry dropped into the recliner and told them about the fingerprints on the murder weapon belonging to Lauri, and that the footprints under Clay's window matched a pair of boots taken with the warrant. Shirlene stared at her slack-jawed.

Kate's expression was sober as she absorbed this new information. "You're sure about the gun?"

Merry nodded.

"How did you come to find out about it?"

Merry told her about Jamie. "He's probably telling me things out of school. It'd be good if you didn't spread around where you got the information."

Kate shrugged. "I'd find out soon enough anyway. This just gives me a leg up. Tell me what else he told you."

"Nothing that would matter."

"Let me decide that."

Shirlene said, "Lauri's going to trial, Merry." Her voice broke. "Please. Anything might help."

Regretting bringing up Jamie's name at all, Merry sketched out what he'd told her, including the information about Gus Snyder and his alibi for the night of the murder. For good measure she threw in what she had gleaned from Anna Knight while giving blood, though much of it was repetitive. Kate wrote on a yellow legal pad as she spoke, scribbling in the weird shorthand Merry remembered from high school. The fan sounded loud in the quiet that followed.

"Well." Kate leaned back. "We still need to work on that bail. I called the courthouse and the hearing is scheduled for tomorrow morning. Once the judge sets bail—and they should unless it's a capital crime—we can figure out where to go from there. I'll meet you at the courthouse at nine a.m. Okay, Shirlene?"

She nodded.

"But if I find out anything before then, I'll call you here, okay?"

Shirlene nodded again, her lips pressed together.

"It'll work out. We just have to take it one step at a time," Kate said. She clicked her briefcase closed and stood. "Merry, can you give me a ride? I walked and I'm running late."

"Uh, sure," she said, but her attention was on Shirlene, who was rubbing her face with both hands as if trying to wash it all away. Her aunt felt her gaze and looked up.

"I'm okay," she said.

"You sure?"

"Yeah."

"I'll come get you in the morning and take you to the court-house."

"Thanks. That'd be good."

She hugged her aunt and went outside with Kate. "You walked?" she asked when they were on the street.

"You thought I made that up?"

"No. Just making conversation." Merry hoisted herself into the Blazer, irritated at how awkward her swollen ankle made her look.

Kate settled in the seat beside her. "Well, I did want to talk to you."

Shit. "Thought you never wanted to talk to me again."

"Did I say that?"

"Oh, yes. You definitely said that."

"Hmm. Probably. But that was a long time ago. Much as I'd like to revisit that unpleasantness, I don't have time right now. But we will, okay? I have some things I need to say about what happened."

Bully for you.

"Take a right here, and—"

"I know where it is," Merry said.

"Oh." Then, "I heard about your mom."

Merry nodded, keeping her gaze on the street ahead.

"I saw her every once in a while. I liked her," Kate said.

"Most people did."

"So how are you doing with it?"

161

"'It' being her death, you mean?"

"Yes. That's what I mean."

"I have my moments."

This time Kate nodded. Then, "I'm going over to meet Lauri, tell her about the bail hearing tomorrow, get her side of things. What's she like?"

Merry shrugged.

"It's possible she killed him, isn't it?"

"Anything's possible. But it's not probable."

"It wouldn't matter, you know. I'll defend her to the best of my abilities no matter what," Kate said.

"I know. That's why I told Shirlene to call you." She pulled to the curb in front of the Hazel Office Mall.

"It was your idea? She didn't mention that." Kate opened the door and got out. Stood on the other side of the open window. "I appreciate your confidence after all these years."

"You were always so determined to be a defense attorney. I figured you must be pretty good at it."

"I am." She leaned one elbow on the door. "Do you have a lawyer up here?"

"No. And I fired my sorry-ass lawyer in Texas, too."

"You're on parole. You might need one."

"Have a lot of faith in me, don't you? I think I can manage on my own."

"Hey, I know you're still angry, okay? But get over it. I'm offering my services, if you should need them. That's all I'm saying."

Merry looked out through the windshield. "I'll keep it in mind."

"Good." Kate turned and started to walk away, then came back. "And we'll talk about the other stuff. Soon."

Merry met her eyes. "I guess maybe we should."

Kate nodded once and walked across the street. On the opposite sidewalk, she turned and looked at Merry, then raised her hand in an uncharacteristically tentative gesture. Merry hesitated, then raised her own hand, feeling that doing so somehow sealed some kind of truce between them.

———

Despite the heat, the huge tangle of copper rose looked fresh and lively against the yellow duplex. The street number hung by the door on the right. Merry wondered who lived in the other side of the dwelling, and if they knew anything about what had happened the night of Clay Lamente's death. The police would have talked with them, she reasoned. Jamie hadn't mentioned that they'd added anything to the investigation.

On the other hand, she didn't trust Rory Hawkins as far as she could kick his flabby butt. She changed direction and went up the neighbor's steps.

After several moments, a young woman holding a baby answered the door. The pungent aromas of garlic and Italian spices wafted through the screen.

"Hi. I'm Merry McCoy. Could I talk to you for a minute?"

The smile that had begun to form on the woman's face faded. "I'm not buying anything, and I already go to church."

Merry laughed. "Well, I'm not trying to sell you or save you. It's about your neighbors."

The baby gazed at her sideways, cheek against his mother's shoulder, blue watery eyes never leaving this interesting newcomer.

The woman opened the door and gestured her inside. Aerosmith thumped through the wall from the other side of the duplex.

The living room was furnished in early-marriage thrift accented with new-baby clutter. The bright plastic toys had seen use, as had the furniture. But the blank television screen and smell of home cooking won Merry over. The woman put the baby in a bouncy baby holder hanging in the kitchen doorway.

"What's this about?" Her dishwater-red hair, clasped in a large silver and turquoise barrette, exploded in a cloud of curls at the nape of her neck. Freckles dusted her light skin.

Merry gestured with her chin. "You know about what happened over there?"

"God, yes. Scared the living daylights out of me."

"I bet. Did the police come and talk to you?"

She nodded, looking curious. "Big guy. Kind of … abrupt, you know?"

Merry knew. "Well, I'm just following up on a few things."

"You work for the police?"

She'd be in a pile of hurt if she impersonated a police officer. "No. I'm doing a study. A research project for a class. About how the police interact with the public."

The woman nodded. "I went to MSU. Accounting." She smiled at the gurgling child, trying to fit his entire fist into his mouth. "But this is good, too."

Merry plunged on. "Did the policeman you spoke with ask you about the night of … the night it happened?"

The woman nodded. "Do you need some paper to write this down?"

"Oh, that'd be great. I walked off without my notebook. Can you believe that?"

Rifling through a kitchen drawer and coming up with a pad printed with kittens gamboling through a basket of yarn, she nodded. "When I was pregnant it was like I had a brain tumor. I couldn't remember anything."

"Well, I don't even have that excuse. Thanks." Merry took the proffered pad and pen and began writing earnestly. "What's your name?"

"Samantha Cisco. But you can call me Sam."

"Okay, Sam. The officer asked you about that night. Did you see anything?"

"No."

"Hear anything?"

"No. Sorry."

"No, no, that's okay. There aren't any right or wrong answers here. How would you characterize the officer when he questioned you?" It was a throwaway question, but she hoped it would fit her assumed character.

Sam hesitated. "Will he hear about this?"

"All the data I compile is anonymous. That way people can be honest in their responses."

"Oh. Good. Well, he seemed like he was in a hurry. Like I said, kind of abrupt."

Merry smiled. "Well, I'll tell you a secret. You're not the only one who thinks that. Did he ask you about the week prior to the crime?"

Sam shook her head.

"If he had, would you have had any information to give him?"

"Not really."

"No unusual visitors next door, no arguments, stuff like that?"

"Well, there was this blonde girl who came over. She drove a Honda. She wasn't there very long, and when she left she looked like she'd been crying."

Lauri. Great.

"And then there was that older man. I'd seen him before a few times. He and Clay, the one who, you know, got killed? They got in a shouting match. I could hear it through the wall."

With effort, Merry kept her tone mild. "Could you hear what they were saying?"

Sam shook her head, looking apologetic again.

"How long before the, uh, incident did this happen?"

"Oh, it was that same day. In the morning."

Merry scribbled furiously, thinking. Harlan? Or maybe Bo?

"Was the other resident home at the time?"

"Denny? His van wasn't there." She grimaced. "And I can usually tell when he's home by the music."

Merry looked up. "He plays it that loud all the time?"

"My husband has gone over a couple times to ask him to turn it down, but that only lasts a day or so. Me and Quinn just try to ignore it," she said, smiling at the baby again. Quinn bounced a couple times and started working on his other fist.

This woman was too good to live. Merry felt bad lying to her.

"Can you think of anything else?"

"About that week? No."

"What about your interaction with the officer who questioned you?"

"Not really. Like I said. It didn't take very long."

"Well, I sure appreciate you talking to me."

"Oh, no problem. Would you like a cookie? I just baked them this morning."

———

The music vibrated through the all-weather siding, and she had to pound with her fist to be heard. The volume lowered, and Denny Teller opened the door. His stringy blond hair flowed down over a black T-shirt. Long toes gripped leather flip-flops below the hem of his faded blue jeans. He was deeply tanned and muscles roped over his arms and flexed in his neck. Unfocused blue eyes hazed with red peered at Merry above a sharp nose and thin lips.

He blinked at her. "Yeah?"

"I'm Merry McCoy."

"So?"

"I want to talk to you." She didn't offer her hand.

"What about?"

"Can I come in?"

"No. It's a bad time." He started to shut the door.

Merry stuck her cane in the doorway just in time. Denny said "Hey!" and continued to push on the door. She pushed back, hard, and the door flew open as he let go and stepped away. She walked into the living room. The air held the unmistakable skunk smell of pot smoke.

Denny backed into the room. "What the fuck do you want?"

"For one thing I want to talk to you about Lauri Danner."

His eyes narrowed, and a calculating smile crept onto his face. "Hey, you're the one just got out of jail. So McCoy's your name, killer?" He said the word as if it were an endearment.

Feeling as if a cold hand had snaked inside her chest, she stiffened. "I've heard about you, too, Mr. Teller. And believe me, it ain't all good."

He laughed, his teeth flashing. "Hoowee! Simple question sure got me some flutter. Well, Miz McCoy, I ain't no Hatfield, so you can go ahead and lower your gun. I don't mean no harm."

I'd rather just lower my aim.

"You Lauri's sister or something?"

"Cousin."

Denny barked a laugh. "Well, Cuz, what do you want to talk about li'l Lauri for?"

"She's pregnant."

"Don't I know it. She kept trying to pin it on my poor roommate. He's dead now. I'm in mourning, you see. So maybe you could come back later."

"Lauri says it's yours."

"Shee-it. That's not my kid."

"She says it is."

"Then she's lying."

"You know, I don't think so. And it'll be easy enough to prove."

Denny swaggered to the battered recliner sitting in front of the TV and flopped into it, one long leg hanging over the arm.

"It was one time, just one of those things. She told me she was on the pill. She wanted me bad, and I try not to refuse the ladies, you know what I mean?" He winked at Merry.

He reminded her of Zeke and his patter and obnoxious come-ons when he'd had a few beers. She fought the urge to run right back out the door.

She forced herself to look him in the eye. "Well, she's pregnant. And you're the lucky guy, Denny."

"Man, that is one crazy girl. How can you believe what she says? She could have slept with anybody. Everybody."

A lot of people would buy that, but he'd already admitted he could be the father, and that was good enough to start with.

"There are tests once the pregnancy is well enough along. We'll find out for sure then. And then you'll be legally bound to pay child support after it's born."

"Fuck that. Lauri'll probably be in prison, anyway."

"I'd heard you were kind of an asshole, but I had no idea."

He looked bored. "Yeah, yeah. No one's keeping you here."

"Did Clay know you got together with Lauri?"

"I'm not stupid."

"You're proving that every time you open your mouth. What would he have said if he'd known?"

"They were long over, man, and he had a new little hottie."

"Why didn't you tell him about you and Lauri, then?"

"Never came up. Besides," he looked embarrassed, "he was kind of a holier-than-thou type, you know? If I'd a known that, I never would've answered his ad for a roommate. Had to have a place to stay while I'm working, though, and he was working the Hi-Sho, too. Thought he'd be cool."

"So he wouldn't have approved on principle."

He shrugged.

"Bet your wife wouldn't be very impressed, either."

"Hey, man, that's none of your business. My wife and me, we have, like, an understanding, you know? She does her thing and I do mine."

Maybe. And maybe your thing is to sleep with every female you can wrangle around whatever job you're working, and her thing is to put up with it.

"It's a shame about Clay."

"Yeah …" He shook his head, an exaggerated movement. Merry wondered just how high the guy was.

"I hear you were right here when he died that night. And that your gun killed him."

He rolled his eyes. "Nice try."

She swallowed. "Doesn't it creep you out to be in a house where someone was murdered?"

He shrugged.

"Aren't you afraid they might come back?"

"Man, you are something else. Why would anyone want to kill me?"

She turned and twisted the doorknob. "Funny. I can think of a couple reasons with no trouble at all."

Denny shot out of his chair, slamming the half-open door shut and grabbing her wrist.

"And you're just the one to do it, is that it, killer?" He hissed the words at her.

"Let go of me." The words grated out around her panic, and she knew she'd do whatever she had to in order to get away from this guy. It must have shown on her face, because his eyes widened and he stepped back, releasing her.

"Go. And don't be coming back here, honey. That'd be a mistake."

But the threat was a weak one, and she left with a feeling of victory that lasted until she reached the Blazer. Then she realized how willing she had been to hurt the guy. Really, really hurt him.

What was wrong with her?

FIFTEEN

As much as Merry wanted to go home and saddle up Izzy, she had one more errand in town. Harlan's comment about Clay had been bothering her more and more. Since Shirlene hadn't been able to enlighten her, she could think of only one person who could.

Eyes adjusting to the dim light in the hardware, she followed the aisle to the rear door. Out on the loading dock, heat crept through the afternoon air, intensifying the woodsy fragrance from a pile of cedar bark off to one side. The subtle scents of oats and sweetened corn from the sacks nearby tangled in the breeze. Behind it all lurked the not unpleasant odor of composted manure.

Harlan stood at the edge of the platform, gazing out at the horizon beyond the edge of town. He turned in response to the sound of her footsteps behind him.

"Merry! What can I do you for?"

"Something's been bothering me. Thought you could help me out with it."

"Well, shoot. I'll sure try."

"The other day when I was in here and asked if you knew Clay Lamente, you acted like he was the scum of the earth. You want to tell me what that was all about?"

Harlan reddened and turned away. "Not really."

She waited.

After a few moments he turned back, determination on his face. Still he didn't speak.

"What?"

"Merry, did your mama tell you about us?"

"About you?"

He toed a wooden plank. "We were seeing each other."

Her mouth opened in surprise. "No … she never mentioned it." Why hadn't she? "You didn't say anything when I was in here before."

"I thought about it. I did. But, well … it would have been awkward right then."

Like it wasn't awkward now.

"I guess I just had to think how to handle it."

"There's nothing to handle. You had a fling with my mom. Big deal."

His voice was gentle. "It was a little more than a fling."

Merry blinked. "How long?"

Harlan looked miserable. "Since not long after your father died, actually."

"What?" She couldn't keep the sarcasm out of her voice. "You sure it wasn't *before* my father died, Harlan? Were you having an affair when he was still alive?"

"No. Absolutely not."

"Really." Unsure whether she believed him or not. "So. How did you two meet up?"

"Oh hell, you know we'd known each other forever. We went to junior high and high school together, for God's sake."

She waited for a better answer. Eventually it came.

"I just called her up and asked her out. It was a few months after the funeral. You were at college, and I knew she was all alone out at the ranch. I thought she might like some company, maybe even have some fun."

"It was right after the funeral, Harlan!"

"I said it was a few months after. Maybe four. But I didn't really call her for a date or anything. We were just two old friends getting together for dinner and an early show at the movie theater. All we did was pal around for a year or so before things started getting serious."

"She could have told me."

"She could have, sure. She didn't, though. You were so busy, you hardly had time to talk to her in those days. It just didn't come up. And then she didn't know how to bring it up later, after it had been so long."

She stared, her face flushed. "So it's my fault?"

"It's nobody's fault." He met her gaze. "Doesn't it help to know your mother wasn't alone when she was sick? I really loved that woman. I still do. And I miss her." His voice broke.

Merry walked to the edge of the platform. When she turned back, Harlan was gazing out toward the horizon again.

"What about Clay?" she asked.

"One evening me and your mama were in Chewie's Bar. She was hungry for a hamburger. I would've flown in Maine lobster if she'd

174

wanted it, her appetite was so poor from the chemo, but she only wanted a hamburger. So we went to Chewie's."

He turned and looked at her. "All her hair had fallen out, but she wasn't one to wear a wig or one of them turban things. She had on a baseball cap. So she's sittin' there in the booth, and I'm up at the bar getting us something to drink when I hear someone say, 'Hey, Kojak.' I turn around and it's that little prick Clay Lamente."

Merry paled.

"She was so embarrassed, I could see her getting red from clear over where I stood."

"Oh, God."

"So she turns around and looks the sonofabitch in the eye. Well, then *he* starts getting all red in the face. He's mumbling and fumbling around, and I go up to him and tell him he'd better apologize to the lady or I'm gonna hand him his nuts on a platter."

"Did he?"

Harlan gave a little shrug. "Well, yeah. He did. All over the place. Said he was supposed to meet some buddy a' his in there, and the guy didn't have any hair. Said the guy's nickname on the rig was Kojak."

"So it was a mistake, him calling her that."

"That's what he said. I didn't buy it. Your mama did, though. Told him not to worry about it. Actually laughed, thought it was kinda funny." His expression said Harlan still didn't find the incident the least bit amusing. "Next day he comes in here looking for a washer to fix his faucet, but I wouldn't sell it to him. Told him to get himself gone and not to darken my door again."

"I don't suppose you went to visit him the other day, did you?"

Harlan looked puzzled. "Now, why on earth would I do that?"

175

Merry knew Chewie kept the light in his bar down low, and it sounded like Clay had been contrite about the misunderstanding. She found it oddly touching that Harlan still hated a man he thought had insulted the woman he loved, even after both of them were dead.

But he wouldn't have killed Clay over it. Sighing, Merry thanked him and left.

So who had argued with Clay the morning before he'd been murdered? It had to be Bo. Denny's nice neighbor had said she'd seen him several times. It could have been anyone, of course, but it made sense if the "older man" had been Clay's own father. But why had they argued? She remembered Shirlene mentioning Bo and the woman in the Hungry Moose. The more Merry found out about Clay the more sanctimonious he sounded.

Could this whole mess have started because Bo Lamente had been having an affair? With Anna *Knight*?

The thought made her brain hurt.

———

The next morning Merry picked up Shirlene and they drove to the courthouse. Another squall had passed through during the night. The sunlight swooped through the freshly washed air and glinted from the wet pavement.

Her aunt wore a linen suit the color of lime sherbet, with a crisp white blouse. She fidgeted on the short ride, pulling her hem down, fussing with her cuffs.

"Olivia is holding a memorial for Clay and Bo this afternoon at two thirty. I know Lauri would like to go."

Merry glanced over, surprised. "That seems fast."

"Not really. Your mother's funeral was two days after she died. They haven't released the, you know, bodies yet, but Olivia wanted to go ahead with the memorial." Shirlene tugged at her hem again.

"You can smoke if you want to."

Her aunt began rummaging through her purse. By the time they pulled into a parking space, she seemed calmer.

Inside the building, they went through a metal detector, and the guard indicated the day's court schedule posted on the wall. There was only one courtroom, though it looked like both judges worked out of it. Lauri's name was third from the top of the list. Merry turned and saw Kate approaching them.

"When is she up?" she asked, not bothering with a greeting.

Shirlene turned worried eyes on her. "She's third. What time will that be?"

"It all depends on how quickly the other two cases go. How are you holding up?"

"I'm okay."

"Good. I saw her this morning, took her the clothes you gave me."

"Is she okay?"

"Well, she's not very happy—the morning sickness didn't help— but she seems better than when I finally got in to see her yesterday afternoon. She was pretty upset about the other women they put her in with when they first arrested her. By the time I talked to her, she'd been moved into a more private cell, so at least she managed to get some sleep last night."

"Will she be able to come home with me this morning?"

Kate shot a glance at Merry. "If we're lucky we can pay the bail today."

"But you said…"

"I said this was our chance to get bail, Shirlene." Kate's voice was kind. "We drew Judge Magnuson. He's usually pretty reasonable, though a little, um, unpredictable. He'll grant bail, but even so it's bound to be a lot of money. It's not something you can just write a check for and take her home."

"So I'll call a bail bondsman. I won't let her stay in jail."

Kate nodded. "I know a good bondsman. But let's focus on this step for now. Are you ready to go in?"

"Is there time for me to go outside real quick?" Shirlene was already fumbling her cigarettes out of her bag.

"Sure," Kate said.

When Shirlene was out of earshot, Merry asked Kate, "What's the deal with the bail? How much are we talking about?"

Kate looked grim. "It'll be at least eighty thousand, could be as much as a million."

"Jesus! Does Shirlene know that?"

She nodded. "I told her, but I don't know if it registered. And by law he has to set 'reasonable' bail, and most people around here don't make that much money."

Her aunt walked back in, chewing on a breath mint. Kate gave her an encouraging smile and they moved toward the courtroom.

Merry had expected a starkly lit, functional space. Instead, they walked into an old-world atmosphere. Dark paneling lined walls that stretched up three stories. High windows rimmed the room, and incandescent fixtures along the walls augmented the abundance of natural light. The Montana state seal took up much of the back wall, and the state and U.S. flags hung in the rear corners of the room. On the right, an old-fashioned recessed gallery looked over the courtroom. Around them, the seats held a sprinkling of observers. People spoke to one another in muted voices, and Merry breathed in the smell of wood oil.

The judge entered, and everyone popped to their feet. A door to the left opened, and two men and Lauri walked in and sat in the plastic chairs. Merry heard Shirlene's intake of breath and saw Kate reach over and take her aunt's hand in her own. All the defendants wore street clothes. Lauri's modest sundress and fresh-washed face projected youth and vulnerability. Merry realized with a shock that her cousin was quite beautiful under all the pancake makeup she usually wore.

The first case was a drunk driver, and it was soon obvious this wasn't his first trip to court. Judge Magnuson's questions showed common sense, and his ego didn't constantly peek around the edges of his statements. A good sign. He sentenced the man to jail time—not such a good sign. The next defendant had beaten the crap out of his wife. He had a mild face, pale with a scrubby beard, and was obviously wearing the same clothes he'd slept in. His wife threw a wrench into things, denying he had roughed her up. She said the bruise that ran all along one side of her face was from a spill she had taken down the back steps of their home. The judge took the couple back into his chambers.

Voices raised in conversation while they all waited. Shirlene waved to Lauri, who smiled painfully back. Her aunt popped another breath mint, and Merry knew she wanted to bolt outside and smoke a quick cigarette, but didn't dare leave. Then the judge returned without the couple, and the bailiff called Lauri's case.

Kate hurried up front as Lauri was led out of the enclosure. They spoke a few moments, and then the judge banged his gavel. Kate argued hard for Lauri's bail to be low, and the county attorney asked for three hundred thousand. Kate spoke of Lauri's ties to the community and the fact that she lived with her mother.

"Bail is set at three hundred thousand dollars," Magnuson said and rapped his gavel against its wooden block.

"Your Honor," Kate said. "I ask you to reconsider—"

"We're done here, Ms. O'Neil."

Kate pressed her lips together, but didn't argue.

The county attorney began shuffling papers while the judge took a break. Lauri was taken back through the side door to return to her jail cell. Shirlene watched her go, then left the courtroom. Kate and Merry followed her out to the sidewalk, where two other people stood smoking.

Shirlene took a deep drag. "You did a great job. Thank you."

"It's what I'm here for," Kate said.

"So who's this bail bondsman?" Shirlene asked.

"He's in Missoula. We have to go up there to see him."

"Can you go right now?"

"Hang on. Let me call him first. You'll need some collateral." Kate shot a look at Merry. "And cash."

"How much?" Merry asked.

"Ten percent is the going rate."

"I need thirty grand? I don't have that kind of money!" Shirlene looked like she was going be ill.

"Do you have any equity in your house?"

Shirlene gave a slow nod. "And I know the president of the bank," she said. "Worked with him on the committee for the new library. He'll light a fire under the loan officer."

Kate agreed and headed back to her office to call the bail bondsman. She told Shirlene to call when she had news.

―――――

Standing in line at the teller's window, Merry could see Shirlene talking with a tiny guy in an outdated blue suit behind the window of a glassed-in office. He was wiry and hyper, and his head bobbed constantly as her aunt talked and gesticulated.

"May I help you?"

Merry stepped forward to the teller and told the woman what she wanted, praying Shirlene wouldn't pick that moment to turn around and see her.

―――――

That afternoon they met at Shirlene's again. The bank president had pulled some strings to get the second mortgage approved and she already had a check in hand. She could use her dry cleaning business as collateral, but even with the equity she had in the house Shirlene was still short of the cash required to post Lauri's bail.

"I wonder what my truck would sell for?" she said.

They were sitting at the wooden picnic table in her back yard. A gray squirrel chattered at them from the neighbor's tree. Kate had her briefcase open again out of habit, but she hadn't touched any of the papers it contained. They didn't even need a yellow pad to add together the chunks of money they were talking about.

"Don't do that, Aunt Shirlene," Merry said, and handed her a rectangular piece of paper.

"What's this?" she asked. "Oh, no. No, no, Merry, I can't let you do this."

She held a cashier's check. Merry had cashed out her mother's savings account.

"The hell you can't. If it makes you feel any better, it's not really my money. It's Mama's. And you know damn well she would have insisted on giving it to you."

Shirlene started to cry.

Kate gently took the check and looked at the amount. "This takes us over the top," she said. Shirlene nodded, unable to speak.

"Shall we head up to Missoula and take care of this? If we hurry, we can still make it to the courthouse in time. Lauri will be glad to sleep in her own bed tonight."

Shirlene took a deep shaky breath and wiped her face. "Let's go." Together they walked around to the front of the house.

"You need me to go with you?" Merry asked.

"No, of course not. Kate'll take good care of me."

Merry looked at Kate. "I'm going to let her, then. I think I'll go to the Lamentes' memorial."

"That's good. You tell Olivia I'm thinking about her," Shirlene said.

"I'll do that."

Shirlene slid into Kate's Volvo. Kate said, "That was a really nice thing you did."

Merry shrugged. "No big deal." She limped across the street and climbed into the Blazer, glad she hadn't told Shirlene about Frank canceling his leases. Her aunt would have never taken the money then.

———

Small groups clustered on the lawn in front of the Methodist Church. Merry parked across the street, still wearing the black slacks and beige silk blouse she'd worn to court that morning. She'd been comfortable enough in the air conditioning, but the old church boasted no such convenience.

Inside, mourners shuffled into pews, talking in low voices. She slid onto a seat with a pang of angry regret as she thought again of missing Mama's funeral. Up by the podium an easel held two enlarged photos of Clay and Bo Lamente, both candid grinning shots. The family resemblance was obvious. In the afternoon heat, a profusion of roses overwhelmed the intense odor of more traditional lilies.

The murmuring quieted, and Merry looked up to see the pastor mounting the step behind the pulpit. The man, youngish and pale, adjusted the height of the microphone as if from long practice and turned it on. A horrible whine erupted, and he hurried to turn it off. A collective sigh of relief rippled through the congregation.

"I think we can do without the added volume, don't you? Can everyone hear me?"

No one spoke, but heads nodded.

Later, she couldn't remember the specifics of what the pastor had said. It seemed to be the same formulaic, memorized script. When they stood and sang, she did the best she could with the unfamiliar hymn.

Olivia delivered a eulogy. She choked up, but continued despite her tears. She spoke of Bo with deep affection, recounting how they had met at a livestock auction in St. Onge, South Dakota. He was managing a cattle ranch over by Spearfish and was looking for breeding stock for the land he owned outside Hazel. She was looking for breeding stock, too, in hopes of starting her own horse farm, but in those days it was still a pipe dream for Olivia.

"Despite our age difference, we knew right away we belonged together. Clay was just thirteen then. He loved the horses, and he was a hard worker." Her voice broke and she took a few minutes to regain her composure. "He grew up to be a fine young man. We started the training stable and bred thoroughbreds. In another couple years we would have finally been in the big leagues, supplying horses to champion riders all over the U.S. I don't know how I'll manage to do it without Bo, but I'm going to try. Because that's what he would have wanted me to do." She ended simply, "I miss them both so much."

Olivia returned to the front pew, next to Barbie. On Barbie's other side sat another woman. A woman with long dark hair. Anna? The thought was incongruous, and Merry couldn't believe Bo's wife and lover would be sitting together at his memorial. She craned to the side, trying to see the woman's face beyond the swath of blue-black hair. The man sitting next to Merry cleared his throat. She glanced up to see him scowling at her. With an apologetic moue, she sat up straight again.

Hazel's mayor addressed the group next. He praised Bo's involvement in the community, from serving on the library board to mentoring disadvantaged kids. And Clay had begun working with the same group of kids, organizing them into a softball team and acting as their coach.

Swiveling her head, Merry saw several youngsters in the seats around her.

The pastor returned and gave them a few parting banalities. They ended by singing "Amazing Grace," and she found it not only familiar, but surprisingly comforting. Row by row, the pews emptied into a neat double column as mourners exited the church proper.

In the large vestibule, she waited to go through the receiving line. She heard Olivia muttering thanks over and over as the mourners shuffled forward. Then Merry stood in front of her.

The girl standing between Olivia and Barbie was about sixteen years old with soft brown eyes and smooth toffee-colored skin framed by her straight black hair. Definitely not Anna Knight.

"I'm so sorry," Merry said. "And Aunt Shirlene and Kate O'Neil wanted me to pass on their sympathies." She didn't mention the reason the two women couldn't attend the memorial was because they were busy bailing out the only suspect in Clay's murder. "Please let us know if there's anything we can do."

Olivia nodded, but Merry didn't warrant thanks. Merry couldn't blame her. The police would have told Clay's stepmother that they'd arrested Lauri.

"Hi," she said to the girl.

The teenager's eyes widened. "Hi."

Barbie, standing on the other side, said, "This is Delores Little Wolf. Bo was tutoring her in math. Delores, this is Merry McCoy."

Merry nodded. Little Wolf was an old Cheyenne name. "It's nice to meet you."

Delores's manners won out. "Nice to meet you, too." Her voice was soft as butter.

"I'm very sorry about Bo. And Clay." She directed this to both Delores and Barbie.

The girl stared at her, but Barbie said, "Thank you," and managed a strained smile. The short hair set off sharp features and gave her an elfin look. She wore little makeup, and her skin was fine and unblemished, though still inflamed along one side of her face. The bandage by her ear was smaller than it had been two days ago.

"You'll let me know if you need anything?"

Barbie nodded and turned to the next person in line.

Bo hadn't been having an affair at all; he'd simply met the girl he was tutoring in the Hungry Moose, and Herb Paysen had jumped to conclusions. So what had Bo and his son argued about the day of Clay's murder?

SIXTEEN

That evening, after a long, restorative ride on Izzy, Merry returned her fishing gear to the basement. In the dim light of the single bulb swinging from the ceiling cord, she fitted the tackle box back into its outline on the shelf, a neat rectangle delineated by fine gray dust. Around the edges of the room, leaning towers of overflowing containers held sentimental or still-useful odds and ends. Lifting and prodding, she finally found the box that held her old leather crafting equipment.

Metal instruments clanked and muttered within the cracked cardboard as she lugged it up to the kitchen and set it on a chair. She unfolded a terry dishtowel onto the table, and spread out the tools, wiping each item with a damp cloth. The scent of leather permeated the room, mingling with the smells of coffee and dust.

She rocked a round knife through a scrap of goatskin lacing, checked the edge, put it to one side. Next to it, she arranged an all-purpose knife, a rotary cutter, and a pair of shears. She found an embossing wheel with a loop pattern, modeling tools, stamps with animal heads: a horse, a buffalo, a wolf, and a steer skull. A beveller and a large punch emerged from the box last. At one time there had been more stamps, and she remembered at least one other embossing wheel. Another beveller and a couple of punches seemed to be missing, and there weren't any edgers or awls in the gleaming row of implements.

A carefully wrapped bundle opened to reveal an array of odd-shaped leather scraps. The meager selection included a strip of crinkly-grained steer hide with a two-toned, pebbled surface. Then a piece of dark indigo calfskin, oblong and rough-edged, and under that, a length of pigskin suede. Finally, a handsome specimen of top-grain, vegetable-tanned cowhide the color of caramel, fine-textured and inviting design. She had used some of this for her last project years ago, a wallet for her dad. The leather, smooth against the pads of her fingers, bent with ease. In her mind, a pattern she could work into the hide began to develop, inspired by the steer skull stamp and Mama's overgrown roses now perfuming the warm night air drifting through the open kitchen window.

She glanced at the clock, surprised to find it so late. After eight and Shirlene hadn't called yet. She picked up the phone from the kitchen counter and punched in the number.

Her aunt answered on the first ring, as if she'd been sitting by the phone.

"Hey, Shirl. You get the bail all taken care of?"

"Oh. It's you. Yeah. I've hocked everything I own, but it's done."

Merry closed her eyes. "I bet Lauri was glad to get home."

"She was." Something in her voice.

"What's wrong?"

"She's gone."

"What do you mean she's gone? Gone where?"

"I don't know where. After dinner I went to check on her and her room was empty. Some of her clothes were missing and so was a suitcase."

Damn. "She take her car?"

"It's still in the driveway. I've called her friends, I even called some of the motels around here. I don't think she could get very far without a car."

"Jesus. And you didn't see her go?"

"No, Merry, I did not. If I had, I would have stopped her."

"I know. Sorry. Is there anything I can do?"

"I don't think so. I'll call if I find anything out."

"Maybe it's nothing and she'll be back by morning. You never know."

But as they said their goodbyes and hung up, she could tell her aunt thought Lauri was gone for good. Her cousin had dug herself into a mighty deep hole, and now she was dragging Shirlene into it with her. Along with all of Mama's meager savings.

———

Merry packed up her leatherworking equipment, no longer inspired to begin a project. She limped through the house, picking things up and putting them back down, tired but restless. She stopped in front of the sideboard and traced the elaborate silver curlicues decorating Mama's black-lacquered cinerary urn. Resisted the temptation to remove the lid and look inside.

Her foot didn't hurt as badly, and her head hadn't ached all day. She didn't feel like staying home alone. She wanted to be around other people, if only to watch them. After dreaming for so long about solitude, she now found she had less tolerance for it than she used to.

She grabbed her keys and jacket.

On the far end of Hazel, the gaudy magenta neon sign flashed THE LUCKY LOWDOWN CASINO into the night air. Inside, she slipped onto a stool at the bar. She ordered a shot of Scotch and turned to observe the crowd. Sipping her drink, her eyes moved over the dancers and the backs of people facing the machines lining the walls, hunched over video poker and no-armed bandits, feeding in their money and punching electronic buttons. The palpable belief the next game would be the winner hovered around them like auras. Digitized gambling was a vice so sterile she couldn't fathom its allure.

The gamblers persisted despite the zydeco pounding out of the speakers above. Unexpectedly, it was Cajun Night at the Lucky Lowdown, and dancers swarmed the open floor. Some of them displayed impressive ability, two pairs in particular capturing her attention with their skill.

She watched for a while, holding each sip of peaty single malt on her tongue and then allowing it to slide gradually down her throat. The bartender reached over and poured her another drink.

"It's on her," he said, pointing toward a small round table in a corner off the dance floor.

She looked, and Anna Knight waved at her. Barbie sat next to her roommate, her shorn hair looking pathetic under the dull lights. Merry waved back, pretending not to understand Anna's gesture to join them. She sipped and watched some more. Anna alternated between flirting with passing men and directing sorrowful looks at Barbie while patting her arm. Occasionally Anna would speak, but Barbie sat staring at the feet of the dancers, blinking and swallowing from the glass in front of her with clocklike regularity.

When their waitress walked by, Merry asked her what the two women were drinking and bought them a round. When the drinks arrived, Anna gestured her over again. She wove her way to them through the tables. Anna flashed a high-wattage smile, all white teeth and pink tongue and dark red lips. Barbie looked up as Merry approached, and a small smile replaced her wan expression.

"How're you doing?" Merry asked.

She sighed and shook her head. "I just can't believe it."

"Is Olivia still staying with you?"

"Yeah," Anna said. "She's kinda bossy, you know?"

Barbie glared at her.

"Anyway, I thought it'd be a good idea to get Barbie out of the house," Anna said. "She needs to have a little fun, take her mind off things!" But her voice was hollow. She obviously didn't know what else to do. "Do you like to dance to this stuff? It's a blast. Barbie's really good."

Barbie gazed at her roommate with exasperation. A tall man in black jeans and a shiny black shirt came up to Anna and asked her to dance.

"You don't mind, do you?" she asked.

"God, no," Barbie said.

They sat in the zydeco-filled air for a few moments. Anna and the man in black made a striking couple as they swirled and swayed.

Merry took a chance. "It's hard to lose someone you love."

Barbie's eyes jerked to hers, then fell away again. "Your mother died recently."

She nodded.

"I liked her a lot."

She nodded again. "I hear it gets better."

"Does it?" Barbie said after a pause. "I suppose it must. I just don't know if I can get over ... what a damn waste it is, I guess." She took a swallow of her gin and tonic, then shook her head. The movement was a little off, and Merry wondered how many drinks she'd had.

Barbie looked at the dancers, then back at Merry. "Why would your cousin shoot him like ..." she trailed off.

Merry sighed. "She didn't."

"The police arrested her."

"The police are wrong."

Barbie shifted her red-rimmed gaze toward the dance floor again.

"All I know is no one should ever have to go through the hell you're going through."

Still staring at the swaying bodies, Barbie's eyes filled with tears.

Merry sighed. "I meant to be comforting. But it doesn't help, does it?"

Barbie shook her head. "But it's nice to know you tried."

Merry had come over to the table hoping to ask her questions about the night Clay died, but Barbie wasn't in any shape to answer them. This was real grief. Or guilt. Sometimes the two were hard to separate.

She drained her Scotch. "You want a ride home? I'd be happy to drop you."

Barbie looked hesitant. "That's okay. I'm sure Anna will want to leave soon."

Merry looked out on the dance floor. Anna was dancing with a new partner, a cowboy who was two-stepping her around the floor to the lilt of a Cajun fiddle. Her head was thrown back, her mouth open in laughter. Barbie followed her gaze.

"She doesn't look quite ready to leave," Merry said.

Barbie sighed again. "Yeah, I guess I'd better take you up on that ride. Thanks." She donned her short jacket, a canvas and corduroy affair, and made her way out to the dance floor to talk to her roommate. She spoke, and Anna nodded and said something back, then waved at Merry. They headed out to the parking lot.

———

Barbie gave directions to her house. Merry liked the small white dwelling, or what she could see of it in the dark. She thought of it as a "grandma" house, probably because her own grandmother had lived in a similar one when she was a child.

Merry got out when Barbie stumbled on the front sidewalk, following her and holding the screen open while she unlocked the door. When the knob twisted, she turned to go.

"Wait." Barbie stood framed in the light from inside, miller moths fluttering around the porch light above her head. "Thanks for the ride."

"No problem."

She stood looking at Merry, something unreadable in her eyes.

"You going to be okay?" Merry asked.

She shrugged. "I don't ... I don't want to be around all those people. But I don't want to be alone, either. You want to come in?"

Merry nodded. "Sure, I can come in for a little while."

Inside, the house was nothing like Grandma's. The floor was maple hardwood, the walls a seafoamy color that proved to be a neutral background for the impressionist prints hanging on them. Monet. Manet. The air smelled of bleach.

Barbie saw her looking at the prints. "Anna's collection. It always struck me as odd, that she'd like all the blurry stuff when she seems so sharp."

"Sharp like smart?"

"Like well-defined."

"Maybe she likes the contrast."

"Maybe. I don't mind them."

Merry started to move a folded quilt and bed pillow to one end of the couch so she could sit down, but Barbie grabbed them and took them to a room down a small hallway.

When she came back, she said, "My waterbed blew a gasket or something. Flooded my whole bedroom. I've been sleeping on the couch until I get it taken care of. Olivia's asleep in the guest bedroom." She held her finger to her lips.

Merry lowered her voice. "Anna told me someone intentionally sliced up the bed."

"Anna has a big mouth. This probably isn't a good subject for us, so let's just talk about something else, okay? What do you want to drink? What were you having at the Lowdown—whiskey?"

"Scotch. But I think I'm pretty much done for tonight. I don't suppose I could talk you into a cup of coffee?"

"Yeah, I can do that. I'll join you. Hate to drink alone and all that."

She began measuring and pouring in the tiny kitchen. Merry moved to a tall stool at the breakfast bar and watched her through the opening. At the Lowdown their grief had mingled, serenaded by fiddle and accordion. Here Barbie seemed more awkward. Maybe alcohol had lubricated their previous interaction, and now she was sobering up.

Or maybe she wanted to talk and didn't know how to start. Merry plunged in, having no idea if she was saying the right thing. "How long had you and Clay been going out?"

Barbie looked up, disconcerted. "What?"

"You and Clay. Going out. How long?"

"I heard you. It just... everyone else has avoided talking about him altogether."

"Might help to talk. If you don't want to, just tell me and I'll back off."

"Well. No, you're right. I've wanted to, I guess. But I don't know if I'm ready to yet. I'm still so goddamned pissed off."

"At him, for dying?"

"No, not at *him*. At your fucking cousin." Barbie turned away and brought her hands to her face. Her shoulders shook, and she made small snuffling sounds.

Shit, shit, shit. Merry went around to the other side of the counter and found a glass, filled it from the tap. And waited. Finally, Barbie let out a long, shaky breath and wiped her eyes with the back of one hand, holding it over them for a moment as if she wanted to hide in the comfort of the dark.

She sniffed, and when she moved her hand, Merry was holding a paper towel out to her. She smiled a little and blew her nose.

"Sorry."

"That's okay. You needed to do that."

"Yeah. Maybe I did." She paused. "He slept with her, you know?"

"Lauri?"

"Yes, *Lauri*."

"But he didn't." At Barbie's look, she held up her hand. "No, really. She told me the father of her baby is Denny Teller."

"Well, she sure changed her tune," she said with bitterness.

"Denny admitted they had sex."

Barbie paled. "Oh, God." She poured a cup of coffee, running her teeth over her lower lip. "I was so damn mad at Clay. For nothing."

God, no wonder she's such a mess.

"I know about what you did."

Merry's head jerked up. "What?"

"I heard. You killed your rapist."

Stunned at the abrupt turn of conversation, Merry stared at her.

"I just want you to know, I think what you did was really brave. More women should take control like that."

"No, not like that. There wasn't any control in what I did." Talking about it with a relative stranger like this felt like opening a vein.

"I'd do it. I'd kill to protect myself if I could. You shouldn't feel bad about it." Barbie's head bobbed emphatically.

"Did you?" Merry asked.

"Did I what?"

"Kill to protect yourself."

Barbie looked puzzled, then sudden comprehension dawned. "What? You think *I* killed Clay?"

"I didn't say that."

"You didn't have to." Her face had flushed a deep scarlet, and her voice shook. "I can't believe I thought we could be friends. Jesus Christ."

Merry held up her hands. "I—"

"Get out. Just get out."

The very air had soured. As Merry limped to the front door, Barbie spoke from the kitchen. "You know what I said, about thinking you did the right thing?"

Merry turned and looked at her.

"Well, I was wrong. You're a murderer, just like that tramp cousin of yours."

Olivia, wearing a battered terry cloth robe, emerged from the hallway. The glare she directed at Merry could have stripped the skin off a moose. She hurried to Barbie, put both arms around her. "It's okay, honey. It's okay."

Merry left.

Out on the street, she paused and took a deep breath, trying to fill the void that seemed to have opened in the pit of her stomach. She climbed into the Blazer and started it.

Less than two blocks away she was shaking so badly she had to pull to the curb and dowse the lights.

SEVENTEEN

CLOSING HER EYES, MERRY concentrated on slowing her breathing, on not thinking, but it didn't work. Zeke's visage rose in her mind.

His lank dishwater-blonde hair, the sharp features that reminded her of a rat. The swagger, and the high-pitched giggle that sounded like a girl's. She'd disliked him the minute she'd laid eyes on him. He'd been a high school buddy of Rand's, had latched onto his coattails and ridden them through five or six jobs in Daddy's oil exploration company. A sycophant, fawning over Rand and agreeing with everything he said while gazing after him with calculation whenever he left the room. Rand had loved having the guy around, and would hear nothing against him. The only time her husband had ever threatened to become violent had been when Merry and he were fighting over Zeke's constant presence in their lives.

By that time, she'd realized what a vast mistake it had been to marry Rand in the first place. They argued constantly, bitterly.

She'd already made the decision to leave him when Zeke came over that afternoon.

Merry had told him Rand had a business meeting and wouldn't be home for hours. He'd gone into the kitchen and helped himself to a beer. She couldn't bodily remove him, so she tried to ignore him, going about her business as best she could. At one point, she'd contemplated going out and running errands. But she didn't trust him and hated the thought of leaving him alone in her house.

Zeke settled in front of the television and kept drinking. He made it through one six-pack and started in on another. Then, coming into the laundry room from the back yard where she'd been deadheading the spring flowers, she found him waiting for her, a strange look on his face. He blocked the doorway into the kitchen, glassy-eyed and grinning.

"Excuse me, Zeke."

He belched in her face, filling the air between them with a roiling miasma of half-digested brew.

She waved her hand in front of her, disgusted. "You're such a goddamn pig. Let me by."

"Ah, Merry. Don't be like that. Why don't we be friends?" A leer replaced the sick grin.

Her eyes narrowed. "I don't think so."

"Bitch."

She looked into his eyes and saw the jealousy, the loathing. But it took a few more seconds to finally recognize her danger. She rotated on one foot to run out the back door, but he grabbed her and pulled her back.

"C'mon. You and me're gonna have a little fun."

"No!" She yelled it into his face and twisted in his grasp, moving her arm against his thumb and breaking his hold. But scrambling backward, she wasn't fast enough to escape his other hand, which shot out and caught her arm again. He coiled his fingers in her shirt and yanked her toward the kitchen. She screamed as loud as she could, hoping one of the neighbors might hear. Infuriated, he punched her in the face, and her head cracked back into the doorframe. The pruners she'd been using in the yard went flying.

Struggling to remain conscious, she kicked and scratched and bit. She kept thinking she should be able to get away from the scrawny little bastard, but his strength, even against her high-adrenaline panic, unnerved her. The entire time they fought he kept muttering.

Bitch. Whore.

He dragged her into the kitchen and shoved her to the pantry floor. She tried to crawl away, but there was nowhere to go. He fumbled with his belt, and, for a moment, hope flared that he might be too drunk to go through with it.

As he concentrated, she aimed a kick and let fly. But she had no leverage from her prone position, and at the last second he turned enough so her foot only bounced off his thigh.

He hit her again, in the stomach, and her resistance leaked away as she retched. He got her shorts down, scratching her with ragged fingernails, pinned her to the floor and forced her legs apart. He tore into her then, a ripping, distorted conglomeration of pain and humiliation, punctuated by waves of crippling terror as he muttered in her ear with each thrust.

"Interfering whore … making life hell … no one … will miss you … stupid … interfering … bitch … make … you pay … shut up … shut up … shut up!"

She'd known he was going to kill her then, was trying to tell him she was leaving anyway, but he wouldn't listen, wouldn't pay attention, he was so concentrated on his vengeance.

Fury bloomed within her, fueled by both her fear and an overwhelming sense of self-preservation.

And that was when she'd seen the pruners had fallen inside the pantry. She turned her head and pretended to close her eyes, going limp beneath him. Still he labored away, swearing at her. But her eyes were open enough to see the sharp, pointed little blades of the dead headers. She slid her right hand over. Couldn't quite reach. Wiggled a little to get closer.

"Oh, now you're liking it, aren't you bitch? Gettin' into it, yeah."

Her fingers touched the short, wicked blades of the pruners, and she teased them into her hand. Turned them so they lay across her palm. And in one sweeping motion, jammed their sharp points into his neck.

He stopped driving into her, unsure, and then roared in pain and anger. She stabbed him again. And again. Over and over until he slumped on top of her, pants around his ankles, hot blood gushing out of his neck onto her face and chest and arms. She kept stabbing even after he had stopped moving, needing to be sure, out of control, hatred incinerating her reason.

That was what no one knew. That she'd kept doing it even after he was unconscious, possibly even after he was dead. That was what haunted her, made her doubt her own sanity at three o'clock in the morning.

Rand had been livid. In court, he'd testified that he thought Merry had seduced Zeke and had taken out her anger at him on his friend. He'd lied, saying she liked rough sex, had begged him for it, and he was sure she'd convinced Zeke to play along.

The jury hadn't believed him altogether, or she would have been convicted of a worse crime than manslaughter. But he had swayed them enough that they didn't believe she'd killed Zeke purely in self-defense. They thought she'd started it.

———

The air inside Chewie's Bar vibrated with music from the jukebox squatting by the door, something slow and aching. A couple swayed over the wood plank dance floor, and patrons leaned onto small tables, talking and watching and drinking. Through an empty doorframe, a man and woman played pool at the table in the back room. The fierce odors of beer, bodies, and pungent aftershave mixed in the air.

Chewie clanked an empty into a bin below the bar. Merry grinned to herself as she flashed on Han Solo's hirsute friend. She caught a glimpse of red and black under the thick hair that covered Chewie's arm as he guided a towel over the bar, methodically wiping up any spills and polishing the dark wood. It was the tattoo of a bull's-eye he'd had for twenty years, commemorating his first marksman competition win. Trophies from subsequent victories were tucked in among the liquor bottles lining the mirror behind the bar. The most meretricious of these was a gold-plated rifle that stood more than two feet tall.

The bar hadn't changed much. A crisp new sign hung on the wall over the jukebox. CAPACITY: 72 PERSONS—THANK YOU, HAZEL FIRE DEPARTMENT. The lower corner had a computer-generated picture of a block-figured man putting out a small fire of exactly five flames with a hose. It looked like a well-endowed fat man pissing on a fern.

Those firefighters working the fire at the Lamentes' deserved a better logo.

Chewie's delighted voice rumbled. "Hey, Merry! Welcome home! What're you drinking tonight?"

Her eyes raked over the tap handles. "I'll take a Moose Drool. No, wait." To hell with it. "Make that a whiskey ditch. Not a lot of ditch." She felt a righteous drunk coming on.

After a couple attempts at drawing her into conversation, Chewie shrugged and moved down to a spare old man who seemed more than happy to take advantage of his devoted ear. But the bartender seemed to know her intentions and kept the drinks coming. Three whiskeys later, Merry stood up to go the bathroom and had to put her hand on the bar to steady herself. She'd always been a bit of a lightweight, but four dry years in the joint—ha! the joint, what a stupid fucking term—had badly undermined her capacity for alcohol. 'Course, it might have something to do with all that extra blood she was sure Anna Knight, that lip-licking angel of mercy, had drained in the name of public service. Or the two shots of scotch she'd had at the Lowdown.

She felt better, though. Lots better. Mostly because she didn't feel much at all.

After the hazy but otherwise uninteresting trip to the bathroom, she settled onto her stool again and raised her finger to Chewie. He frowned but lumbered her way.

A voice behind her spoke. "How 'bout a Coke this time around?"

She whirled and had to catch herself again. Yvette Trager, wearing a hot pink satin running suit, hitched herself up on the stool next to her.

The older woman gestured at the glass sitting in a pool of condensation on the bar. "You making a habit of that these days?"

"Not so far. But I gotta say, I'm liking this so well I might do a lot more of it in the future."

Yvette nodded. "Plenty of folks decide it's a good way to go."

Merry nodded back at her. "Glad to hear you approve."

"Oh, honey. I don't approve. Just because a lot of people do it doesn't mean they're right. You do much drinking before you went in?"

"Nope." She drained the glass. "So I've got a lot of catching up to do."

"Uh huh. Well, if you want to be stupid about it, I can't stop you. Problem is, the stupidity tends to spread. You keep it up and I'll bet ten to one you'll be back inside prison within a year."

"Oh, right. I wasn't drunk when I killed Zeke. *He* was, but I wasn't."

"Hon, you don't have to *kill* anyone to go back to prison. You just have to break your parole."

"Well, don't you worry about me, Yvette. I'll be a good girl." She turned away, dismissing the woman, and signaled for Chewie again. "I'll take another."

"The hell you will. Chewie, give this girl a Coke. We'll be over there in that booth."

He nodded and fished for a glass under the counter.

Traitor.

Yvette grasped her arm in a surprisingly strong grip and pulled her off the stool. She wasn't prepared for it and almost fell.

I'll be embarrassed about this tomorrow. But for now she didn't much give a rip.

Yvette led Merry, protesting, to the booth. "Oh, for Godssake. I was just kiddin'. Just havin' a little post-release celebration. Little party for myself."

"Okay. Come sit with me for a while. We'll make it a girls' night out."

Merry grimaced. "Tried that already. Over at the Lowdown. Didn't go so good."

"Ah, so you're making the circuit. Love that zydeco they have over there."

Imagining the woman who was depositing her into one of Chewie's Naugahide banquettes prancing around to a Cajun beat in that glaring pink running suit made Merry laugh.

"What?"

"Nothin'. Never mind."

Chewie brought over a couple Cokes, and Yvette paid for them. She took a sip, watching Merry over the rim of the glass.

"What's going on with you?"

"Told you. I'm celebrating."

"Bullshit."

"Oh, fuck, Yvette—" She winced at the other woman's sharp expression. "Sorry. Anyway, nothing's going on."

Yvette considered her. "How's the detective work going?"

Merry took a drink. Damn stuff was too sweet. And fizzy. "Not so hot. Lauri's been arrested. And now she's—" She remembered in time that Yvette, as an officer of the court, should not be told of Lauri's sudden departure.

"She's what?"

"She's not guilty, that's what. They're going to put her in jail for something she didn't do."

"Like they did you?"

"Oh, I did it. Never claimed not to. Even if I didn't exactly have a choice." Barbie's words came back to her. "Everyone thinks I'm a murderer, and you know what? They're right."

"So Lauri's different."

"Yeah."

"Is it just the teensiest bit possible that she did do it?"

The idea wended its way through the whiskey cloud. No one seemed to know what Lauri was capable of, how she thought, or what to expect from her. Hope laced Merry and Shirlene's perceptions, self-defense against the idea that someone they knew, someone who was family, could have killed a man in cold blood with no rational provocation. And if she was innocent, the thought of wrongly accusing her became equally untenable, so they—Merry and Shirlene at least—veered away from considering Lauri's guilt. They seemed to be the only ones, though. Everyone else appeared quite willing to believe her capable of murder.

What if they were wrong? What if Lauri *was* that cold-blooded? Would anyone, especially her mother, identify what amounted to severe mental illness in her cousin?

And all this time Merry had been endangering herself, getting into it with pretty much everyone she knew, in defense of the little brat. And now Lauri'd run off. That flat-out pissed her off.

"I'm going to get another drink, Yvette. You can wait here or you can leave, but I'm having another whiskey."

"Sheez, listen to yourself. Whatever you've got stuck up your butt, it's not about Lauri. I mean, sure, her situation's bugging you, but I don't think that's what has you in here tonight. This thing with your cousin's been a cause for you. As far as I've heard—and believe me, I've got ears everywhere—you're not doing yourself any real harm by trying to find out what happened. At least you're not moldering away out at your ranch. And who knows, you may be right about her."

Merry stared at her. "You think I'm doing the right thing?"

"I do. Just don't get in over your head. And if it turns out she did kill her boyfriend, well, be ready to accept that."

"But she didn't. I know she didn't." And this clarity, she realized, she should trust. Her earlier thoughts had just been booze-induced whining, looking for an excuse to stop trying to find out what really happened to Clay Lamente. One positive word from the former high-school secretary, and she was ready to try some more.

Problem was, she didn't know what else to do.

"Okay. So that's not the issue," Yvette said. "Are you having trouble with anyone else since coming back, about what happened down in Texas?"

"Oh, for crying out loud. Of course I am. People don't take kindly to a murderer coming home to roost among them."

Yvette nodded. "Either the comments are piling up, or some-one said something in particular that got to you. Well, hon, I am here to tell you, and this is as a woman and a friend—yes, a friend, whether you like it or not—that you are not a murderer. You killed someone, and you did it because you thought you had to. If your rotten ex-husband hadn't testified against you in court, the jury would have ruled self-defense. They should have anyway. But they didn't, and you've had to live with that. You'll have to continue to live with it. But don't let it eat away at that core of strength that allowed you to keep yourself alive. You do that, and your rapist and your ex and all the sonsabitches who would prefer that women stay soft and pliant and defenseless will have won."

Merry gaped at her.

"All that is, of course, off the record. And on the record, I don't recommend using physical violence to solve your problems in the future."

The Cokes were gone. Her liver had been laboring away, and she now felt steady and only a little fuzzy around the edges. She didn't want to be drunk anymore, and that seemed to have an effect, too.

"Yvette?"

"Yeah?"

"You're one hell of a parole officer, you know that?"

"Why yes, honey. I do." And she smiled.

———

But she wouldn't let Merry drive home, despite her protestations. Yvette took her back to her house and made a bed on the sofa. It was a lumpy old thing, but Merry fell asleep in seconds, warm and more relaxed than she'd been since returning to Hazel.

She awoke at four a.m., muzzy, dry-mouthed, and intensely embarrassed about making a fool of herself the night before. At least she hadn't danced on any tables. Yvette's kindness had been welcome at the time, hell—it was still welcome—but watching the window in her living room brighten to a lighter shade of night, Merry felt exposed. Vulnerable. In prison she'd carved out a place for herself among the other women with great care and self-control, keeping the reality of who she was private. It was the only private thing she'd had for four long years. Her self-concealment had served her well for so long that now it was hard to give up.

She folded the blankets neatly and stacked them with the pillow on the end of the sofa. Then she wrote Yvette a note and let herself out the front door. It was only a three-block walk back to Chewie's, where the Blazer nosed up to the side of the building. She climbed in and drove home.

At the ranch, she stepped to the ground and swung the door shut with a solid thunk. She leaned her back against it. She'd forgotten how pleasant the dawn could be here. Wind had blown an earlier shroud of cloud to the east, and the pale illumination from a sliver of moon low over the foothills allowed a luminescent spoor of twinklings overhead. She watched them wink out, one by one. A cacophony of birdsong and the sound of the wind rustling through the leaves of the maple by the barn filled the yard. The flat odor of dew-damp dust, pine, and sage merged with the slightest hint of wood smoke in the air.

Inside, she crawled into her own bed and fell back asleep.

———

Merry awoke, less muzzy and more dry-mouthed, a little after eight. Her early morning slumber had been plagued by strange dreams she couldn't remember, and the overall result was a general grumpiness, despite the promise of beautiful weather and the anticipation of riding Izzy.

In the kitchen she poured coffee, and some of the hot dark liquid splashed onto the counter. Swiping at it with a dishtowel splattered some of it on the front of her yellow tank top. Swearing, she went back into her bedroom to change.

She took her coffee out to the barn and turned her mare out to graze, then came back and settled on the front porch, propping her feet up on the railing. At least her ankle had reduced in size enough to allow her to wear her boots again. She sipped the pungent caffeine and let her eyes wander. The morning was cooler than normal, though only a few high shreds of white accented the incandescent blue above. A sea of golden grass rippled in her peripheral vision, and the air carried the scent of clover from a field further away.

She was thinking of breakfast when they came. Eggs and sausage and chunky fried potatoes with onions. A veritable cholesterol fantasy.

First she saw the plume of dust, then the blue and red flashing lights within it. Three Crown Victorias barreling down the ranch road like the place was on fire.

Well, hell. There went breakfast.

EIGHTEEN

RORY HAWKINS AND LESTER Fleck emerged from the first car, the sergeant's hand hovering near his unsnapped holster. Merry stood with her hands visible on the railing and didn't move as he approached. Lester sauntered behind him. The county sheriff had pulled up behind the Hazel Police cruiser. He got out and leaned against the driver's door, seeming reluctant to join the festivities. Jamie followed last, shutting off the engine and hopping out.

"Gentlemen," Merry called. "What can I do for you?"

Hawkins stepped up onto the porch. "You can get into the car without giving me any guff."

"What's this about?"

"We'll discuss that down at the station."

Lester leaned against a porch support and shoved his hands in his pockets. Jamie stopped next to him. Merry's blood thudded in her ears and her vision narrowed. She reminded herself to breathe.

"Let me get my keys." The words warbled a bit as she spoke them, and a flash of satisfaction crossed Hawkins's features.

"You won't be driving."

"I need to lock up."

Hawkins looked unhappy but nodded. He followed close on her heels as she went in the front door and through to the kitchen. Her keys lay on the counter. She picked them up, and he held his hand out for them. She glared at him and went back outside. When he came out behind her, she shut the door and locked it, putting the keys in her pocket.

Jamie watched but wouldn't meet her eyes.

"Am I under arrest?" Merry demanded.

"Soon enough," Hawkins said.

Merry struggled with a horrible feeling of déjà vu. *Soon enough.* Should she resist? Or would that only get her into trouble later? Numb, she allowed herself to be led to his cruiser and deposited into the slick vinyl backseat.

No one spoke on the ride into town. Merry turned around once and saw Jamie driving behind them, but the sheriff had left the procession by then. She guessed he'd only been along because the ranch fell within the county's jurisdiction.

At the station, Hawkins led her inside and put her in the same room where they'd questioned Lauri. Lester veered to another part of the building, but Jamie came in and sat at the opposite end of the table.

Hawkins shook his head. "Gutierrez, go find something else to do."

"I'd just as soon sit in."

"Too bad."

Stony-faced, Jamie got up and left the room.

Hawkins shut the door and turned to her. "Where were you last night?"

"I want my lawyer."

"In good time."

"Am I under arrest?"

"You don't have to be. We'll just keep you here until you answer our questions."

"Not without my lawyer, I won't."

The hatred she'd witnessed upon first meeting him flared to life behind his eyes. He turned and walked out of the room. The lock clicked.

She was hungover and hadn't eaten since lunch the day before. Her hands tingled and her head felt like it was floating—she'd managed to hyperventilate during the trip into town.

Voices raised outside the door, then it opened and the tall man Nadine had identified as the chief of police stepped into the room.

"Who's your lawyer?"

"Kate O'Neil." Her voice felt raw.

"We're calling her now."

"Thank you."

He nodded and closed the door again. The lock didn't click.

"Excuse me?" Merry called, hoping someone would hear her. If she dared to open the door, Rory Hawkins would likely shoot her on the spot. She tried again. "Hello?"

The door opened again.

Hawkins pooched his lips. "Whadaya want?"

"Could I get some aspirin?"

"Got a little headache? Poor thing."

She had a little everythingache, but she didn't feel it necessary to enlighten Hawkins. "Yes. A couple aspirin would be great. Tylenol, ibuprofen, whatever."

"I'll get it." Jamie's voice wafted in from someplace behind the sergeant.

Hawkins turned his head. "The hell you will. We're not a goddamn pharmacy."

"Oh, for God's sake, Sarge—"

"This isn't your case." He turned, and the door drifted behind him but didn't close all the way. "You're too close to her. Might be sleeping with her for all I know."

Jamie, Hawkins, and Chief Matthews all started talking at once. The chief's voice rode above the rest.

"*Quiet.* Gutierrez, he's right. The sergeant is handling this case. It's not like there isn't enough for you to do."

Jamie's retort came too fast. "Think maybe a murder investigation's a little too big for me to get involved in? Or maybe you're afraid investigating all aspects of this case instead of forcing evidence to fit your version of things might put a real criminal in jail? You might end up having to cover up something one of your hunting buddies got themselves into. Like last fall."

Oh, God. Don't do this. Please, don't do this.

A long, taut silence followed Jamie's words.

The chief said, "Officer Gutierrez, as of this moment you are suspended without pay for insubordination. Your badge and gun." Another long silence. Then: "Good. Now leave the building."

Merry buried her face in her hands. She'd only wanted a couple of aspirin. Why had he said those things? Even if they were true— and no doubt they were—why would he say them now?

She waited, sans painkiller, for over three hours. When Kate finally arrived, the first thing Merry did was demand to go to the bathroom. She'd been crossing her legs for over an hour but hadn't wanted to give Hawkins the satisfaction. When she returned, Kate shut the door behind them and sat down with her.

"So what's this all about?" she asked once Merry had swallowed two ibuprofen and most of a granola bar Kate had pulled from her purse.

"I don't know."

"No idea at all?"

"None."

Kate frowned. "Well, let's get this party started, then." She rose and opened the door.

Hawkins entered, a frown creasing his florid face. "You done dancing around?"

Kate inclined her head. "You can ask my client all the questions you want, Sergeant Hawkins. And she will consult with me prior to answering any of them."

She shot Merry a look as she spoke, and Merry responded with a grave nod. She felt tremendous relief at having someone she trusted navigating the shark-infested waters with her.

Hawkins settled into a chair across the table. "Where were you last night?"

"Don't answer," Kate said. "Sergeant, can you be more specific as to time?"

"I don't know the exact time. Why can't she just tell me where she was all night? It's not that tough a question."

"If you don't know the precise time for which you are asking my client to be accountable, then may I suggest that you explain the circumstances that prompt your asking in the first place."

Merry stared at her. So did Hawkins.

"Sergeant?"

"There was a guy shot dead last night. And *Ms.* McCoy here didn't get along with him so well."

Holy shit. They thought she'd *killed* someone last night? "Who was it?" she asked.

Kate sent her a look, and she shut up. "Yes, who was the victim?"

Hawkins grimaced. Glared at Merry. Sighed. "Denny Teller."

Kate raised one eyebrow. "So? Why would my client have anything to do with it?"

"Her mother's gun was found by the body." He said it with great satisfaction. "Another thirty-eight revolver."

Mama's gun? The one she'd had forever? Merry had forgotten all about it.

Wait a minute. She murmured in Kate's ear. Kate nodded, looked up at Hawkins. "How do you know it was Elsa McCoy's gun?"

His smile was smug. "Had her name engraved on it."

"Mama sold that gun."

"Who to?"

She looked down at the table. "I don't know."

He leaned forward. "Right. Unless you can show me a bill of sale, that poor kid was shot with your gun. I already know he got your cousin pregnant, and you got into it with him yesterday and threatened to kill him. And now you don't seem to have an alibi."

Kate shot Merry a questioning look.

"I never threatened—" she began.

"But threatening wasn't good enough for you. Or maybe he blew you off. So you went home and thought about it and got pissed off and decided to do something about it. Decided you'd show him. Did you mean to kill him when you went over there, or were you just going to scare the crap out of him? You know what I think? I think you did mean to kill him. You got a taste for it now. I'll tell you one thing—you're never getting out of prison again after this."

No. This could *not* be happening.

"Knock off the bullshit, sergeant." Kate's matter-of-fact voice brought Merry back from the hysteria gabbling in the back of her mind.

The nails on her clenched fingers had left red, half-moon indentations on both palms.

Kate continued. "We're not interested in your fantasies, sergeant. Is my client under arrest or not?"

"Not yet. But—"

"We're leaving, then. And next time? Don't even think about trying to question Ms. McCoy without my being present."

Hawkins stood. "I think it would be better for her to cooperate with this investigation."

"Sergeant Hawkins, I thought I made it clear: I don't really give a rat's ass what you think."

————

Merry followed Kate out past the desks and through the front door. They kept walking until they reached the tiny Hazel Veterans' Memorial Park, half a block from Kate's office.

She turned to Merry. "Did you kill him?"

"Christ! Of course not."

"Were you at the ranch last night?"

She shook her head. "I was in town."

"How late?"

"I drove back out to the ranch about four a.m."

Kate quirked an eyebrow. "Really."

"No, nothing like that. I was at the Lucky Lowdown, and then at Chewie's. A friend made me stay on her couch, didn't want me driving after drinking. I woke up early and went home."

"Who's this friend?"

"Yvette Trager."

"You stayed last night with Yvette *Trager*? Your *parole* officer? Merry, that's perfect!"

"Hang on. I left awful early, and she wasn't awake. I wrote her a note, but didn't say when I left. She can't vouch for me being there all night. And we still don't know when Denny was killed. I'm not in the clear yet."

"Okay, you're right. No good getting ahead of ourselves. I'll call Yvette and see what she can tell me. Now, what's this business about you threatening Denny Teller?"

Merry sighed. "Lauri told me he'd fathered her baby and that he wouldn't give her any child support. So I went over there yesterday to talk with him."

"Yeah, and how did that go?"

"Badly. I let him know we wouldn't let him off that easily. He got ... aggressive."

"Aggressive how?" Kate's voice was sharp.

"Aggressive like guys with big heads and little dicks get aggressive. Bark, not bite." She almost felt casual as she said it, but there

218

must have been something in her expression because Kate narrowed her eyes in disbelief.

"Did he threaten you?"

"Well ... sort of."

"Did you threaten him?"

"Not exactly. I said it seemed strange that he wasn't afraid to be in the house where Clay died. That someone might want to kill him, too."

Kate looked aghast. "You said that? Who else was there?"

"We were alone."

"Alone. With that little creep. Jesus fucking Christ, Merry. After everything that happened to you, what in holy goddamn hell were you thinking?"

"I—"

"You weren't thinking, that's what. Don't do *anything* like that again, do you understand me?" Kate was almost shouting and looked like she was about to grab Merry by the shoulders and shake her.

"Okay." She held up her palms. "Okay, I'm sorry."

Kate took a deep breath and watched a mother pushing a toddler on a swing in the kiddy playground across the park.

She turned to Merry again. "If no one else was there, then Hawkins is getting his information secondhand. Denny told someone about your visit. But they can't testify about what you said—that's hearsay."

"Who would he have told?"

"I don't know. But whoever it was has Rory Hawkins's ear."

And quite possibly, whoever it was had taken Denny's life.

NINETEEN

Kate drove Merry back out to the ranch. "I wish you'd called me when the shit hit the fan in Dallas. I didn't find out about what was going on until it was too late for me to do anything."

Merry's brow furrowed. "You made it clear you hated my guts. Why would I have called you?"

"I know I said a lot of stuff back then. I was angry about Rand. I thought you'd intentionally seduced him. I didn't realize he was just a cheating asshole."

"I was pretty flattered that he'd picked me. I'd always thought of you as the one who had it all together, the one who got the guys."

"You did?" Kate laughed. "I always thought that about you."

That gave Merry pause. "Well, you ended up the lucky one, Rand-wise." Her tone was bitter.

"I know."

"Not that you would have stuck around as long as I did. You would have realized right away and left him."

Kate shook her head. "Don't beat yourself up. He's a charming bastard. And if I'm so damn discerning, why did I blame you instead of him when he broke up with me?"

"Well. There's that."

Kate looked sidelong at her. "We okay now?"

Merry nodded. "Yeah."

Kate smiled. "Good."

Jamie's Jeep was parked in the round drive in front of the ranch house when they arrived. Wearing jeans and a T-shirt, he sat on the porch in Mama's rocking chair with his feet up on the polished log railing.

She got out of Kate's Volvo and hurried toward him. "Jesus, Jamie. Why did you mouth off like that?"

"Something I should have done a long time ago."

"When will the chief let you go back to work?"

"I don't know if he will. Don't know that I'll go back even if he does."

"Hell. You can't give up your job over... well, you just aren't going to do it." She had been going to say "over me." Like Jamie couldn't control himself where she was involved. And that, as their brief physical encounter by the river had proven, simply wasn't true.

His next words bore out her thoughts. "I can do any damn thing I want to, McCoy. I've been working for that prick Hawkins for three years, and he's the sorriest excuse for a lawman I've ever seen. When the old chief retired and they brought in this new guy, I thought things might change. Turns out, even though he's from over by Butte, he's well connected in the old-boy network in this county. You know, the ones not too fond of people with last names like mine—doesn't matter a damn whether I was born and raised in this county or not."

"So he's a racist, and he's corrupt. Can't you lodge a complaint?"

Jamie exchanged knowing looks with Kate. "With the mayor who appointed him? Or the city council made up of his cronies? My best bet is to find something else to do."

"But you love being a cop."

Distress crossed his face, and he looked away.

"Listen, I've got to get back into town and uncover an alibi for you," Kate said, breaking the mood on the porch.

As she was climbing into her car, Merry called to her. "Kate." Their eyes met. "Thanks."

Kate nodded. "I'll call you later, after I talk to Yvette."

Merry waved and watched the Volvo leave, pulling a plume of road dust behind it toward the highway. She turned to Jamie.

"You hungry?"

"What did you have in mind?"

"That cutthroat I caught. It's a day old, but—"

"That'll do."

They walked inside and Merry set about fixing the trout. She salted the interior cavity and layered slices of lemon and onion and dabs of butter in and around the fish, then folded the whole thing into a foil packet. While Jamie fired up the barbeque, she assembled a salad, sliced strawberries, and whipped the cream for strawberry shortcake.

Check two items off the list.

When the food was ready, they loaded their plates and returned to the porch, Merry in Mama's rocker and Jamie sat on the top step. She closed her eyes as she took a bite of trout.

"God, that's so good." The words came out almost a groan.

She opened her eyes to find Jamie watching her with an odd expression on his face. Maybe not odd so much as changing, the messages in his eyes warring with one another.

"What?" she said.

"Nothing."

"Something."

"Just ... for a second there, you looked so ... I don't know."

She suddenly knew exactly what she'd looked like, savoring that first bite. And he'd recognize that look, not from a meal eaten on a front porch but from long moments of a different sort of pleasure altogether.

She finished eating without comment. They went in to get the shortcake and returned to the porch. The talk turned to Denny Teller's murder. Jamie didn't have any information Hawkins hadn't already imparted, and Merry updated him on everything she'd told Kate. Inside, he helped her put away leftovers and wash the dishes. When they were done, a sudden awkwardness descended between them, and she led the way back outside in order to escape it.

"Does Gayle know you're suspended yet?"

Jamie shook his head.

"You want to call her?"

Holding her gaze for a long moment, he shook his head again. Then in two long steps, he closed the distance between them, sliding his arms around her shoulders and pulling her to him. She stiffened, half afraid to respond, half afraid not to. His arms tightened, and one hand shifted to her neck, fingers tangling in her curls. He eased her head back so she could see his face.

There was no mistaking the message in his eyes now.

"Jamie," she whispered, giving a slight shake of her head. "You can't—"

He bent his head, brushing his lower lip along the length of her upper one, an almost-kiss, soft as goose down. Tentative. Teasing.

The seed of desire that had germinated by the river exploded through her veins, licking at the inside of her skin, seizing her breath and forcing a small moan. His lips moved across her mouth, firmer now, demanding and seeking. Then his tongue found hers, and all pretense of being on the verge of stopping vanished.

She closed her eyes and pressed against him. She wanted to slide inside his clothing like liquid, glide across his skin, surround him, dissolve and soak through his pores. Lose herself in tasting his otherness, receiving without judgment or even thought. She wanted to rip his clothes off, climb him like a monkey, and fuck his brains out.

She slid her hands under his T-shirt, raking her thumbnails over his nipples. He grunted and his hips jerked against hers. Pushing her against the porch railing, he slipped her tank top over her head and leaned her backwards, licking along the inside curves of her breasts as his fingers worked off her bra. She watched through half-slit eyes as he tongued one erect nipple, then covered it with his lips, sucking and pulling, each time a little harder. He scraped his teeth over the sensitive skin, whipping her need into a blistering demand.

Pushing him back and scrabbling at his shirt, she drew it over his head and reached for his belt. He grabbed her wrists and stepped forward, holding her arms to her sides as his mouth sought hers and plunged into another probing kiss.

She broke away, releasing a long shuddering breath. One last attempt at reason. She closed her eyes, forcing herself to concentrate.

"You're married," she managed to get out. What was her name again? "Gayle."

Jamie went still, and she looked up into his steady brown gaze. He kissed her again, their eyes open, watching each other.

He drew his head back, his fingers now entwined in hers by their sides, his chest hot against her breasts. "I love her. But I can't stop loving you because of that. You're my ... well, you're my Merry." Smiling, he moved a hand up and ran his thumb along her jaw. "It's like you and I are something outside of things. Rules don't exist for us. They just don't apply. Even jealousy is silly. Because no matter who else we might be with, it slides off whatever you and I have."

She wanted to believe him so badly it made her throat ache. She wrapped her arms around his neck, tugging at his earlobe with her teeth.

He nibbled her jaw in response, then trailed upward to her temple. She arched her neck, and he licked across the hollow of her throat, lingering on her collarbone for a moment before kneeling in front of her.

He pulled her boots off, first the right and then the left. Still kneeling, he unbuckled and unbuttoned and unzipped, drawing her jeans down and tossing them toward the end of the porch.

If anyone drove up now, they'd get one hell of a surprise, Merry thought, standing by the railing, stark naked in the slanting sunshine as Jamie stripped off his own jeans. She grinned at him, and he grinned back.

They moved together with informed ease. She scraped practiced fingernails down his back, and he hissed with pleasure. He smoothed his hands across her hips, cupping her ass and lifting her to the porch railing. Wrapping her legs around him, she arched one eyebrow and urged him forward with her heels. He resisted, pausing to slide his fingertips along the nerves behind her knees, smiling as her eyes widened.

He pushed into her then, with slow, savoring strokes, their tongues entwined. Each exquisite sensation building like an incoming tide. The railing groaned and creaked beneath her as their tempo took on a driving urgency.

They abandoned their kisses, their faces inches apart, eyes locked. The cords in Jamie's neck stood out, his teeth clenched and his face flushed as he waited for her. Her beginning spasms spawned his own, and they clung together until the convulsions faded and their heartbeats slowed. An alfalfa-scented breeze cooled their sweat-covered skin.

"Good God," Merry said.

"Uh huh."

After several moments they disentangled, and Merry staggered inside. She returned with two couch cushions and placed them on the floor of the porch. They curled together there, watching Izzy graze in her pasture and listening to a Steller's jay complain from the depths of the big maple.

She turned her head to murmur in his ear. "Thank you."

He looked down at her with an expression of mild surprise, pulled her closer. "Jesus. All the shit you've been through. And nothing I could do to help."

If he only knew. She wanted to tell him, but her throat was too clogged with relief and gratitude. They sat and watched the sun sink beyond the Bitterroot Mountains, Jamie running his fingers slowly through her hair while silent tears ran down her face.

TWENTY

Kate called that night, after Jamie had gone home to attempt to explain to his wife why he might not have a job anymore.

"Yvette confirmed that you spent the night on her couch and said you left around four in the morning. Apparently you weren't as quiet as you thought when you left."

"That's good, right?"

"As long as Teller was killed before then. Otherwise it puts you in town when you shouldn't be."

"How soon will we know?"

"Tomorrow, I'm guessing."

"Let me know when you find anything out."

"Will do."

"So, Kate? I guess I should ask what you charge."

"Don't worry about that now. We'll figure something out."

———

The next morning Merry drove to the bank, armed with the key to the safety deposit box she'd found in Mama's desk when she'd searched it unsuccessfully for the bill of sale for the revolver. Going through the contents of the box depressed her. Her birth certificate lay on top, as if Mama had looked at it recently. Below, she discovered birth certificates for Drew and for both Mama and Daddy. Daddy's death certificate. Three old silver dollars, an elaborate filigree ring that had belonged to her grandmother and, at the bottom, four old stock certificates from a company that had long gone out of business.

Mama had had a life insurance policy, the proceeds of which would obviate the inheritance taxes on the ranch. But there would be no more money from Frank Cain's leases for the annual property taxes and day-to-day expenses. Time to look for another job.

Employment pickings were lean in Hazel. But surely the Hungry Moose would have some turnover.

Janelle Paysen said they didn't have openings right then but gave her an application to fill out. Seated in a window booth, Merry looked out at Hazel's Main Street traffic. Nine-to-fivers took late morning coffee breaks, and summer tourists littered the sidewalks, wandering in and out of shops and stopping to look at the real estate ads plastered on the inside of Hazel Realty's plate glass window. Merry wondered if that was where T. J. Spalding worked.

Three gray-haired couples ate their early lunches in the other window booths and a lone woman sat at the counter eating a taco salad and reading a book. A group of four men, all wearing wifebeaters, stained jeans, and seed caps so filthy you couldn't read what they advertised, came in and sat down at a table near Merry. They could have been brothers: the same longish dark hair poking out around the edges of their caps, the same disregard for laundry facilities, and loud, loud voices that mingled with the smells of coffee and Danish, hamburger grease, and onions.

She didn't want to work here, inside all day, dealing with stupid sonsabitches pinching her ass and making comments. But she filled out the application carefully, and she knew she'd take any job Herb Paysen offered.

Beggars can't be choosers.

———

"Rory Hawkins graced me with a visit today." Shirlene leaned her elbows on the table and directed a worried look at Merry.

After giving the job application to Janelle, she'd stopped by Kate's office. Kate told her she had bypassed Sergeant Hawkins's game playing by calling a friend at the state medical examiner's office. Denny had been killed between midnight and two a.m. She'd called Hawkins and informed him that Merry's parole officer was willing to provide her alibi. He'd responded by shifting his suspicions to Lauri.

But that morning, when he and Lester came by the house to pick her up for questioning, Shirlene had to tell them she had no idea where her daughter was. Now she and Merry were seated in the back room of her aunt's dry cleaning business, plowing through the tuna melts Merry had picked up at the Moose. The air inside was heavy with humidity and the sharp chemical odors of solvent, detergent, and chlorine. A dryer droned in the back room.

"He threatened to arrest me—which is no surprise, really—for obstruction of justice or some damn thing. Man watches too much television if you ask me."

"He thinks you know where she is?"

"Naturally. I'm her mother, so I must know, right?"

"Do you?"

She rolled her eyes. "No, Merry. I do not."

Merry didn't smile. "Just checking."

Shirlene sighed and tossed the remainder of her sandwich in the trash. "I wish I did. I've looked every place I can think of."

Merry ate her last onion ring and wiped her mouth. "So Hawkins decided if I didn't kill Denny, Lauri must have done it."

"He said Denny told him he got Lauri pregnant, which somehow, I don't know how, means she killed him. Make any sense to you?"

"No. Hard to get any child support from a dead man." But it did explain how Hawkins had known about her visit to Denny Teller; he'd likely learned it directly from the victim himself. Which meant they had to be friends—or something like it. She remembered Hawkins's threat about finding drugs in her truck, and the smell of pot in Denny's living room.

The evidence in Denny Stand's murder pointed to Merry, but she hadn't shot him. The evidence in Clay Lamente's murder pointed to Lauri. Was someone framing her, too? But she admitted to being outside his window the night he died. And she also admitted to touching the gun, accounting for how her fingerprints came to be on it. Not quite a frame, then. At least not a premeditated one.

Merry leaned back. "Do you know who Mama sold her gun to? The thirty-eight?"

"You mean the one she kept in the kitchen drawer?"

"That one."

"She sold it to Bo Lamente."

A tiny shiver whispered across her neck. "When?"

"Oh, God, I don't know. Three, four years ago. She only had it for the coyotes when she had those chickens. Harlan tried to give her a newer model, but she liked that old thing."

"Yeah, thanks for telling me about Harlan and Mama, by the way."

Shirlene set her jaw. "It wasn't my place."

"Still." She took a sip of soda.

"Anyway, she never used the gun. After she stopped keeping the chickens, she sold it with all your daddy's hunting guns. Only thing she kept was that old shotgun of our dad's." Shirlene's face softened as she remembered her father, several years deceased.

The shotgun. Merry had forgotten about that old thing. An ancient Remington twelve-gauge, it had always been tucked in the mudroom cupboard. Just having it on the ranch was a parole violation.

"You know if Bo still had the thirty-eight? Apparently it was used to kill Denny Teller."

Shirlene's hand flew to her mouth. "So that's why they picked you up? Bo bought and sold guns as kind of sideline to everything else he did. He could have sold it to anyone. Or kept it. I don't know."

"Olivia might know."

"She might. You should have Kate ask her."

"That's a good idea." Merry cocked her head to one side, studying her aunt. "You seem … better."

"Hon, I gotta say, I feel like I got a second wind. I may lose the house since Lauri's taken off, and now she's being accused of another murder, but she's not in jail, and if they don't find her she's not going back. I know it sounds wrong, but I don't want them to find her." She paused. "I'm sorry about your money, though."

"Kate's a good lawyer."

"I'm sure she is. And we may have to face a trial, I know. But for right now I'm going to live my life and hope my daughter's safe, wherever she is."

"Wherever she is, huh."

Shirlene rolled her eyes and stood to dump out a bag of dirty work clothes. "So, what's the deal between you and Kate?"

Merry shrugged. "We knew each other in college."

Shirlene looked over her shoulder. "Right. You were a mess the other day when she was at the house."

"I was not."

"You were. But you don't have to tell me."

Several seconds passed. "We knew each other in high school, and then in college we got to be really good friends. Then this older guy, well, not that much older, but out of school, out in the world, came into the picture. They began dating. Then he left her for me."

"Ouch."

"It was Rand."

Shirlene winced. "Double ouch."

"Yeah."

"But you two seemed okay after that first time I saw you together."

"We've worked it out."

Shirlene loaded the clothes into the washer and added detergent and Borax. "You should go talk to Harlan."

Merry almost choked on her iced tea. "Why?"

"Because he's miserable. And he thinks you're angry at him for dating your mom."

"How do you know I'm not?"

"Because you're not an idiot, Merry."

Well, when she put it like that. "I'll think about it."

"Yeah. And then when you're done thinking about it, go talk to the poor guy."

———

At the ranch, Merry found two cars blocking the circular drive. She'd never seen the Land Rover, but the Cadillac was familiar. That damn real estate doofus was around here someplace.

She climbed out of Lotta—she'd dropped by Shirlene's house and traded the Blazer for the old pickup—and heard voices coming from the direction of the barn. She slammed the door and strode toward them, ignoring the twinge in her ankle. In the paddock outside Izzy's stall, a woman stood stroking the mare's neck and talking to her in a high-pitched voice better reserved for babies and Pomeranians.

"Oh, and aren't you a sweetheart? What a pretty girl!" Izzy nibbled at her fingers. "Is you hungry? Does the pretty girl want a little snack?" With her other hand she reached into her pocket.

Merry walked through the open gate and up behind the woman. "Don't even think about feeding my mare. And don't ever offer your fingers to a strange horse unless you're willing to lose them."

The woman whirled, then laughed. "Oh, you scared me. But don't worry—this little darling and I are no strangers. We met just the other day."

Smooth blonde hair capped her skull, framing a heart-shaped face. Small-featured, tan and pretty, the effect was marred by her thinness, so extreme that her head looked too large for her body. She couldn't have weighed more than ninety pounds.

"She is a girl, isn't she?"

Merry sighed. "Yes. Most mares are." She studied the woman. "So you've been here before."

"Mr. Spalding brought us out the other day, but the owner wasn't here—is that you? We looked around a bit. The house was locked, so we couldn't see the inside, but we were able to check out everything else. Including this sweet horse." She turned and hugged Izzy.

"You tried to go in my house?"

"Well, of course. After all, if we're going to buy the property, we have to be able to see what we're getting."

"You're not going to buy the property. It's not for sale."

The woman took a step back, a small frown creasing her brow. "It's not?"

"No. It's not. You're trespassing. *And* you endangered my horse by leaving the gate open so she could get out the last time you were here nosing around. She might have run away, or injured herself. Of all the thoughtless—"

"Hey now, hey now, no need to fly off the handle there. You are a prickly one, yes, you are." T. J. Spalding and another man approached through the gate and walked toward them. His companion, tall with a thatch of dark unruly hair and an open face, watched them.

Izzy pushed past the blonde woman and came to Merry, who walked her into the stall and shut the half door.

She heard the woman whisper behind her. "Look how that horse follows her. Can you teach them to do that?"

Merry gestured the trio out of the paddock before closing the gate. As she latched it behind them, she shot a pointed look at the woman, who blushed. Spalding had reached the porch and had his hand on the door before he noticed Merry and the couple had stopped in the middle of the yard. He jogged back to them. The few steps of exertion left him panting.

"Now listen here, Ms. McCoy—" Spalding began, but the other man held up his hand.

"I'm Thomas Brentwood, and this is my wife, Theodora."

"You can call me Tee."

She gave a little nod. "Merry McCoy."

"Ms. McCoy, you own this property?" Brentwood's mellifluous voice sounded like it had been aged in an oak casket for twenty years.

"Yes. And you're trespassing."

Brentwood raised his eyebrows. "We've been given to believe that this property is on the market."

Merry narrowed her eyes at Spalding.

Brentwood looked displeased. "Apparently that's not the case. Perhaps Mr. Spalding here was mistaken."

"No," Merry said. "I was very clear."

"I see." Brentwood shifted his gaze to the shorter man beside him. "T. J.?" A vein of iron ran through his smooth voice.

Spalding blanched. "Well, I ... of course she's going to sell." Regaining his cockiness, he spoke to Merry. "Sure you are, sure you are. Your mother is unfortunately deceased, and you don't want to stay around here where everyone knows what happened down in Texas. You're a pariah. Why would you keep the place when you

have buyers standing right here in front of you that are very—
very—interested and able to take it off your hands?"

"T. J.," Brentwood said.

"Exactly what do you think happened 'down in Texas,' Mr. Spalding?" Sarcasm laced Merry's tone.

"I asked around," Spalding said. "I know."

"I just bet you do." She turned to the other man. "Listen, Mr. Brentwood, I'm sorry you wasted your time coming out here, but I'm not selling."

"I won't say I'm not disappointed. We really like the place." Brentwood smiled.

Merry smiled back. It wasn't his fault Spalding was such a little prick.

"Oh, you're being downright unreasonable, Ms. McCoy," Spalding said.

"T. J., please wait for us by the car," Brentwood said without looking at him. Reluctant, Spalding drifted to stand by his vehicle, a big sulk all over his soft little face.

"Honey," Tee Brentwood said. "You made him mad."

Brentwood shrugged. "Sorry about all this, Ms. McCoy."

"Merry is fine."

"Okay. And I'm Thomas. You don't have to worry about us bothering you again."

"Thank you. Now if I could just get it through to Mr. Spalding that his time is wasted here."

Brentwood frowned. "I have some friends on the real estate commission. I'll see what I can do to help you out with that."

"You don't need to do that. He should take the hint this time."

"It's just a phone call. And maybe you'll let me know if you hear of any property coming up for sale that we might like." He reached into his pocket and handed Merry a card. "Needless to say, we just lost ourselves a real estate agent, and while we love this country we don't know the area very well."

She considered the card. The phone number had a Montana area code, but she didn't recognize the prefix. Probably a cell phone. There was no address.

"What exactly is it you're looking for?"

His wife answered. "Enough land to get a taste of open country. I've lived in the city my whole life, and now I want to live in some of this wonderful untrammeled space you have here. Keep some animals—I love horses, but as you've already guessed, I don't know much about them. I'm really very sorry about letting that one out the other day."

"You just have to use common sense with animals. Helps if there's someone around who will answer questions, too. Are you looking for a vacation place?"

"No," Brentwood said. "I'm retiring. We want to live here full-time, be a part of the community. Maybe even get some cattle."

"Why were you looking at this place? It sounds larger than what you want."

"T. J. told us smaller plots weren't available. And I wouldn't mind having a good-sized chunk of land."

"Well, I'll keep your number. You never know."

She shook both their hands, and the couple walked to where the real estate agent waited. Merry watched Spalding's irritation turn to something like fear as Thomas Brentwood spoke to him. He jumped into the Cadillac and jerked it into drive, spraying gravel as he drove away. Tee Brentwood said something to her husband. Brentwood smiled and kissed her on top of her head.

The Land Rover worked its way around a couple of potholes before picking up speed. Merry would think long and hard about recommending a place to Brentwood. Like most Montana natives, she didn't like the idea of a bunch of rich outsiders moving in, the preponderance of Hollywood types buying up land for vacation homes they rarely visited having long ago jaded those who lived and worked here. At least the Brentwoods planned to stay year round and had a lot of money, some of which they'd spend locally.

And for some reason, Merry kind of liked the guy.

TWENTY-ONE

MERRY'S FIRST CALL WENT through to Barbie's voicemail. She hung up without leaving a message and tried the Quikcare Clinic next. A woman answered after four rings.

"Hello? I'm looking for Olivia Lamente."

"This is Olivia."

"Hi. This is Merry McCoy."

Silence.

"Listen, I was going through some of my mother's papers, and she has a note here that she sold a gun to Bo a few years back." She was surprised at how easily the lie came to her.

A pause. "Yes?"

"Listen, I know it's a bad time, but I was wondering whether he kept it or sold it to someone else."

"Why?"

"I was, uh, kind of hoping to buy it back if I could track it down."

Another pause. "You're allowed to have a gun?"

Uh oh. "If I permanently disable it, so it won't work. Then it's okay. I don't want to shoot it. Only have it because … because it was Mama's."

Sorry, Mama.

"What kind was it?" Olivia said finally. But her tone was softer.

"A thirty-eight."

"I'm sorry. I don't really know much about guns. What did it look like?"

Merry described the revolver in general terms. "And it had her name on it." She hoped Olivia hadn't heard about the gun that killed Denny Teller.

She didn't give any indication she had, saying, "I think I remember seeing it."

"Did he sell it?"

"I don't think so. If it's the one I'm thinking of, he taught Barbie how to shoot with it."

The tiny shiver traveled up Merry's neck again.

"But it was probably lost in the fire, along with everything else. I'm sorry. I know about wanting to keep things that belonged to those we've lost."

"I know you do, Olivia. I'm sorry, but I had to ask."

"I understand."

After they said goodbye Merry sat looking out the kitchen window for a long time, trying to put it all together.

———

Merry spent the next few hours catching up on mundane chores. She cleaned Izzy's stall and spread clean bedding. She did her laundry, picked up the house a little, and watered the bushes running rampant in Mama's rose garden.

She remembered the shotgun as she came in the back door to the mudroom. Sure enough, it was leaning against the back of a cupboard there. The exterior surface was finely pitted with rust, but it looked clean enough inside. She'd take it apart and oil it down sometime soon. The box of ammunition tucked on the shelf below might have been purchased by her grandfather; the shells inside were old, wrapped in stained cardboard rather than brightly colored plastic. Tucked in with them was a metal box that held three chokes designed to screw on the end of the barrel in order to narrow or widen the shot spray, depending on the prey.

Merry grabbed the box and gun and took them out to the barn. She climbed the ladder to the hayloft and stuffed them into a gap between the floor of the loft and the wall. As a teenager she'd used the space to hide contraband cigarettes, tequila, and the occasional joint. This, too, was contraband for a felon on parole.

Back inside she was folding a load of laundry when the phone rang. She sighed. Having free access to a phone wasn't as great as she'd remembered, and it didn't help that Mama hadn't believed in Caller ID. But she gave in to its trilling demand in case it was Shirlene or Kate calling, trying to ignore the excited, piping voice in the back of her mind that hoped it might be Jamie.

"Hello?"

A pause and then a voice cutting in and out.

"Hello?"

"… wasn't home."

"Lauri? Where are you?"

The connection cracked again, allowing only spurts of her cousin's voice.

"I can't hear you." Merry tried to hide her exasperation. "Are you on a cell phone?"

"I was over there the night he died. She wasn't there."

What the hell was she talking about? "Who wasn't where?"

"Barbie wasn't there."

"At Clay's?"

"No! At home."

Wait a minute. "She wasn't home the night Clay died? You're sure?"

"*Yes.*" Now Lauri sounded frustrated. "Janelle told me she said she was home, but I went inside … slashed …" Her cousin's voice faded out.

Slashed. That was the night Lauri had punctured Barbie's water-bed. Of course. Merry tried again. "Where are you? Are you okay?"

A few seconds passed, and Merry thought the cell connection had given out. Then, "I'm all right."

"You need to come back home."

"No way. It's not safe."

A part of Merry agreed with her cousin, though reason screamed that Lauri was making it harder on herself by running away.

"At least tell me where you are."

"Will you *listen* to me? Barbie wasn't home."

"Okay, I get it. But damn it, Lauri, tell me where you are."

The connection abruptly ended. Merry stood with the phone still pressed to her ear, a pair of tube socks dangling from her hand.

Shit.

After lunch Merry headed back out to the barn. Leading Izzy to the center of the aisle, she hooked her halter to the crossties and began brushing her coat with a round rubber currycomb, scrubbing in small circles. The mare's hair sloughed off as she worked her way from neck to rump. Then she did it all again with a stiff-bristled brush, and a final time with a soft-bristled brush, smoothing the horse until she gleamed.

So before peeping in Clay's window in the hope that she could seduce him and then convince him he was the father of her baby, Lauri had gone over to Barbie's, walked in, and vandalized her waterbed. The house had been empty, even though Barbie and Olivia had supposedly been busy with WorldMed-related work.

Was her cousin telling the truth? Merry thought so. Why hadn't she told someone earlier? She said Janelle Paysen had told her about Barbie's alibi. Which meant she might not have known before. She hadn't exactly involved herself in discussions about her own case. Though, now that Merry thought about it, Lauri might have known about Barbie's alibi for a while. If she didn't want to admit she'd borrowed her mother's boots because she'd get in trouble, she sure wouldn't want to admit she'd taken a knife to someone's property.

Either way, Olivia had lied to provide Barbie with an alibi. She seemed so protective of the younger woman, a regular mama bear. She'd always taken in strays—horses, dogs, people. Even Barbie had mentioned it the day after the fire when she'd come to see Merry, though she certainly hadn't seen herself as one of Olivia's rescue projects. Still, Clay had been Olivia's stepson. She couldn't know she was protecting a murderer.

Merry brushed Izzy's face and combed out her dark brown mane and tail. She lifted each hoof and pried it clean of debris with the curved metal hoof pick, then placed pad and saddle on her back. The mare opened her mouth to accept the bit, and Merry gently bent her ears forward to fit the headstall over them. She led her out of the paddock and mounted up.

Despite the horse's eagerness, Merry held her back to a walk at first. They made their way east, toward the rolling foothills that rose up on the edge of the ranch. Out on the flat beyond the barn, she eased into a jog.

Had Denny known Barbie's alibi didn't hold up? Maybe he and Anna had stopped by her house and no one had been home. But Anna hadn't seemed unsure about where her roommate had been when Merry talked to her at the bloodmobile. Then again, as Jamie said, anyone can lie.

Denny, flopped in that awful recliner, talking about Clay's new little hottie. Barbie, her face alive as she'd said she'd kill to protect herself.

At the base of a small rise half a mile away, Merry slowed to a walk again, and she and the mare picked their way to the top.

Where she and Rand had lived in Texas, the constant flat horizon defined a perfect saucer of ground where the light fell hot and pale. Here the altitude, low humidity, and the contrasting richness of undulating purple-blue mountains enriched the sunlight to a generous ripeness. A cloud shadow poured across waving grassland.

An unreasonable sense of nostalgia assaulted her without warning. Izzy's ears twisted back as she swung down under a windtwisted pine, looping the reins over the stub of a lower branch. Squatting on her haunches, she surveyed the meadow down slope through a veil of yearning. She inhaled the spice of willow and timothy hay, wild roses and equine musk: a plethora of memories mixed together in the still, dry air and deposited into her soul for consideration.

Izzy whuffled softly in her ear, offering the warmth of her breath, her animal concern, the whisper-soft touch of her tender nose against skin. Merry stood and stroked the big horse's neck, mounted, and continued east.

Why did Barbie feel so many had to die? Jealousy, maybe, for Clay. But Bo? Maybe his death really had been an accident.

Denny could have known why she killed Clay. That might have been enough for him to confront her. Merry suspected he wouldn't want to turn Barbie in so much as get something for his knowledge. Blackmail. Because if he'd wanted to turn her in, he would have. He'd obviously had some kind of truck with Sergeant Hawkins.

Avarice had done him in. Not that Merry could say she'd miss him much.

What about Anna? She was the link between Denny and Barbie. Was she next on Barbie's hit list?

Merry and Izzy rambled along a circuitous route, ending at the Lamentes'. The mare picked her way among the charred ruins of the smaller outbuildings. Where one had stood, the fire had left behind only a small, blackened pile of wood charcoal surrounded by a rough square of singed earth. The house had fared little better, reduced to a scorched skeleton leaning precariously against the sky. In the open, stark interior, Merry could see the wreck of barely recognizable furniture protruding from the mess. Izzy nosed a piece of seared countertop lying in the front yard and shied away from the stink.

Merry dismounted and looped the reins over a piece of broken fencing. She loosened the saddle girth and walked to the half-burned horse barn.

———

Lauri squinted at the *Glamour* magazine Janelle had lent her, the light from the kerosene lamp growing dim. Something wrong with the glass thingie that fit around the flame. She sighed, and wished for the forty-second time that day for electricity.

No TV, no telephone, no microwave, and worst of all, no hair-dryer. So not only was she stuck in a tiny dark cabin in the middle of bum-fuck nowhere, she had to look like shit, too.

Janelle said she believed Lauri was innocent. But even so, Lauri couldn't tell her about following Barbie Barnes. Janelle would say it was too much of a risk, wouldn't like Lauri using her car to do it, and wouldn't get why she was doing it at all. Lauri couldn't tell her the whole truth either; however much Janelle vowed to be on her side, she wouldn't understand what Lauri had done to the waterbed. Wouldn't matter how much she tried to explain it. There had been too many other situations like that, too many other people who gave her that look when she'd only been trying to tell them what they'd asked to know.

So she hadn't told her. Janelle worked all the time, so she wouldn't see her own car in town, and if someone else saw it and asked Janelle about it, Lauri would tell her that she'd had to come into Hazel to get something or other.

At least she got out once in a while. It was hard to follow Barbie during the day in a town the size of Hazel, so she only did it at night. She'd dyed her hair dark like Janelle's and added a variety of hats and a pair of big ugly sunglasses like Janelle would wear—that girl had the *worst* taste—and no one had taken a second look. At least, she didn't think they had.

And at night Lauri could get close enough to see what Barbie was doing in her house. Persistence pays off, her mother always said. Lauri was just waiting for that to happen. She was getting pretty tired of waiting for Merry to catch on, though. She'd been going great guns there for a while, tracking down clues like Nancy Drew and generally making a pest out of herself. Then she'd kind of dried up, like she'd hit a dead end. Plus, she'd started hanging out with Barbie Barnes.

At first, Lauri had thought it was because she knew what Barbie had done and was trying to prove it, but that quickly went out the window. Drinking together, getting all chummy, and crying on each other's shoulders. Made her sick, having to watch that garbage through the kitchen window. Seeing how everybody liked sweet little Barbie so much. Only Lauri seemed to know what a bad person she was.

And why didn't they all like *her* like that? What was it that the Barbie had? How did she fool them all so easily?

She was worried Merry might have heard her when she took up her nighttime watching place, high in the branches of the big old tree in the yard next to Barbie's house, just as her cousin stormed out. It was cold at night sometimes, but not too bad, and Janelle had lent her some pretty good outdoor clothes.

Clay had certainly made the wrong choice in women, but Lauri would make sure Barbie got what she had coming. She had to pay for killing the man Lauri loved, the man she was going to have a family with. And besides, if she didn't, everyone would continue to blame Lauri. She couldn't imagine going to jail for Clay's murder, she just couldn't. And she didn't want to be running her whole life either. She sure as hell wasn't going to be sitting in this nasty cabin that belonged to the Paysens when it came time to have the baby.

Then Denny died and Sergeant Hawkins blamed Merry. So now she had even more reason to find out what really happened, didn't she? Lauri had hated doing it, but she'd finally made the cell phone call. Merry wasn't working fast enough on her own, and it was pretty clear no one believed anything Lauri had tried to tell them.

No one but her cousin. So she had to come through. She just had to. Lauri had seen the hunted look in her eyes that first day when she'd barged into the police station, before Officer Gutierrez asked all his questions. Merry hated that place.

Now Lauri got it, even after just one night in jail. It sucked, and she had no intention of going back.

TWENTY-TWO

SUNLIGHT STREAMED THROUGH THE gaping hole above. The smells of dead smoke and molding hay made Merry's nose itch. Eight stalls marched along one side of the aisle. Along the other side, falling sections of roof had crushed five more. At the far end, an open area held tack. Saddles hung on the racks jutting from the rear wall, and bridles, hackamores, and halters from the pegs on either side. Under the pegs, built-in cubbyholes held everything from fly spray to curry combs, brushes, and hoof picks to padded boots and leg wraps. Soot cut by rivulets of water streaked everything.

Merry stepped past the tack to the closed door on the other side. It revealed a makeshift office, most of the space taken up by a desk made from an old door and two filing cabinets. A folding chair leaned against one wall. She stepped to the file cabinet on the right and opened the top drawer. The files contained printouts of forms and client information from the Lamentes' business. These would be copies for easy access, while the computer containing the electronic copies remained in Bo's burned-out den. If Olivia really planned to continue training horses, she'd need all this.

The last drawer held WorldMed brochures and several copies of a direct mail piece asking for donations. Merry fingered the edge of the paper, considering. Shirlene had said she spent the majority of her volunteer time on the library, but WorldMed kept coming up over and over. Olivia and Barbie had supposedly been working on something for the organization, though now that appeared to be a lie. Shirlene had said that even Anna volunteered with WorldMed, though she really didn't seem the type.

Merry tucked the brochure into her pocket.

Barbie could have killed Clay in simple rage. After all, she had believed he was sleeping around. But that felt ... off. WorldMed was the common theme among the suspects in Clay's murder. Well, not all the suspects. It seemed odd that the evidence seemed to center on Lauri, yet she was the one person who didn't have anything to do with the organization.

So could WorldMed be involved? How?

Merry shook her head. *Good Lord. Look at yourself, suspecting a nonprofit that gives desperately needed medications ...*

Medications. *Narcotics.*

Her mind scrambled around the thought. She'd instantly discounted Sergeant Hawkins's statement that there was a drug problem in town when he'd pulled her over in the Blazer. However, what if he'd been telling the truth? Not about receiving a tip about her, of course, but about there being a problem with illegal drugs in the area. Even so, the usual suspects in small-town Montana were meth, maybe some pot—easy enough to access since the law allowing medical marijuana had passed. And Gus Snyder had apparently had access to cocaine.

On the other hand, prescription drugs were hot stuff, especially with kids, though Merry had known a few women whose addictions to pills like Oxycontin had landed them in jail.

If something was catawampus with WorldMed, it had to have something to do with prescriptions.

Clay had hated drugs—enough to harp on his roommate about them and enough to get Gus Snyder fired from the drilling rig. Shirlene had said she didn't have anything to do with the controlled substances, but as a nurse—and the main organizer, it seemed—Olivia would know how the narcotics were handled for WorldMed. However, asking her about an old gun was one thing—asking her to look for evidence against Barbie, another.

Merry swung up on Izzy's back and pressed her legs into her sides.

She would have gone to Jamie with what she knew if he'd still been on the case. As it was, Rory Hawkins probably wouldn't be interested in anything she had to say, and she didn't know Lester Fleck well enough.

Jamie would kill her if he found out she'd gone to talk to Barbie face-to-face suspecting she'd killed both Clay and Denny. And maybe even Bo. But that wasn't why Merry decided to call instead of going to Barbie's house or trying to track her down at the clinic. For one thing, if Olivia were around it would be more difficult for her to run interference on the phone. The second reason lay in Olivia's earlier reaction to Merry's call. Something about talking to a disembodied voice asking for help was less confrontational than looking someone in the eye.

And maybe the same story would work. Only Barbie would know why Merry was asking about Mama's gun. She'd be putting herself in danger. She'd be bait.

Bait for a trap. Not a bad idea, actually. But not yet. Merry would tell Barbie that she'd come around, that now she blamed Lauri for the murders. It wasn't that far of a stretch. Everyone else thought she did it.

Back home, Merry sluiced down Izzy's sweat-streaked back and let her out to graze in the near pasture. She humped the bulky western saddle into the tack room and gave the leather a quick wipe down, then shook out the saddle pad and returned it to its peg.

Inside she treated herself to a tall tumbler of sun tea, listening to the popping of the ice cubes as she rubbed the condensation that had formed on the outside of the glass across her forehead. She eyed the phone, thinking about what to say before she picked it up and dialed the number that had gone to voicemail that morning.

Barbie answered on the first ring. "Hello?"

Merry took a deep breath. "It's Merry. McCoy."

A beat while that hung in the air. Then Barbie said, "I don't know any other Merrys."

"Listen, I'm sorry about the other night."

The other woman hesitated. "You shouldn't have said that. About Clay."

"I know. I'm sorry. I'm at my wit's end here."

"Your cousin killed him. I'm sorry, but that's what happened."

Bingo. "I'm starting to believe that myself. And Denny Teller, too. She was out on bail, after all."

"There you go."

Merry felt her way. "He was shot with my mother's gun."

"Oh, my God. She stole it?"

"Not exactly. In fact, Mama had sold that gun."

"Who to?"

"To Bo."

Another hesitation. "Bo? I don't understand."

Oh, but you do. "I asked Olivia, and she said she'd seen it. She said he taught you how to shoot with it."

A pause. "She told you that?"

Merry kept her tone light. "It was a thirty-eight revolver. Had Mama's name engraved on it. Do you remember it? Can you think of how Lauri might have gotten a hold of it?"

A long silence from the other end.

"Barbie?"

"Sorry. I'm here. I just … no, I'm afraid I don't know how your cousin got that gun."

"You sure? It would help put things to rest. I don't like being framed." The last sentence came out with a hard edge to it.

"Framed? No. No, I bet you don't." She sounded thoughtful.

"Well, let me know if you think of anything, okay?"

"Yeah. Yeah, I'll do that."

Merry hung up and grabbed a towel. Mopping the puddle that had formed under her tea, she thought about Barbie's reaction. What had she expected? A tear-stained telephone confession? Of course not. But still, she felt a little disappointed.

———

Olivia was leaning on the counter cleaning a pair of reading glasses when Merry entered the Quikcare. She looked up and blinked.

"More Tylenol?" She didn't sound hostile so much as tired.

Merry smiled. "No, thanks. I'm trying to cut down. But I have some questions about that relief agency you work with, WorldMed."

"You're interested in volunteering?"

"I am. Shirlene has told me a lot about it, of course, but I got to wondering how you handle the narcotics that you send overseas."

Olivia studied her. "I don't know that I should talk to you about this."

"Well, you should know that any rumors you've heard about me, anything about my being in jail? None of any of that had anything to do with drugs."

A ghost of a smile crossed the other woman's face. "I know what happened. Or a version of it. But that's not what I'm talking about."

"Then what's the problem?"

"Unless we're talking about a regulatory agency I don't see that our drug policy is anyone's business."

"Oh."

Olivia narrowed her eyes. "What's this about?"

Merry reached for a lie. "Anna Knight. I heard something about her being involved with drugs." Okay, good. That wasn't even a lie, really.

"Bah. Anna? I don't think so. Besides, what would that have to do with WorldMed?"

"Maybe nothing. I'm just trying to find connections."

Olivia shook her head. "You're still trying to clear your cousin, aren't you? Well, you just leave Anna out of it. She's a good girl."

God, she sounded just like Shirlene. And if she thought Merry was still trying to clear Lauri, she'd tell Barbie.

"You know what? Lauri probably did it. Okay? I get that. But will you at least look at your records, see if there's any discrepancy? What I heard about Anna has me curious."

She hesitated, then dipped her chin. "Okay. I'll take a look."

"And you'll call me if you find anything."

"No. I'll call the police if I find anything." She didn't sound happy about it.

It was the best Merry would get from her. "Is Anna around?"

"Anna's gone. She left this morning to go visit her grandmother. I guess the old girl's not doing so well."

No kidding, considering Anna had as much as told Merry her grandma had died. If, of course, it was the same one who Shirlene reminded her of. God rest her soul.

"I see. Well, I hope she gets to feeling better. You mind if I use your phone?"

———

"Hello? Shirlene?"

A loud click sounded in Merry's ear as the phone dropped back into its cradle. She hit redial, listening with impatience to the number replay musically in her ear. After a dozen futile rings, she slammed the phone down, then had a thought, grimaced, and picked it up again, jabbing at the buttons with her finger. Olivia flashed a glance at her from the far end of the counter.

"Hi, is this Gayle?" Merry asked when the woman answered.

"Yes."

"It's Merry McCoy. I need to talk to Jamie."

Her tone turned cold. "He's not here."

Merry lowered her voice. "I really need to talk to him."

"He's on leave from the police department for a while. I don't think he can help you."

"I just have a procedural question," she said. "Can you ask him to call me?"

Jamie's wife made a noise in the back of her throat. "I guess. I'll tell him when he gets home."

"As *soon* as he gets in."

"I said I'd tell him. Does he have your number?" Her tone was sarcastic.

What had Jamie told her? Merry tried to wipe the guilt from her voice as she left the number of the ranch.

Damn.

Merry thanked Olivia again and ran out to Lotta. Thunderheads piled upon the horizon, and the wind began to pick up. The light turned gray as more clouds obscured the sun. Distant rumblings, fair warning of the impending storm, followed a faint flash from deep inside the growing mountain of moist air.

She pulled into Shirlene's driveway, ran up the walkway, and pounded on the door. No one answered. Circling the dwelling, she peered in the windows. No one was home. If it hadn't been for someone picking up the phone when she called, she would have let it go.

The back door was unlocked.

She walked through the darkening house, flipping on lights and calling out. Upstairs and down, she looked in all the rooms. Clothes were scattered on the floor of Lauri's room and two of the dresser drawers gaped open. Either someone had been through her things, or her cousin was a terrible slob.

Then something caught her eye. Two one hundred-dollar bills lay folded on the dresser. Merry fingered them, then put them back.

She checked the cluttered, cobweb-festooned basement, finding footsteps in the dust, but no indication of when they had been made. Probably Shirlene's. She shut off the lights and locked the back door on the way out.

The wind had turned colder, and she shivered as she got back into her truck. Darker clouds reached Hazel, creating an early twilight. She guided Lotta to Shirlene's Dry Cleaning on Main. A CLOSED sign hung in the window. A bleak fluorescent nightlight illuminated the rear of the shop.

She cruised through town, wishing she had a cell phone and chiding herself for overreacting while she peered into the gloom hoping to spy Shirlene's red Toyota pickup. She checked her aunt's church, the library, the grocery store, the clinic, the park, and the Hungry Moose. At the Dairy Shack, three teenagers loitered, eating ice cream and talking to another teenager behind the food counter.

A thought occurred to her, and she drove to the alley in back of the Hazel Office Mall. Maybe Shirlene was in Kate's office.

No luck.

What had begun as a combination of mild concern and curiosity gradually turned to dread as her search efforts turned up nothing. She made one more circuit before heading back to Shirlene's.

The sky loomed above, packed with volatile potential. A few fat drops of rain splatted on her windshield. The clouds built momentum, negating the best attempts of daylight saving time to hold onto the fading summer light. A sudden flash rent the rumpled gray flannel overhead, and the accompanying roll of thunder followed almost immediately.

Merry pulled up in front of her aunt's house again. Still dark. She'd leave a note. Around back, she turned the doorknob before remembering that she'd locked it.

The door swung open.

"Shirlene? Are you in here?"

Silence. Thoroughly spooked, Merry edged into the kitchen and turned on the light. Flipping light switches in all the rooms, she passed through the house again but didn't find anything different.

Except in Lauri's room. The money on the dresser was gone.

———

If his wife bothered to give him the message, Jamie would call Merry at home. But she wanted to talk to him now. An electric scent quivered in the air as she walked across the asphalt to the entrance to Chewie's Bar.

Early Friday evening, already the floor vibrated from the loud music and people getting started on the weekend. Once she elbowed her way up to the bar and caught Chewie's attention, she shouted over the cacophony. "Have you seen Shirlene tonight?"

Chewie put one hand behind his ear and pointed to a beer bottle with his eyebrows raised in question. She shook her head and gathered breath to shout again, but he turned to take another drink order.

She waited as he filled a pitcher, perusing his trophies scattered among the liquor bottles behind the bar. She squinted to read the base of the huge gold-plated rifle. Team shooting. John "Chewie" Ueland and—

She pushed her way to the end of the bar, offering an absent apology as she stepped on one drinker's foot, and went around behind. Stood in front of the trophy, unbelieving.

"Gosh, Merry, you don't have to serve yourself." Chewie stood next to her with a puzzled grin on his face.

She pointed at the rifle. "You won this with Olivia?"

Chewie shrugged. "Hell, I taught that woman how to shoot. She wanted to go to a competition, so I dragged her along. Turns out she's a natural." He smiled again. "Surprised the hell out of me when we won that thing."

"She said she didn't know anything about guns!"

"Well, now, I think you must be mistaken there." His eyes widened. "Merry? You okay?"

"What about Barbie Barnes? Do you know if she knows how to shoot?"

"I don't know. She sure didn't seem interested when she was around and Olivia and I were training. You want a beer? You look like you could use one."

She waved him off. "I gotta go."

Making her way through the bar crowd, she felt a tug on her sleeve and turned to find Shirlene standing beside her.

"You looking for me?"

"Yes!"

She grasped her aunt's arm and pulled her to the door. The sky grumbled again as they exited to the parking lot.

"What's the matter?" Shirlene asked in alarm.

"Did you hang up on me?"

"What? When?"

"About an hour ago. I called your house and someone answered and hung up on me."

"I came over here after work for a bagel dog. Chewie stocks them for the weekend from the Schwan's truck."

"Shit. Shirlene, you knew she was going to come by. You even left the back door open for her."

Her aunt's eyes grew round. "Did you see her?"

"No. I saw the money you left on her dresser. And then, when I went back, it was gone."

Shirlene sagged against the rough brick of the building. "Thank God. She's okay, then."

"You really don't know where she's staying?"

Shirlene shook her head. "No. But I hoped she hadn't gone too far. I wanted her to have money for food or whatever she might need."

"Jesus. If she goes shopping, she'll be back in jail in no time. Not that that would be a bad thing."

Shirlene set her jaw. "I can't believe you're saying that."

"Hasn't it occurred to you that she might be in danger?"

"Sure. From that bastard Rory Hawkins."

"Not Hawkins. Olivia. Olivia killed Clay. And his roommate. Lauri told me her alibi isn't right. Well, she told me Barbie's alibi isn't right, but that's the same thing. God, why didn't I realize when Olivia gave Barbie an alibi, she gave herself one, too?"

Her aunt turned white. "You think..." She swallowed. "He was her *son*, Merry. Parents don't kill their children."

"Stepson," Merry said.

Shirlene shook her head. "You must be wrong. I can't believe Olivia would do that." She froze. "Wait a minute. You talked to Lauri?"

"She called me."

"She called you? When? Why didn't you tell me?"

"It was this afternoon."

"Was she all right?"

"She sounded fine. The connection was bad. I think she was on a cell phone."

The wind whipped Shirlene's hair around her face, and she hugged herself. "Shit. I wish I knew where she is."

"So do I. I take back what I said about her being safer in jail. Wherever she is, I hope she stays there until we get this figured out."

"Figured out! Even if you're right, the police won't do anything! Jamie was the only one on our side, and Kate said he's been suspended."

"I know. But I may have a way to make them pay attention."

———

Merry hurried home, after eliciting a promise from Shirlene to call her immediately if she heard from Lauri. She'd been home for fifteen minutes when Jamie called.

"I heard you were looking for me." His tone was strained.

"I think I know who killed Clay and Denny."

"Who?"

"Olivia. I think we can flush her out. I want to use myself as bait."

Several seconds passed. "Are you out of your mind?"

"Maybe. Are you in?"

"Of course not. I'm not going to let you do something that stupid."

"Okay. Just checking whether you'd back me up. Guess not. Gotta go."

"Merry, wait."

"That woman killed Denny and Clay, and probably her husband as well. She tried to frame me, and my cousin has been arrested and is hiding from Rory Hawkins. Olivia lied to provide Barbie an alibi so she'd have one, too. I'm going to do this. You're either with me, or you're not."

"Don't do anything foolish. You're at home?"

"Yeah."

"I'm coming out."

TWENTY-THREE

"So what's this Jessica Fletcher plan of yours?" Jamie sat on the couch, scowling, arms crossed over his chest.

"I haven't quite worked it out yet. That's why you're here." Merry leaned against the fireplace mantle across the room from him.

"Gayle's furious with me."

She winced. "She seems to really hate me. You didn't tell her anything, did you?"

"About yesterday? Are you nuts? But she knows we were involved back before I met her. Who knows what else she might have heard."

"I'm sorry. Maybe you should go home."

"And let you pull some loony stunt by yourself? I don't think so. What's got you pointing at Olivia?"

She hesitated, then plunged in. "Olivia gave Barbie an alibi, probably telling her that she'd automatically be suspected. Barbie bought it, and then when Lauri so conveniently showed up and put her finger and footprints all over the murder scene, couldn't take it back."

"And how, exactly, do you know the alibi's bogus?"

"Lauri told me."

Jamie rolled his eyes.

"No, listen. She was not only peeping in Clay's window that night, but she'd made an earlier stop by Barbie's for a little evening vandalism."

He raised his eyebrows. "That waterbed thing?"

She nodded. "Right."

"Hmm. Barbie said that happened earlier in the day."

"Well, it didn't. It happened when Barbie and Olivia were supposed to be working on WorldMed stuff."

"So where was Barbie?"

"I don't know."

"Maybe they did it together."

She looked thoughtful. "You're right. They could have."

"Or maybe Barbie killed Clay, and Olivia is trying to protect her."

"I wondered about that, too. Until I found out Olivia lied about Mama's gun. She said she didn't know anything about guns, and managed to imply that Barbie not only knew how to shoot, but how to do it with that particular revolver."

"Why do you say she lied?"

"Because John Ueland and Olivia Lamente won a team shooting competition last year."

"Chewie?"

"Yeah." She shifted against the mantle. "I called Barbie and asked her about the gun. She sounded surprised that Olivia had told me she'd used it. Seemed distracted for the rest of the conversation."

"Oh, please. That's what you're basing this craziness on?"

"You didn't hear her."

He grinned. "Women's intuition?"

"More than that, smartass. And Olivia is a viable suspect, even if Clay *was* her stepson."

"But why would she kill him?" Jamie asked. "You don't have a motive stuffed up your sleeve, do you?"

She let out a breath. "Maybe. You know how Clay was so against drinking—and drugs?"

"Sure. His mother died from a drug overdose when he was a kid. Bo married Olivia a few years later." He made a get-on-with-it gesture.

"I'll be damned."

"What?"

"Well, I don't know for sure. I think there might be something hinky about the drugs that WorldMed dispenses. If Olivia was stealing them and Clay found out, he'd be furious." She nodded. "I guess I would, too, if my mother had died from an overdose."

Jamie sat back and looked thoughtful.

Merry toed the brick hearth. "Uh, I kind of screwed up."

His eyes snapped to hers. "What do you mean?"

She took a deep breath. "I asked Olivia to take a look at the World-Med documentation to see if there are any discrepancies. I said I suspected Anna Knight of being involved with drugs, and wanted to make sure it didn't have anything to do with WorldMed. I was really looking for information about Barbie."

"And that was a big, big mistake," Olivia said from the doorway into the kitchen.

Merry's head jerked up, her mouth open. Jamie's hand went to his hip for a gun that wasn't there.

"Because," Olivia examined the forty-four she held. "That means I have to kill you, too." She sighed. "Goddamn it, why couldn't you just let it go, Merry? Now your crazy little cousin is going to be blamed for even more death."

Merry heard a muffled thump out on the porch, but Olivia didn't seem to notice. She tried to stall. "So it *was* about the drugs. Why did you kill Denny?"

Olivia's forehead creased. "Clay told him, and the little bastard thought he could blackmail me into letting him in on the operation."

Being right about Denny's greed didn't make Merry feel any better right then. Olivia was trying to act like she had everything under control, but she was obviously a mess. Her unbound hair straggled in greasy wisps around her pale face, and she wagged her head in an exaggerated fashion, which made Merry wonder if she'd been sampling her own product.

"This sure has turned into a mess." She sounded apologetic as she pointed the gun at Merry.

Jamie spoke for the first time. "Did Bo find out you murdered Clay? Is that why you killed him?"

Olivia covered her mouth with one hand, tears brightening her eyes. Her hand dropped away from her face as she said, "Bo tried to talk to Clay, tried to convince him not to turn me in for the drugs. But it didn't work, Clay wouldn't listen to his dad. So I went over to Clay's myself. He got really nasty, wouldn't listen to sense. Then I made the mistake of offering him money, and he completely blew up. I didn't even think, just grabbed that gun from the living room and shot him." The tears spilled over and streamed down her face. "I couldn't tell Bo. I knew what it would do to him, and I loved him too much. But after a couple days he got suspicious, started asking me questions. When he finally came right out and accused me, I told him the truth. I told him I'd shot his son."

She slumped, leaning one shoulder against the doorframe. Merry could see her shaking. "He came after me. My sweet, gentle husband came after me with a pitchfork." A choking sob made her next words almost unintelligible. "I had to defend myself. I didn't mean to kill him. I didn't." Her eyes pleaded with Merry.

"But once he was dead you set the fire in the barn to cover it up." Merry's voice was flat.

Olivia pushed away from the doorjamb and swiped the back of her hand across her wet cheek. Her other hand tightened around the gun. "Shut up. You don't understand."

Jamie said, "You're only making it worse. You can stop it, right now."

She pointed the gun at him. "No, I can't." There was a finality in the three words that arrowed new terror through Merry.

Then a familiar fury erupted, as if something exploded in her gut and only her skin held in the red heat. Merry fought it, afraid of the prickling of her scalp, trying to control the urge to rush the other woman and pummel the life out of her for all the death and grief she'd caused. She couldn't do that again. There had to be a better way. There had to be.

The shot was deafening. Jamie lurched against the back of the couch as the bullet angled through his chest. He blinked at Merry, a small gesture that seemed to take forever, then slumped forward.

Merry gaped. "No!"

Not Jamie, please not Jamie.

The gun swung toward Merry. She dove through the doorway to her bedroom as the gun went off. The bullet pinged off the stone fireplace chimney, spraying shrapnel as she sprawled on the floor. Another shot percussed the air. She kicked the door shut, reached up, and turned the lock.

A bullet ripped into the door by the latch, scoring Merry's arm as she regained her feet. She grabbed a ladder-back chair from against the wall and jammed it under the now-wobbly doorknob. Racing to the window, she threw it open and tried to punch through the screen. Her fist bounced off the screen. Knuckles burning, she drew back to try again, then realized it would be quicker to unfasten it and pop it out. In seconds, it fell to the ground outside.

Olivia had stopped shooting. Merry heard the faint creak of the front door opening. The other woman had heard her trying to get out the window and was moving to cut her off.

To cut her down.

Merry went to the door and eased the chair from under the knob, then stood to the side and opened it with slow care. The living room was empty except for Jamie, who had fallen to his side, one hand clutching at the shirt in front of the bullet wound. His eyes were closed. His blood soaked the green velveteen of the couch, turning it a dark brown.

She bolted through the living room to Jamie's side. He was still breathing. A noise came from the porch. Merry jumped up and dashed into the kitchen. If she'd miscalculated, and Olivia was in there, Merry would at least have the element of surprise.

It was empty. The door to the backyard off the mudroom was wide open. Still moving, Merry reached for the cordless phone. The kitchen window shattered as the big gun boomed again, blending with a hollow *punk* as the bullet punctured the side of the refrigerator scant inches from her head.

She abandoned the phone and dashed out the open back door. *Have to get help for Jamie. Have to stay alive to do it.*

Pressing her shoulders against the rough, weathered boards of the house, she sidled quickly along the stones of the foundation toward the rose garden. Olivia would already be on her way around the house, and Merry couldn't be sure which direction she'd come from. She ran across to the deer fence and hurried to the back side of the garden. She crouched down, screened from the house by the tangle of overgrown rose bushes, and tried to keep her breath shallow.

Light flickered through the seething clouds above, and thunder muttered soon after. She strained to see the back of the house.

If she could make it down to the trees, she could circle around, approach the barn from the front. But there were eight hundred yards of open meadow between her and the wooded area. Still it was dark, and maybe she could…

A sudden flash of lightning illuminated the house and yard— and Olivia standing by the back door, looking in her direction. Merry held her breath, ears poised for sound, waiting for her eyes to readjust after the brilliant strobe of light.

"I know you're out here. We can do this all night if you want. I've disabled the phone, and I've got your keys. And Merry? I know your mama sold all your daddy's guns. Give it up, and we'll do this quick."

But Mama hadn't sold all of *her* daddy's guns.

"You know what I think? I think you're behind those roses."

A bullet ripped through the foliage four feet to Merry's left. Olivia couldn't see her, or she wouldn't have missed by so much. Hell, given that trophy in Chewie's she wouldn't have missed at all.

Merry eased all the way to the ground, lying flat. The sharp edges of the bunchgrass that had sprung up around the garden bit into her arms as she watched Olivia through the petals of a drooping flower head. She thanked providence she'd chosen a navy T-shirt to wear with her jeans that morning.

Olivia approached. Merry coiled her muscles and dug the toes of her boots into the ground, ready to jump and run or attack if the opportunity arose.

Her adversary paused on the far side of the garden, squinting into the roses. Merry found herself praying to some indeterminate deity.

Make me invisible.

Let her get closer. Let her stumble onto me before she knows what's happening.

The sound of metal striking metal rang out from the front of the house.

Olivia whirled and ran, gun at the ready. Merry sprang after her, veering around the opposite side of the house, cutting to the right before she reached the front and angling behind the old garage.

Lotta was parked in the circular drive, the Lamentes' rust-colored Ford pickup snugged up behind it. No other cars, but someone else had just slid into the equation.

As she reached the corner and prepared to dash across to the rear of the unused chicken coop, Merry heard running footsteps. She froze, watching. A figure, mere shadow, moved under the maple tree by the barn.

"Hey!" Olivia shouted from the direction of the house.

The shadow disappeared around the back of the barn. Olivia went after it.

Who else was here? Friend or foe?

Izzy whinnied from her stall. Fear stabbed through Merry all over again at the sound.

It began to rain, huge drops that raised puffs of dust as they cannonballed to the ground. She ran to the barn entrance, silent on the balls of her feet. It was pitch black inside, the smell of horse strong. Feeling her way along the stalls, she struggled to hear, but the rain on the roof drowned all other sound. As a child, the barn had been her favorite place during rainstorms; now the cacophony was a nuisance.

Or maybe not. If she couldn't hear Olivia, Olivia couldn't hear her either.

She touched the wood of the loft ladder. Her hand slipped as she swung up to the first rung, and a chunk of wood slid under the skin of her palm in the same place that she'd taken the splinter moving the wood at the Lamentes' fire. It stung like a sonofabitch. Climb, she chanted to herself. *Climb.*

She ascended into a dark that was, if possible, even blacker.

Panic gripped her as she moved into the loft, her eyes wide open but completely blind. She closed them and concentrated on the throbbing furrow Olivia's bullet had made in her arm.

No time for panic now. She was too close. The shotgun was right ... over ... *here.*

Her hand closed on the barrel, and she finger-walked along the crevice until she felt the box of shells. Pulling them and the gun out of their hiding place, she allowed herself a small feeling of satisfaction.

She set about loading the gun. The sound as she slid the antique pump action cracked through the loft, even with the drumming on the roof.

She fumbled a shell out of the box and dropped it. Felt around, but it had rolled beyond her reach. With care, she extracted another and, feeling to make sure the metal cap was on the right end, slotted it into the gun. She couldn't remember how many shells the Remington would take. Three? Or would it take more? There wasn't a plug in this old thing, but it had a relatively short barrel. Urgency made her impatient, and when it seemed full at three, she rose from her hunched position to her knees and ratcheted a shell into the chamber.

Armed and more than ready, Merry made her careful, crouching way back to the ladder. She reached the edge of the loft without incident and lay down with her head hanging over. The dim rain-soaked light from the square of open doorway looked like the entrance to nirvana after those long moments of blindness. Still, it didn't illuminate any of the barn.

Olivia could be down there. Waiting for her.

A chance she'd have to take.

Climbing down the ladder took longer than going up, encumbered as she was by the twelve-gauge. The extra shells she'd slipped into her jeans pocket weighed against the fold of her hip. She lost count of the rungs, wasn't positive how many there were anyway. She cursed herself. How many times had she climbed them? How many times had she looked at the ladder in passing? Maybe eight rungs. Maybe ten.

Her weak ankle gave out, and her foot slipped on the slick, well-worn wood. Pinwheeling, she fell backwards and hit the floor of the barn's central aisle with a thump. Izzy snorted from her stall.

She'd only been a couple of rungs up, and while falling had twisted away so as not to stick her foot through and break her leg. The shotgun remained in her grasp.

Things could be worse. Get the hell up.

She rolled to her side, pushed herself to her knees, and stood. At least Olivia wasn't in the barn; despite the drumming on the roof, she would have heard Merry's fall and come at her.

Creeping to the door, she peered around the edge into the pouring night. The rain was letting up, but the wind whipped at the maple, filling the air with the subtle roar of wet, slapping leaves. If she were Olivia, where would she be waiting? Not inside—too easy for Merry to go cross-country. Someplace where she'd have a good view of the area around the ranch. There were no good options for that, and in this downpour seeing very far was moot. So she'd be on the move, trying to outthink her.

Merry had to find Olivia before she found Merry.

Better yet, wait in the barn until Olivia came looking for her here. Ambush her.

Jamie doesn't have that kind of time.

As she watched the shadows for any hint of movement, a scream pierced through the wind and rain.

A figure stumbled from behind Lotta. Another strode purposefully behind. Neither was looking toward the barn, and Merry slipped out, running to the thick trunk of the maple. The bulb over the porch, though weak against the heavy night, provided enough light to see them.

"I'll kill her, Merry," Olivia called in a rough voice. "Get out here or I'll do it."

The figure turned, then. Merry could see the white, frightened face sixty feet away.

Barbie.

Olivia looked wildly around the yard, her face pale under the rain-soaked strands of hair plastered to her cheeks. She grabbed Barbie by the collar of her jacket and pressed the gun against her temple.

"No," Barbie said. "You don't know what you're doing. Olivia, you don't want to hurt me, I know you don't. I love you."

A sob ripped from Olivia's throat. "I know, honey. I know. But it's totally out of control now. There's nothing else I can do."

The revolver looked huge in Olivia's hands, and Merry could have sworn they were shaking. Without warning, she switched her hold on the firearm and hit Barbie, an arcing blow of the gun butt on her left shoulder. Barbie cried out and crumpled to the ground next to the truck. Merry brought the shotgun to her shoulder, sighting down the barrel as she steadied herself against the tree trunk.

"Come on, Merry," Olivia called again and let go of the gun with one hand to wipe at her cheek. "There's no reason to draw this out."

Merry pulled the trigger.

Or tried to. Nothing happened.

The safety, stupid, the safety.

As she fingered the button under the trigger guard, she realized it was a good thing the gun hadn't gone off. In her impatience to get the thing loaded, she'd forgotten to screw a choke on the end of the barrel and Olivia hovered too close over Barbie. A blast from this far away with the unfettered scatter shot would injure, perhaps even kill, them both.

Barbie came up fast, driving her shoulder into her tormentor's stomach. Olivia spun to the side as Merry crowed in approval and ran toward them.

"Damn it!" Olivia panted through gritted teeth, her face twisted in pain, but she didn't fall. She pointed the gun at Barbie.

"No!"

Olivia looked up to see Merry fifteen feet away, pointing the shotgun at her. She turned but kept the huge revolver pointed at the woman at her feet. Regret settled across her features. She grimaced and Merry knew Barbie only had a moment before Olivia pulled the trigger. She took the shot.

Nothing.

Olivia's eyes widened in surprise.

Barbie grabbed her leg.

Olivia stumbled, and Merry ejected the dud shell, shuffling awkwardly forward and cursing humidity and time for ruining the powder. Olivia raised her gun again as Merry worked the pump and paused to pull the trigger again, only a dozen feet away.

The sound put all the thunder to shame. A dinner-plate-sized wound bloomed in Olivia's abdomen, but somehow she staggered backward without falling. A part of Merry marveled; the force of the blast should have knocked her flat.

Olivia looked down, then back up at Merry, a question in her eyes. Barbie scrambled around the back of the truck. Slowly, Olivia looked down at the gun in her hand. Watched it drop from her fingers into the mud. Her eyes rose to meet Merry's.

She smiled and something like gratitude flickered in her eyes before all the light went out. She collapsed to the ground, a puppet without strings.

Merry crept forward, still leery. But Olivia was thoroughly dead.

Barbie joined her. "Thank God." Her voice quavered and tears streaked her face. "Thank God."

TWENTY-FOUR

DROPPING THE SHOTGUN, MERRY wrapped her arms around Barbie. "It's okay," she murmured.

Jamie.

She released Barbie and loped to the house.

Jamie still lay slumped on his side. Merry touched his neck and felt a weak, thready pulse. She ran into the kitchen. The phone was gone.

Back in the living room, she eased him back a few inches so she could see the damage, afraid to move him, afraid not to.

Barbie pushed her aside. "Here, let me look at him."

They'd have to get him in the truck—no, Olivia said she'd taken the keys, too. They'd be in her pocket. Have to go get them. Or, wait—

"Barbie, where's your car?"

"Down the road a little. I didn't want Olivia to see it."

"Give me your keys. We've got to get Jamie to the hospital."

Barbie fished in her jeans pocket. "Moving him right now could kill him."

"He'll die for sure if we don't." Merry stood and started for the open door, only to see her cousin, now with dark hair, walking up the steps. She had a cell phone clamped to her ear.

"*Lauri*? What are you doing here?"

"Hello? Yes, someone's been shot. The McCoy ranch. You know where that is?"

"Tell them a police officer's been wounded."

Her cousin's head jerked up. "Um, and a police officer has been wounded . . . I don't think so." She moved the phone away. "Is it bad?"

Merry, giddy with helpless fear, shot a look at Barbie.

She nodded. "They'd better hurry."

Lauri said, "Tell them to hurry."

Merry knelt next to Jamie. The bullet had entered on the right side of his chest. Barbie slid her hand along his back, careful not to move him. Her hand came back slick with red.

A bubble of blood appeared at the corner of his mouth and popped. His shirt was saturated dark maroon where Barbie pressed her palm against his chest.

"What can I do?" Merry asked.

Barbie frowned. "I'm pretty sure his right lung collapsed, but he's still breathing so the left one's okay." She looked up and saw something in Merry's face that made her say, "Here. Apply pressure here, where my hand is."

Merry quickly complied. A ghost of a wince crossed Jamie's unconscious face as she pressed down.

I'm so sorry, baby. I'm so sorry.

"What happened to your arm?" Barbie reached as if to pull her hand away from Jamie's chest.

"It's fine," Merry barked and shrugged away from her.

"I remembered to call 911 this time." Lauri stared at Jamie, dazed. "I forgot at Clay's, but I remembered this time."

Merry felt the hysterical burble of laughter in her throat, and swallowed it back down. If she started now, she might never stop.

"What are you doing here?" Barbie asked Lauri.

"I followed you. I thought you killed Clay. I never thought…" She indicated the body in the yard with a slight movement of her chin.

"You've been here this whole time?" Barbie sounded shrill.

"Yeah."

"You should have called for help right away!"

"I was way out by the road! I didn't think anyone was hurt until I heard the shot in the yard. Even then it took three times for the call to go through. Your cell reception sucks out here."

Merry glanced at her watch. Only a few minutes had passed since Lauri had called. She had a sudden, terrifying thought.

Jamie, what if you were right? What if Olivia and Barbie were partners in carnage?

"Barbie, why are *you* here?"

"When you called and asked about that gun of your mom's? You said Olivia had told you Bo taught me how to shoot with it. Well, I've never seen it, and she knows that. So I got to thinking about why she'd say that, and I realized what she'd done. I was going out to her ranch to confront her when I saw her turn in on your road. I thought she might be coming after you."

Merry shifted her position to provide more leverage on Jamie's chest. "So you figured out that she killed Clay."

"And gave herself an alibi when she gave me one."

Lauri squinted. "Where were you that night?"

Barbie looked unhappy. Sighed. "I guess it'll all have to come out anyway. I was at the clinic. Packaging up drugs for our dealer in Billings."

See, Jamie? I was right. I told you I was right. Wake up so I can say I told you so.

"You were in on the drug skimming, too."

"You know about that?"

"Not all of it. But why else would Olivia kill Clay? He was going to turn her in, wasn't he?"

Barbie took a deep breath. "Big-mouth Anna found the Billings dealer for us, but then she blabbed to Denny and Clay. Clay lost it when he found out Olivia was involved. Probably wasn't too pleased with me, either, but I never got a chance to talk to him about it. He called Bo, and he went over there, and they had a big fight about it. Olivia told me about that."

"Did Bo know about the drugs?"

Barbie hesitated, then said, "Yeah. So I don't know why she'd kill him."

Because he found out about Clay. Right, baby?

Jamie sighed beneath her hand. His face swam in her vision, and she bit down hard on her lip.

"She killed her stepson." She nodded toward Jamie. "She shot a police officer, and she was sure as hell going to kill both of us. But before she shot Jamie she said she killed Bo by accident."

"By...? But she wouldn't burn down her barn. The whole reason she got involved in selling narcotics was because she needed the money to make it big in the training business. She really wanted to deal with the high-end horse people."

The mink-and-manure crowd. But Olivia couldn't blame Lauri for Bo's murder, could she, Jamie? She'd needed to cover it up. And I bet she was well-insured.

Lauri cocked her head at Barbie. "So how come you stole drugs?"

"I couldn't buy back my family's land on a nurse's salary. I needed the money, too."

A siren sounded far away. Merry looked in the direction of the county road, willing them to hurry.

"Would you have killed Clay, too?" Lauri asked her rival.

Barbie's chin rose. "Of course not." Tears welled in her eyes as the ranch yard filled with flashing lights.

———

A dank, rotting smell nudged into every crevice of the aquamarine cinderblock walls, every splinter of the smooth-worn bench, and reflected off the dull iron bars. It wafted up from the drain in the aisle between the cells as if the jail had a direct subterranean connection to a massive locker filled with gangrenous meat.

Merry hadn't been surprised when the sheriff had led her to his car and made her wait in the backseat after she'd answered his initial questions. Barbie and Lauri had gone into two other cars. Renegade women. Protect the horses, men.

Suspected of two murders in two days. One she hadn't committed. One she had.

No. Olivia had been self-defense. There was no question. Except the authorities had questions anyway.

In the cruiser she'd been swamped again by déjà vu. They would decide it hadn't been necessary to kill Olivia Lamente. Forget her big-ass gun. Forget the string of murders she'd committed. Forget that she'd shot a police officer. They'd decide Merry had used "unnecessary force." Again.

They'd look at the evidence and somehow know, as she did, that retribution played as large a part in Olivia's demise as did self-defense.

And until they did, she'd sit here in jail. Rory Hawkins had already visited her once to gloat.

No one would tell her anything about Jamie. She didn't even know if he was still alive. But he'd been breathing, his skin clammy beneath her hand, when they'd taken him from her, rushing through the mud to the gaping doors of the red and white van that screamed down the road toward the waiting helicopter.

She'd shown the bloody groove in her arm to the sheriff as evidence that Olivia had shot her, then she wrapped it with gauze from the medicine chest without mentioning it to the paramedics. She wanted every bit of their attention on Jamie. Now the wound throbbed as if her heart lay directly under the damage. Her jaw clenched with each painful beat as she stared, unseeing, at the crosshatching of her cage.

Beside her, Lauri sighed. "When are they going to let us out of here?"

The sheriff was talking to Barbie upstairs.

The palm of her left hand had swelled an angry red around the piece of wood still embedded there from the ladder in the barn. It ached, a dull mirroring of her arm.

She unwound the gauze, wincing as it pulled away dirt and dried blood. Her throbbing hand moved to her arm, and she squeezed. Gritting her teeth, she did it again.

"Merry," Lauri said.

The gash began to bleed freely. She bent her head as tears filled her eyes. A sob broke free and then another. Blood ran between her fingers and dripped onto the gray slab floor, streaking her boots.

Lauri looked on with wide eyes. Merry sensed one hand reaching out to touch her, but it drew back. She wanted to run her bloody hand over her face, through her hair, in imitation of some tribal grieving ritual.

Jamie. I should have stopped her.

"Oh, Merry. This will never do."

Her head jerked up, the tears surprised out of her. Yvette Trager stood outside the cell. She wore jeans and a sweatshirt and her gray curls were flattened on one side of her head as if she'd just crawled out of bed.

Merry hiccupped. Swallowed.

"I heard one of my parolees got themselves in trouble." Yvette began with a light tone, as if ready to chivvy her charge toward right thinking. But the half-smile slid off her face as she stared at Merry. "Are you okay?"

"Fuck no. I just blew a huge hole in Olivia Lamente with my Bampa's shotgun." She wiped her nose against the still-damp shoulder of her T-shirt. "Just having it is a parole violation, right?"

The other woman gave a reluctant nod.

"Using it like I did, well, that's going to land me in prison for more years than I ever had coming before. Not a lot you can do about that." Merry's angry gaze pushed at her to leave, but Yvette fielded her animosity with kind eyes, cracking her ire like an egg. Yvette grasped a bar in each hand and yelled over her shoulder.

"Nick!"

A short, overweight man hustled down the stairs. "Yes, Ms. Trager?"

"Why hasn't this woman seen a doctor? Look at her arm."

"I don't know, ma'am. She came in with the deputy like that." He looked closer. "Well, it didn't look that bad."

"It's okay," Merry said. "I kind of hid it from them so they could concentrate on Jamie."

Her voice quavered as she spoke, and Yvette's gaze sharpened. "Jamie Gutierrez? What happened to him?"

Merry gaped. "You don't know?"

Yvette motioned to Nick, apparently the graveyard shift's Nadine. "I want to talk to her upstairs. Let her out, and get me a first-aid kit."

With alacrity, he bent to the keys dangling from his belt and unlocked the door. Apparently, being a parole officer held some clout around here. Or maybe just being Yvette Trager did. Merry stood.

Lauri followed. "Hey, what about me?"

"In a little while, honey," Yvette said.

"No! Not in a little while. If Merry gets to go, so do I. I didn't even shoot anyone!"

Merry turned pleading eyes on her cousin, who either didn't understand or didn't care, and whose rising voice continued to complain as they climbed the stairs to the main level of the police station. Yvette ignored her, and Merry tried to.

Nick shut them in the conference room Merry knew so well by now. Moments later he opened the door again to hand in the first-aid kit.

"Where's Barbie?" she asked.

"Went back out to your ranch with the sheriff."

Yvette began with the groove in her arm, gently wiping the dirt from the deep slash with a sanitized towelette. Merry winced as the disinfectant worked its way into the wound but didn't pull back.

"What happened?" her parole officer asked.

Grime and blood had worked into her cuticles, into the tiny crevices of her knuckles, and into a fine webbed pattern in the skin on the backs of her hand. Brown-gray smudges of mud daubed her arms and stained her clothing.

Tangible.

Evidence.

It had all really happened. Her mind, playing the defensive tricks minds do when faced with untenable situations, had been distracting her with her own pain and guilt.

Now, as she prepared to relate the earlier nightmare at the ranch, she faced it all over again. Oh God. Jamie could really die. She was really going back to prison. She'd lose the ranch. The grim dominos lying down in all directions from this night filled her interior vision. Fear unfurled in her chest, and her hand began to tremble in Yvette's. The older woman unscrewed the cap on a tube of Neosporine, watching her face.

"Merry?"

Somehow, she held it together enough to tell what had happened. When she'd finished her story, Yvette had finished cleaning and bandaging her hand and arm. Neither hurt as much as before, numbed by antibiotic ointment and the ibuprofen washed down with a bottle of water Yvette extracted from her giant handbag.

Merry gestured toward the bandages. "Thanks."

Yvette nodded.

They sat back and considered each other.

"You saved a man's life," Yvette said.

"I don't even know that! He might have died."

Yvette got up and left the room without a word. Merry waited, unsure.

After about five minutes she returned. "He's not dead."

Relief gusted through her. Short lived. "So he could still die."

"He's stable. Critical, but stable. From what Nick said when he called the hospital, the bullet chewed him up pretty good inside, but it could have done a lot more damage."

"Is that a clinical diagnosis?"

"Layman's terms are all I have. Point is, you can go ahead and hope for him."

Merry looked out at the night through the window.

"Are you afraid wanting so badly for him to be okay will somehow jinx his recovery?"

Merry hesitated, then inclined her head a fraction. As much affection as she'd developed for her, this woman was a little spooky. "I'm sorry."

Yvette cocked her head to one side, inviting her to continue.

"I didn't do what you said."

"What I said?"

"In Chewie's. About staying strong. I could have stopped her, but I didn't."

"I don't understand. You did stop her."

287

"But not in time. I could have knocked her down, hurt her before she hurt him."

"Really? Could you have?"

"I hesitated. Said to myself we could talk it out. But really, I was just afraid that it was wrong to want to hurt someone the way I wanted to hurt Olivia."

Yvette sighed. "First of all, avoiding violence is not cowardice; it's rationality balancing out something more primitive. Second, you couldn't have stopped her."

"I could have—"

"She had a gun, Merry. A forty-four from what Nick told me before I came down to see you." Merry's head jerked up, and Yvette nodded. "I knew part of what happened, just not about Jamie. I wanted your version. Anyway, I come down and find you sitting in jail beating yourself up because you, unarmed and untrained, didn't take on a crazy bitch with a Dirty Harry gun. How egotistical is that?"

"I—"

"Don't be an ass. She would have shot you. Killed you dead. Killed Jamie. And killed Barbie. But she didn't, because you were smart and because you did what you needed to do when you needed to do it."

Merry was silent, resisting.

Yvette rose. "I'm going to go talk to your cousin, now. You stay here for a little while longer."

Merry waited for half an hour. The door opened, and Sheriff Ellers walked into the room.

"Looks like you all were telling the truth."

She stood. "Jamie regained consciousness?"

He shook his head. "Not yet. But the bullets and guns and the locations of things work out. You can go home. I wouldn't wander too much farther than that, though."

"Can I go to the hospital in Missoula?"

Ellers considered, then gave an easy nod. "Want a ride?"

She heard Rory Hawkins's snort of disgust from outside the room.

"If you can spare the time."

Ellers gestured toward the door. "Let's go then."

TWENTY-FIVE

MERRY LEANED HER HEAD back and stared at the fluorescent lights above. Her arm still ached a bit, even after one of the emergency room doctors had elaborated on Yvette's first-aid handiwork with a few stitches. She'd refused the Vicodin he offered.

The clicking of a computer keyboard, the murmur of voices, the whisper of rubber-clad footsteps, and the occasional muted trill of a telephone combined to lull her tired mind. It was almost five a.m. and the sky was already bright. The cloying floral scent of dusty pot-pourri on an end table failed to override the underlying smells of disinfectant and floor polish.

Merry had found the correct waiting area and slipped onto a chair, fatigue put on hold until she found out what happened to Jamie. Another woman sat across from her, and Merry realized it had to be Gayle Gutierrez. Her dark, gleaming pageboy framed a face that would have been downright stunning minus the red nose and bloodshot eyes from crying. She perched on the edge of an un-comfortable-looking plastic chair, emanating worry for her husband. A quick glance up, then the double take. Merry met her eyes, trying for a smile but feeling it slip around on her face as if she had no control of her own muscles. Anger crowded the distress in the other woman's eyes, and Merry looked away.

She should leave. She knew it but couldn't go before finding out that Jamie was okay. At least she could move to another place to wait. She stood.

"Stay." Gayle's voice was raw.

Merry tried a casual shrug. Struggling to keep her voice even, she said, "Just thought I'd stop by and see if there was any news. I'll check in later."

"He'd want you here." Gayle gestured at the chair, and Merry sank back down, unaccountably intimidated and as uncomfortable as she'd ever been.

Gayle slid back on her chair, eyes still on Merry. "He loves you."

Merry opened her mouth, clamped it shut, then shook her head. "We're just friends, from way back."

Gayle ignored her. "Do you love him, too?"

She had no resources left to draw on. Her throat worked, but nothing came out.

His wife went on. "How could you drag him into your shit like that? He almost lost his job, and now he's in there on that operating table, hanging on with everything he's got, all because of you."

Merry should have left, but now she couldn't. She deserved everything Jamie's wife chose to fling at her, and Gayle deserved the chance to do it.

She bowed her head. "I'm sorry."

Gayle's gaze never wavered. "That's not good enough."

Merry swallowed. "What would be? Good enough."

"If he comes out the other side of this thing, you stay away from him."

She studied the floor.

"No crooking your finger so he comes running. No phone calls pleading for help. No asking him to do things to get him in trouble at work. Just leave him alone."

Merry met her gaze, opened her mouth to speak, and found the words had already run. Because his wife was right. Involving him in her crazy obsession with justice had been pure self-indulgence. Having sex with him on her front porch, for Christ's sake. There was no going back from that. And she could think of only one way to go forward.

Gayle let out a short, barbed laugh. "Can't do it, can you?"

Merry stood up. "But I will. Because you're right. I never should have asked for his help. And I hate that he got hurt." She took a step, then turned back. "I'll never trouble either of you again."

She could actually see the relief wash across Gayle's features. This time when Merry turned to leave, Gayle didn't try to stop her. It had become about something different than what Jamie would have wanted.

———

Harlan lived in a manufactured home set on a concrete foundation. He'd painted it white with forest green trim, and the barn and three other outbuildings reversed the colors. The siding showed wear, and lighter shingles spotted the roof in several places where it had been patched after rough weather. The valley to the northeast funneled wind and winter cold straight to Harlan's small spread.

A few red cows lay in the late afternoon sun, fenced from the road with split rails instead of the ubiquitous barbed wire. As Merry shifted into Park, the brown rheumy eyes of a bony old specimen watched her with calm interest. As her boots hit the driveway, Merry breathed in the familiar scent of horse carried on the warm air, along with a hint of cedar. Chickens gabbled at one another conversationally, bocking and scratching in a large rectangular enclosure built off one end of their coop. A metallic clang echoed from the nearest building.

She strode to the doorway and looked inside. A well-lit and tidy shop greeted her eye. Harlan lay on a roller, installing new shocks on the front of an old yellow flatbed truck. She watched him work for a few moments, unnoticed, then cleared her throat.

He craned his head from under the truck, saw Merry, and returned to the bolt he was tightening. The whine of the impact wrench bounced off the metal walls, and then silence settled over the shop. After long seconds of stillness, he rolled out from under the vehicle and used the grille guard on the front to pull himself upright. Wiping grease off his hands with a scrap of blue flannel, he walked over to Merry. Stopping in front of her, he looked up from his hands and regarded her with steady gray eyes.

"Want a beer?" he asked.

"Sure."

He nodded to himself. "Stay here. I'll go get them."

She waited, eyes roving over the hills beyond, the golden grass drinking in the oblique rays of the sun and butting up against a sky turning blue gray with clouds so smooth she couldn't tell where they began.

Harlan reappeared, an oilcan of Foster's in each hand. He handed one of the lagers to her, and popped the top on his own. Then, eyeing the sling on her arm, he took back the can, opened it, and handed it back.

"Thanks," she said.

They gazed out the door at the hills.

She sipped her beer. Swallowed. "I was kind of a jackass. About you and Mama."

When he didn't respond, she looked over at him and met a gaze that held frank amusement.

"Yup. You were," he said.

She grinned and looked at the floor. Gave a little nod. "Yeah."

He leaned against the workbench running along one wall. "'Course, I've had my share of jackass moments." He took a swallow. "Maybe more'n my share."

"Huh," she said. "Hard to imagine."

They watched the hills do nothing for a few more sips.

"What are you going to do now?" Harlan asked.

A hawk dove into the rectangle of land and sky visible through the doorway, streaking toward the ground and then swooping upward with something small and limp in its beak.

The Texas parole board had allowed Merry to remain in Hazel, under Yvette's supervision. It helped that Yvette had argued on her behalf with the same inimitable verve with which she seemed to approach everything else. That—plus the statement Barbie had given Sheriff Ellers and the fact that Merry had saved the life of a policeman—had been enough for the county attorney to decide Merry had not actually committed any crime. Texas had been willing to go along with his recommendation.

"I don't know what I'm going to do now. Couple named Brentwood are buying the Lamente place. Plan to rebuild the whole shebang, and they want to take over Frank Cain's leases when they're up."

"They know what they're doing?"

"Nope. But Thomas Brentwood is hiring Frank's oldest son to run the place. He'll do okay."

"What're these Brentwood people like?"

"More money than God. Seem decent enough, though."

"Well, that's better'n a poke in the eye with a sharp stick." He took a swallow and swiped his forearm across his mouth. "Your Mama would've been proud of what you did." Watching her as he said it.

"Maybe. Maybe she would've. I just wish … never mind. It doesn't matter."

"Some things I wish I'd done differently, too." He sighed. "Hard to get through life without some of that. I doubt she holds our shortcomings against us, wherever she is."

"No," she said. "I don't suppose she would. I'm glad you were here when I wasn't."

"Guilt's a useless thing to hold onto, you know."

She didn't respond.

A rooster crowed outside.

"So are you looking for work?"

"Well, I need some kind of job. I suppose I could hire out to help when someone needs it. Fix fence. Whatever. Don't suppose you need any fences mended, do you?" she asked, trying to laugh.

He pressed his lips together and shook his head.

"Oh, well. I'll find something."

"I've managed to keep up pretty well with the fence work around here," he said. "But I could sure use some reliable help down at the hardware. Don't suppose you'd be interested in doing some indoor work. Some of it'd be in the open, out back with the loading and feed and such. You know. But nothing like ranch work."

She looked at him. "Really?"

"I would dearly love to get rid of that little pissant who pretends to work for me right now."

She recalled the laconic, comic-book-reading youth in the battered John Deere cap.

He continued. "It's not that he's dishonest, but he's such a dipshit I hardly dare to leave him alone. I'd really appreciate if you'd think about it."

She grinned, not certain how he'd managed to turn a job offer into her doing him a favor.

"I don't have to think about it," she said. "It sounds like a pretty good deal to me."

"You don't know how much I'm going to pay you yet. May not be such a good deal after all."

Merry laughed. "Well, you could throw in another beer." She swished the dregs in her Foster's can.

Harlan nodded. "I guess I could do that."

———

Sprinklers defended the grass in the park from the late-July heat, sending occasional drifts of spray under the clump of trees that shaded the big picnic table. It was covered with Chester-fried chicken, egg salad sandwiches, potato and macaroni salads, a quivering bowl of green Jell-O studded with fruit, watermelon cut into chilled wedges, and two pans of pecan-studded, double-fudge brownies made from Mama's recipe.

Shirlene kept an eye on everyone's plate, ready to pass more food to anyone who looked like they were running low. Lauri sat next to her, wearing a loose skirt and top as her nod toward maternity wear. Harlan sat across from Merry, who kept peppering him with questions about the particulars of running the hardware store. Kate O'Neil perched next to her husband, Jack, a quiet, thoughtful sort who Merry took an immediate liking to.

"I'm glad Anna came back," Shirlene said. "She's kind of a ditz, but that clinic needs all the help they can get right now."

Merry nodded, but didn't say anything, rubbing the inside of her elbow where Anna had jabbed at her veins like she'd been playing darts.

"All this has been terrible for WorldMed, though," her aunt continued. "The head office is in an uproar, and all the packaging facilities have been shut down. I just can't believe such a good organization has to suffer like this."

Merry took a bite of potato salad. "The murders aside, I don't think either Olivia or Barbie realized how … how, *evil* stealing those drugs was. Imagine all those kids that dealer in Billings sold to. And the people all over the world who didn't get drugs they needed."

"How could they not know?" Shirlene asked.

Merry shrugged. "Hard telling."

"No compassion," Shirlene said.

"No empathy," Kate said.

Lauri cocked her head at them for a moment, then shrugged and took a bite of fried chicken. Speaking around it she said, "They aren't very nice people, that's all."

TWENTY-SIX

AIR STILL COOL FROM the darkness whispered around Merry, less than a breeze in the predawn light. The ornate cinerary urn she carried weighed more than it had a right to. Mama hadn't been a large woman to start with, and now she was just ashes and a few tiny bone fragments.

She'd awakened early with the knowledge of what to do with her mama's ashes, and lay staring at the square of lighter dark that defined her bedroom window until it turned to gray. In the past months, she'd considered several options, rejecting them all. She'd even talked Frank Cain into taking her up in his Piper Supercub. But when they'd returned to earth, she still had the full urn on her lap. It hadn't felt right. And it needed to.

This morning in the early hours, less dream than memory, it had come to her in that fog between sleeping and waking. Merry had been at the awkward age between girlhood and womanhood, thirteen and starting the eighth grade. She'd come home from school early due to a teacher-planning day but hadn't found Mama in the house or yard.

Drawn by a clank from the workshop, she found Daddy working to patch yet another piece of their aging equipment. He greeted her with a grunt, and grunted again in response to her question.

"She got some damn fool idea about it being a nice day for a picnic. Wanted to go over to the back meadow to eat, for God's sake. Told her I had work to do and to go on ahead. S'pose she did." He turned back to the broken blade on the hay mower.

Merry remembered being angry that Daddy so readily dismissed Mama's desire to go on a picnic. Thinking back, he'd no doubt been right about having work to do, because there had always been work to do. Work that had soured him for so long that the bitterness of it had become more comfortable to him than the company of his own wife.

She'd headed down to the back meadow, so called because the field, always aglow with wildflowers in the spring, fell beyond a narrow belt of trees eight hundred yards behind the house. A very few tenacious October blooms sprinkled the early autumn grass, and along the edge, aspens held out the last of their green and yellow and orange-streaked leaves to the sun. Her mother sat beneath the multiple hues of greens and golds, a sandwich wrapper and empty 7-Up can beside her. She heard Merry approach and turned.

"What's wrong?"

"Nothing's wrong. We got out of school early is all."

She looked puzzled for a moment, and then she smiled. "I'd forgotten. Did you eat lunch before you came home?" She bent to pick up the plastic bag and empty can.

"I ate. Mama? Are you okay?"

She smiled. "I'm fine."

"Something's wrong." Mama's eyes looked wet, and her expression seemed … wobbly. "Is it because Daddy wouldn't go on a picnic with you? I bet he just didn't know …"

She interrupted Merry with a laugh. "No. I'm not surprised your father can't put down his tools long enough to eat a sandwich with me."

"Then why do you look so sad?"

She went still for a moment, then cocked her head and turned her gaze on Merry as if trying to gauge something deep inside her.

"I'm not sad. I'm just too happy for my own damn good."

"I don't understand."

Mama held out her arms, sandwich bag in one hand, green metal can in the other, and turned three hundred sixty degrees. One wrist brushed the top of a fireweed gone to seed, and bits of fluff floated up into the air. Her gesture took in the expanse of meadow, the breeze shivering the gold-dollar leaves of quaking aspens, the snowy clouds piled high into the sky above the foothills, the brilliant blue Stellar's jay chukking from a pine branch.

Merry had forgotten as she grew older, even now was only beginning to remember. But at thirteen, standing there in the tiny back meadow with Mama, she'd understood, and Mama had seen it. Holding hands, they'd walked back to the house.

Now October had rolled around yet again. Autumn had been Mama's favorite season, a time of abundance, of transition, of settling in. From the meadow, Merry watched the sun rise, her exhalations creating thin clouds around her face. Veins of tangerine spread into the pale sky. Violet clung to the undersides of the clouds to the north, intensifying to drastic magenta where the cumulus bunched and folded in on itself.

She waited until daylight glittered across the fine frost on the grasses and weed stalks, and the show of colors dissolved from the sky. Then Merry opened the lid and waited for a breeze. When it came, she tipped the vessel and let her mother shift and swirl into the bright morning air.

THE END

Photograph by Kevin Brookfield

ABOUT THE AUTHOR

K.C. McRae grew up in the West and earned degrees in philosophy and English from Colorado State University. She's had jobs ranging from driver's license examiner in Wyoming to localization program manager for Microsoft. She also writes the Home Crafting Mystery Series as Cricket McRae. *Shotgun Moon* is her first mainstream western mystery. For more information about K.C. and her books please visit www.cricketmcrae.com.